For my cousin, Alison

One

Tilda's plans for revenge were becoming more venomous by the minute. She had never really had these feelings about Seb before, but Tilda realised that she was now enjoying the process of working out how to exact vengeance on her brother, who had always had such an easy life. *There was no rush, though,* Tilda decided, *there would be pleasure in the planning. No one else needed to know until she was ready to act.*

In the past there had been fleeting moments when Tilda had resented her brother. She had hated the way everything seemed to land in his lap, with little or no effort on his part. And now that his studies were complete, Seb was destined to become a partner in the thriving family business. It had never been suggested that Tilda might eventually do the same. And yet she was a high-achiever too, as her results had consistently shown. But for some reason she was nowhere near as highly valued within the family as Seb was, or so it seemed to her. She would redress this balance, by whatever means it took, and whatever the fallout for either of them.

Tilda called across to her brother, who was lying back motionless in an old-fashioned deckchair on the lawn, shaded by an apple tree, 'Seb, would you *please* give me a hand with this weeding? You know we *both* promised Mum and Dad that we'd keep the garden tidy while they're away.'

1

Without so much as opening his eyes, Seb replied, 'Oh, quit moaning, sis, they won't be home for ages yet, and anyway the garden looks fine to me. You keep forgetting that I've got to recover from all the mental exertion of my exams,' he added, although Tilda knew that she would never be allowed to forget that. Seb turned up the volume on his music, and Tilda resumed her weeding, inwardly seething at Seb's self-centredness. But throughout his life Seb had been encouraged to see himself as the brilliantly academic one, the talented sportsman, the gifted musician, while Tilda, nearly four years his junior, had quietly followed in his wake, scarcely noticed.

Tilda usually found gardening a soothing and diverting occupation, but not today. Whilst their parents were away on a celebratory cruise around the Baltic, Tilda was daily becoming more irritated with her brother's behaviour and prospects. She tugged impatiently at the stubborn dandelions and ground elder, at the same time snagging her sleeve on a rose bush.

'Oh, sod it,' she muttered, 'I've had enough of this!' She decided that the gardening would have to wait for now. She started to gather up her tools and gloves to put them in the shed.

'Hey, sis,' called out Seb from his deckchair, when he realised that Tilda was packing up, 'fetch me a beer, will you?'

'Get it yourself,' came the response, much to Seb's surprise.

Tilda had some serious thinking to do. *Why have I always been such an idiot?* she asked herself.

An hour or so later, Tilda was wandering home from a long and satisfying walk with Zeus, the family's ever-energetic dog. Whenever she wanted to sort out problems, or just think quietly about something, Tilda would take herself off through the woods to the local country park with Zeus. He dashed happily around, chasing imaginary rabbits, while she walked and sifted through her thoughts. Today, though, she constantly returned to the same conclusions, and to the same feelings. She was convinced that her increasing resentment of her brother was justified and that she must take decisive action.

* * *

On arriving home, Tilda heard voices in the garden and saw Seb standing, a can of beer in his hand, chatting animatedly with a trendily dressed young man, whom she didn't recognise. She stood silently watching the two of them for a moment, wondering who the visitor could be. Something about the unexpected intrusion added to her irritation with Seb, and she was about to slip quietly away, when he looked over and spotted her.

'Hey, sis, come and meet Luke.'

No escape now, so Tilda sauntered over and casually eyed up the young man.

'Hi,' she said, 'I'm Tilda. I don't remember Seb mentioning you, do you live round here?' Luke gave her a friendly smile and shook his head.

'Actually,' he said, 'I live in London, but I was passing nearby on my way back from an aunt's funeral. I remembered Seb telling me about this place when we were at uni, so I thought it was worth seeing if I could catch up with him. And obviously it paid off, and it's good to see him again.'

Are you sure? thought Tilda, but was surprised to find herself smiling and saying, 'How lovely, I hope you'll stay and have a meal with us. I was about to go and rustle up a bit of pasta and salad.'

She could have added that she couldn't remember the last time Seb had offered to cook a meal, but she resisted the temptation. Luke thanked her and asked if he could do anything to help. But Seb quickly drew him away, saying that Tilda didn't like help in the kitchen and preferred to get on with things her own way.

Tilda went into the kitchen and quietly fumed as she viciously chopped onions, garlic and tomatoes, throwing them into the sizzling pan with rather more force than was necessary. Her plans were beginning to take shape.

She was startled by a quiet movement at her elbow and turned to see Luke watching her with amusement. 'Well,' he said with a laugh, 'thank heavens I'm not an onion.'

Tilda tried unsuccessfully not to blush.

'Sorry,' she said, 'just got a few things on my mind.'

'Well, whatever your brother may say, I think you might like a bit of help with this, so no arguments, please! Have you got some anchovies and capers? I'll show you my own wicked concoction which makes a perfect sauce with pasta. Sound OK?' asked Luke.

Trying not to show how pleased she was that Luke was choosing her company rather than Seb's, she agreed to his offer. So, while Luke was busying himself with whatever he could raid from the fridge, Tilda tried to find out more about his friendship with Seb.

'So, did you two do the same courses at uni then?' she asked casually.

'Oh hell, no,' replied Luke, 'we met at the uni sailing club. Seb was a real star. He spent all his time on the water, which is probably why he flunked all his exams and is going back to repeat his final year.'

Well, well, thought Tilda, *that's all news to me... a bit different from what the family's told me.*

'He really stood out from the rest of us,' continued Luke, 'but the trouble was he just couldn't be a *team* player, which is what the club needed. He was only ever interested in sailing solo and getting accolades for himself.'

Yeah, thought Tilda, *that sounds about right, selfish as ever.*

Tilda slowly set about making a rather elaborate salad, deliberately extending her opportunity to chat with Luke alone. She could see through the kitchen window that Seb had settled himself in the deckchair again. Luke then came out with another nugget from her point of view.

'I'm surprised that the gorgeous Helena isn't here with Seb, particularly as your parents are away,' he said with a knowing chuckle. Tilda's bewildered expression made Luke realise his blunder immediately.

'Hell, sorry,' he said, 'I've obviously put my foot in it, just forget I said anything.'

But Luke's clear discomfort at his disclosure spiked Tilda's curiosity. *Another skeleton in Seb's closet perhaps?*

At that moment Seb came into the kitchen to fetch another beer, and for Tilda the chance of pursuing that subject was past.

While they were eating their meal, Seb seemed on edge and always steered the conversation away from his and Luke's time at university. They appeared to have been good friends, but Seb was uneasy about revealing much to Tilda for some reason. She decided that she would have to keep in contact with Luke herself and find out more from him. Luke was potentially a mine of information which could feed into Tilda's plans.

But how could she manoeuvre a trip to London and a casual meeting with Luke? Taking the plunge, she asked Luke whether he had been to the new exhibition of Roman artefacts, which had had such rave reviews. He hadn't, and his reaction to Tilda's question made it clear that he wouldn't wish to.

So Tilda would have to think again, but time was against her, as Luke would soon be leaving to resume his journey home.

* * *

Following Luke's departure, Seb mercilessly derided Tilda's behaviour, accusing her of blatant flirting. To her relief Seb's phone rang, and from his response he was clearly pleased to hear from the caller. Tilda hovered in the hallway sorting the post that had arrived earlier in the day, but really hoping to overhear Seb's side of the conversation and pick up something interesting.

'That's a great idea, but I really don't see how I can at the moment,' she heard Seb say. Then, 'Yeah, I really miss you too Hun… mmm… I know… let's just give it a few more days, and I'll see what I can come up with.' A silence, then, 'Yeah, speak soon,' and Seb, having ended the call abruptly, strode into the hall.

'What the hell are you doing here eavesdropping?' he demanded angrily.

'As you can see, brother dear, I am sorting out this pile of post,' replied Tilda calmly. 'It's not my fault if you decide to have a loud conversation the other side of an open door. Someone special?' She smirked provocatively.

'None of your business,' he snapped, 'and I'll thank you to keep your nose out of my affairs.'

'Oh, so it's an affair is it?' Tilda seized on the word and decided to keep on needling Seb. It would do him good to be on the receiving end for a change. Seb turned swiftly on his heel and slammed out of the front door, creating a gust of wind that sent all Tilda's carefully arranged piles of letters flying.

Ah well, she thought, as she retrieved them and dropped them carelessly in an untidy heap on the hall table, *at least I won that round.*

* * *

Tilda was puzzled why Seb was being so secretive about this new girl in his life. He had always been in the habit previously of turning up with a different girlfriend on almost every trip home, casually discarding the old for the new on a regular basis.

Typical, selfish Seb, thought Tilda. *So what's different this time?* she wondered. *Obviously something he would rather the family didn't get wind of, at least for the time being.*

Luke had clearly known more about the situation than he had let on, and Tilda had failed to find out much in that short conversation in the kitchen. *How on earth was she going to get in touch with him again?* She briefly contemplated taking Seb's phone, when he wasn't looking, and trying to find Luke's number, but she realised that she had no idea what his passcode might be, so that was a non-starter. She didn't even know which part of London Luke lived in, so it was beginning to look like a 'needle in a haystack' situation.

Tilda yawned and stretched. It had been a long and eventful day, and she was feeling tired. *Seb has doubtless stormed off to the local pub for a few beers,* she thought, *so he won't be putting in an appearance again any time soon.* That was fine with Tilda. She called Zeus and let him out for his last run of the day, before settling him in his bed for the night.

Alone in her room, Tilda mulled over all that had happened today, but, try as she would, she couldn't rid herself of the image of Luke's smiling face with his teasing, crinkly eyes.

Now, now, she told herself, *don't let your imagination run away with you. He was just being polite and helpful, nothing more than that.*

However, he was by far and away the nicest of Seb's friends she had ever met. She couldn't help wishing he lived a bit closer, so that there was more chance of him dropping in again, *purely so that she could find out more about Helena, or 'Hun', of course,* she quickly told herself.

Eventually sleep overtook her, and the next day Tilda was up bright and early as usual, but there was no sign of Seb.

No doubt got a hangover, she thought with satisfaction, and she felt tempted to make a din, clattering kitchen utensils, until her better nature took over. Besides, it was so much more pleasant being alone at this hour. She hummed quietly as she made coffee and buttered some toast to take out to the garden, her favourite place in the mornings, with the birds singing and a lovely view over fields and woodland towards the distant hills.

* * *

Tilda's plans for a peaceful breakfast on the terrace suddenly took a surprising turn, when Luke appeared, out of breath, at the kitchen door. He didn't look happy.

'Rushed to see you,' he blurted out, panting, 'didn't know what else to do.'

Luke looked worried, and he was trembling.

'Got a text from Seb very early this morning… it just said, "Tell Tilda not to look for me". What the hell's this all about?'

Two

'Sorry I'm late,' called out Tony, as he kicked off his shoes at the front door. 'I called in at The Willows on the way home to see Aunt Bea. I haven't seen her for ages, so I left work a bit early. Sorry, should've let you know.'

Chloe appeared from the kitchen, smiling and carrying two glasses of chilled white wine.

'Come on, then, tell me all about it,' she said, secretly relieved that Tony had visited Aunt Bea without her. Tony followed his wife into the conservatory and sank into the soft cushions on the rattan sofa.

'How long 'til dinner?' he asked.

'Whenever you're ready,' replied Chloe, 'it can be flexible. So just give me the quick version of your visit first.'

'Well,' began Tony, 'there was all the usual stuff about her aches and pains, poor old soul, and telling me who'd been taken to hospital or died. And I had a sneaky look in the visitors' book to see if anyone had been to see her recently, but there was no sign of her son's name. I asked her about visitors, and at first she just looked blank, but then she remembered that a vicar had come and had a chat with her, but no one else. So I asked the staff to sort out a wheelchair and took her for a spin around the garden, which she obviously enjoyed. Her memory for the names of plants is quite amazing. She told me she'd learned them from her father who was a keen gardener. And yet she can't remember much from yesterday or last week.'

'Yes,' interrupted Chloe, 'I think that's often the case. Did she... '

But Tony clearly wanted to continue.

'The most interesting bit was right at the end,' he said, 'after I'd taken her back to her room. I could see that she was tired and her eyelids were drooping, when suddenly she opened her eyes wide and looked unwaveringly at me. "Tony," she said quietly, "I want you to promise me something... will you do that?" "Of course," I replied, wondering what on earth was coming next. "Find out about Anna," Aunt Bea said, almost pleading, and I noticed there were tears in her eyes. I must have looked completely bewildered, because she then said, "You know... Anna, my aunt Anastasia... promise me you'll find out what happened to everything." I just nodded, and she leaned back in her chair and closed her eyes. And I kissed her on the cheek and left. So what's that all about? I've never heard of Anastasia.'

Tony sat drinking his wine, waiting for Chloe to say something.

There was a long pause, and then Chloe said thoughtfully, 'Well, you've always been fond of Bea, and I'm sure you wouldn't want to let her down, so I suppose you'd better start by asking around the family.'

Tony sat quietly for a moment with a faraway look in his eyes, as though he was trying to remember something, some detail that was worrying him. Then he suddenly came back to the present and shook his head.

'No,' he said, 'I'd rather keep the family out of this just at the moment. I think I'll try to visit Aunt Bea again very soon, tomorrow even, if I can fit it in, and see if I can jog her memory... ferret out a bit more detail. It may be that she was imagining things, and there never was an Anastasia. On the other hand, she was very convincing, and it might be better to do a little more gentle probing, before I start asking questions that could cause trouble. You know how Bea has never got on particularly well with her son, Jacob, not that he's around much for anyone to get on with these days. Heaven knows where he is or what he's up to. And as for cousin Dennis and his family, well, always a bit of an undercurrent going on there, to put it mildly. His late father George, Bea's brother, was always considered the 'black sheep' of the family, and probably there are things we don't know about.'

Tony paused for breath and smiled apologetically as Chloe sighed.

'Your family is so complicated,' she protested, 'I shall never understand exactly how everybody is related and, even more importantly, who is speaking to whom! It seems like a soap opera at times!' Tony put his arm round her and gave her a gentle hug.

'I know,' he agreed, 'but you've always been brilliant, especially as I don't know that much about the family myself. I've always been on the periphery. But Aunt Bea took to you immediately. My instinct, though, is that we should try and find out a little more about this by ourselves, before we start talking to other members of the family, if we can even find them!'

'We?' asked Chloe quizzically.

'Oh, definitely "we",' replied Tony, with a winning smile, 'you know Bea loves you, and even if you don't exactly enjoy visiting The Willows, you've been very good to her.'

'Hmm,' was all the answer he received.

* * *

Next morning, as Tony was getting into his car to drive to his office in the nearby town of Minchford, Chloe called out to him from the front door.

'The Willows is on the phone, can you come and talk to them? They say they found Bea lying in the garden this morning with a head injury, and it sounds pretty serious.'

Tony ran back into the house and grabbed the phone from the hall table. After a brief conversation he hung up and turned to Chloe.

'I'm going straight to the hospital now. I don't suppose there's any chance you could re-arrange your morning and come with me?'

'Just give me a couple of minutes to make a phone call, and I'll be right with you,' she replied, and, seeing the strained look on his face, she added, 'try not to worry too much... she's a tough old bird and maybe things aren't as bad as they sound. I'll talk to Kate in the office... I'm sure she'll cover for me.'

It took less than two minutes for Chloe to make her call and grab her handbag before joining Tony outside. They sat in silence while Tony drove as fast as the early morning traffic would allow. It was frustratingly slow at times, while worrying, unspoken thoughts kept them both preoccupied. When they eventually drove into the visitors' car park at the hospital, they were both relieved to find a parking space surprisingly quickly.

'Right,' said Tony, hastily locking the car, 'we need to find Ward A6.'

He grabbed Chloe's hand, and they hurried into the Reception area, spotted a sign to the Ward and found a lift. Minutes later they were being given an update on Aunt Bea. The nurse calmly explained that Bea had arrived on the Ward only half an hour ago, having been assessed in the Accident and Emergency Department. She was still very groggy from her head injury, but she was not unconscious. The Ward would arrange a raft of tests during the day, to monitor the nature and extent of her injuries, and she would almost certainly be kept in the hospital overnight.

'We want her to rest for now,' continued the nurse, 'but you're welcome to sit by her bed, just for ten minutes. I can't say whether she'll know that you're there, but perhaps she will.'

Tony and Chloe were taken to a small side room, with just one bed in it, and there lay Aunt Bea attached to a quietly bleeping machine. Tony leaned forward and briefly held her frail hand, but Aunt Bea showed no reaction. After being with her for the permitted ten minutes, Tony and Chloe went to find a coffee and have a chat.

They both arranged to have the remainder of the day off work.

'Thank heavens for understanding colleagues,' commented Tony.

They decided that a visit to The Willows would be more productive in finding out what had happened than phoning the care home. And it might be best not to forewarn the staff of their visit.

'But we must be careful not to make them defensive. You know, there are probably insurance implications if they are found to have let an elderly frail resident wander out into the garden in her nightdress so early in the morning, and she then had a serious fall,' Tony was thinking out loud.

Chloe nodded in agreement.

'But we've never had any reason to doubt the quality of the care she gets there,' she added.

* * *

The Manager of The Willows, Sally Jeavons, ushered Tony and Chloe into her office and offered them tea and biscuits.

'We're all very concerned about your aunt,' began Mrs Jeavons. 'I've just rung the hospital and been told that Bea is resting quietly, and that you've already visited her.'

'Yes,' replied Chloe, 'and we'll be returning there later on.'

Mrs Jeavons seemed to hesitate, but she looked Chloe straight in the eye and asked, 'Do you think that's a good idea? I mean, and please don't take this the wrong way, Bea was very upset after your husband's visit here yesterday evening, before her fall, and she obviously needs peace and quiet now.'

Tony and Chloe could hardly believe what they were hearing, but both remained calm.

And there we were, determined not to put them on the defensive, and damn me if they haven't gone straight onto the offensive and more or less accused me of causing Aunt Bea's fall… the bloody cheek of it! thought Tony, hoping that his face betrayed none of this.

Keep calm, he told himself, *and please, please, Chloe, don't you rise to the bait either.*

Mrs Jeavons seemed oblivious to the maelstrom of feelings she was stirring up and continued, 'My staff tell me that Bea was desperately agitated about what you'd been saying about her Aunt Anna, or Anastasia, or whatever her name was.'

At this, Tony's self-control was beginning to wear a bit thin, but outwardly he remained calm. Chloe bit her lips.

'She's mentioned this aunt a lot recently, but the story gets more and more convoluted and confused. You really should have told us that you had been encouraging Bea to talk about her.'

Tony could take no more of this and decided that the only course of action was to retreat.

'Well, Mrs Jeavons,' he said with a somewhat fixed smile, 'we won't take up any more of your time… I'm sure you've got a lot of forms to fill in. Obviously we'll want to know more about Bea's fall soon, so we'll be in touch. We'll sign ourselves out. Goodbye.'

As they were letting themselves out of the heavy front door, one of the carers whom Tony had spoken to a few times before, Maddie, sidled up to them and whispered, 'It's about Bea, please ring me soon.'

She slipped a piece of paper into Chloe's hand and quickly walked away.

* * *

Chloe waited until they were driving away from The Willows, safely out of sight and earshot, before saying anything.

'I don't know about you, but that visit raised more questions than it answered, and it's left me with a very uneasy feeling,' she finally said, looking at the number scrawled on the crumpled piece of paper from Maddie.

'Uneasy and hopping mad,' exploded Tony. 'How dare that woman insinuate that we were in any way to blame for Bea's accident, and how does she know so much about Anna, and why is she apparently anxious to keep us away from Bea? There's something very strange going on, and I'm determined to get to the root of it.'

'Well,' replied Chloe, 'I'm glad we've come away from that place with pretty much the same thoughts and reactions. I think we must try to speak to Maddie at the first possible opportunity, and find out what it is she wants us to know but daren't speak about where she might be overheard. I would guess that her shift ends at about six o'clock, so no point in trying to ring her any earlier. I'd like to arrange to meet her face to face if possible... phone calls are never as satisfactory.'

'Good point,' said Tony, 'let's get back to the hospital, and see how Bea is, and whether they have any further news on her accident... if that's what it was,' he added darkly.

'Good god,' exclaimed Chloe, 'you're not suggesting somebody tried to bump her off, are you? Isn't that a bit far-fetched?'

Tony was slow to reply.

'On first thoughts, yes, but have you noticed the security at that place? All those heavy old doors with codes on them? Bea wasn't… isn't,' he corrected himself, 'anything like strong enough to open one and take herself out for a walk in the middle of the night. I just don't buy it, but I can't imagine why anyone would want to attack such a harmless old lady… unless there is much more to this Anna, or Anastasia, story than we know.'

They drove on in an uncomfortable silence, each with their thoughts racing.

* * *

At the hospital they quickly made their way to Ward A6 and were relieved to see a doctor speaking with the nurse who was caring for Bea. They introduced themselves, and he took them into another side room.

'It's more private speaking in here,' he explained, 'and I do need to have a word with you about your aunt.'

Three

Half an hour later Tony and Chloe were sitting in the Contemplation Garden in a secluded part of the hospital grounds. The garden was enclosed by a pergola adorned with climbing evergreens, and the central part was an oasis of shrubs and flowering plants with bench seats discreetly placed.

Clearly aptly named, thought Chloe, *and the perfect place to think things through.*

They sat in silence for a few minutes, and then Tony asked, 'Well, what did you make of what the doctor said, Chlo?'

The doctor had only been with Tony and Chloe for a short while before his 'bleeper' had called him away to an emergency, but it had been long enough to be given some useful information. His initial assessment (and he was keen to stress that it was *initial*) was that Mrs Elsworth's, as he referred to Bea, visible injuries were consistent with a fall. He speculated that the cold morning air, after the warmth of indoors, may have caused her to become unsteady and fall. She had a wound to her head, which the hospital would look at more closely, and there was bruising to her face, shoulder, arm and hand. They would be doing tests during the day and keeping her in the hospital overnight.

Whilst all this was reassuring to some extent for Tony and Chloe, the doctor went on to voice other concerns.

'I realise that this is outside my medical remit,' he said cautiously, 'but having heard the circumstances of Mrs Elsworth's fall, I would suggest, unofficially of course, that you make further enquiries about this. Obviously, we will look after her immediate medical needs, but I find the timing and place of her fall quite worrying.' With that, and a quick apology, he was gone.

Tony and Chloe had headed for the Contemplation Garden.

'Well,' said Chloe in answer to Tony's question, 'I'm very relieved that Bea's injuries and general state aren't as bad as I first thought. And I'm sure she's in the right place and will be cared for really well. But I also think the doctor's right about how and why this all happened. We must find out more. We owe it to Bea. Perhaps we could try and get hold of Maddie soon after the residents have been given their lunch and are resting… things should be a bit quieter for her then, and she might be able to talk. She seems to be our best bet.'

'Good idea,' replied Tony, pleased that there was an immediate plan of action. 'So until then, let's go for a walk by the river and an early lunch at that nice pizza place. Come on, then.'

The walk helped them to sift through all that had happened that morning and to get their questions ready for Maddie.

* * *

But the call did not go as they had hoped. Maddie answered her phone, but she was clearly in tears.

'That sod Jeavons has sacked me,' she sobbed, 'some snitch saw me with you two. But I want you to know,' she paused, 'a lawyer went to see Bea yesterday afternoon, before you… word is, it was about her will. Other thing is the door, it's often wedged wide open when the early shift arrive so they can have a fag outside first…', another sob, 'poor Bea… and now I've lost my job.'

Maddie rang off, leaving Tony and Chloe in shock again.

A few minutes later Chloe tried to ring Maddie back.

No connection.

* * *

'I feel so sorry for the poor girl and also horribly responsible for her losing her job,' said Chloe, after trying unsuccessfully for the umpteenth time to reconnect to Maddie's mobile. 'Surely that must count as unfair dismissal or something?'

'I agree,' replied Tony, 'and we must try and help her if she needs to get legal assistance. But in the meantime, we should try to track down this lawyer, who apparently visited Bea yesterday but didn't sign the visitors' book. I ought to be able to remember the name of the family firm, it's something odd and quirky, as though it had come out of a Dickensian novel. Give me a minute, and I'm sure it will come.'

'Snodgrass and Peabody?' suggested Chloe, unhelpfully plucking two Dickensian-sounding names at random out of the air.

'Chloe, be serious,' said Tony reprovingly.

'Sorry,' said Chloe, 'just thought a bit of levity might help to lift our spirits, that's all.'

'Got it!' Tony broke into a smile, 'Brownlow and Noggs!'

'You are kidding me?' Chloe asked, looking sceptical.

'No, no, that's definitely it, and I know exactly where their office is too... in one of the little backstreets in Minchford. Not that far from my own office, as it happens. Rather than trying to explain everything over the phone to a receptionist, why don't we call on them and see if we can get an appointment soon?'

Tony was eager to get things moving, and Chloe could tell that he wouldn't rest until he had found out more about Bea's visitor.

***

Standing in front of the offices of Brownlow and Noggs a while later, they saw that it was not only the name that had Dickensian overtones. The building, one of several half-timbered houses dating back to the early 18th century, sat nestled between an old coaching inn and the minster church of St. Anselm's. *It could be a film set,* thought Chloe.

'OK,' she muttered, 'let's hope the actual solicitors have moved into the 21st century, or we may be in trouble.'

Tony pushed the door open. A bell clanged tinnily above their heads, and while they were wondering if they had inadvertently stepped back a couple of centuries, they saw with relief that they had entered a modern reception area. A friendly, smiling young woman behind the desk quickly checked the diary and was able to tell them exactly who had been to visit Bea the previous day.

'It was Mr Abbott, our senior partner,' she said, sounding confident, 'but I'm not sure that he will be in a position to disclose any details of their discussion.'

'I quite understand,' replied Tony, 'but it would be very helpful if we could perhaps just have a word with Mr Abbott. We are very concerned about my aunt and need to find out how best to help her.'

At that moment there was a voice behind them.

'Then you had better come into my office, young man, and talk to me about it. I am Charles Abbott, and I have been dealing with your aunt's affairs for many years. I think we could talk to one another without breaking any confidences.'

They turned to find themselves face to face with a tall, angular man with thin greying hair. He had a kindly manner, and as they each shook his outstretched hand, they felt reassured. He invited them into a large room lined with dark antique shelving and furnished with an enormous oak desk and stylish green leather chairs.

'Please do sit down,' continued Charles Abbott. 'I am extremely glad that you have come to see me. I know from your aunt how fond she is of you, and that she trusts you above all the rest of her family. Now that she is becoming more frail and forgetful, I feel it may be advisable to formalise that relationship, so that you have legal responsibility for her affairs. I talked to Mrs Elsworth about this yesterday, and she was in full agreement, although I do realise she may have forgotten all about our conversation by now,' he added with a kindly smile.

'Then you don't know,' cut in Chloe, 'about her accident?'

He looked sharply at Chloe.

'Accident, no, what accident?' He looked increasingly concerned as Tony and Chloe detailed the events of the past twenty-four hours, including Bea's insistent plea to Tony about "Anna" or "Anastasia".

'But,' concluded Tony, 'I have absolutely no idea who this person is or was, or indeed what it is that worries Bea so much.'

'Ah,' replied Charles Abbott, 'I think I may be able to shed a little light on that for you, but prepare yourselves for something of an unusual story.'

* * *

Tony and Chloe sat in the coaching inn, clutching neat double whiskies and staring at each other in disbelief.

'How did we never know about all this?' exclaimed Tony at last. 'It's just amazing that nobody in the family seemed to know, let alone talk about it.'

'I agree,' said Chloe, 'it all feels a bit surreal at the moment. And the more I think about what Mr Abbott told us, the more gaps there seem to be. And how sure is he really that the whole saga is true? He admitted himself that Bea's memory is a bit suspect at times.'

'Hmm...' replied Tony, clearly preoccupied, 'but it's what we've got at the moment, and he has known her for donkeys' years.'

'And talking of what we've got at the moment,' said Chloe, 'I think we need to make some speedy decisions. The hospital is saying that they'll keep Bea overnight, but what happens if they want to discharge her tomorrow? What do you think about her going back to The Willows? I've lost all faith in that woman Jeavons, and Bea was allowed to wander around in her nightdress, out into the garden, so is it still the right place for her? If not, we're going to have to move bloody quickly!'

Tony agreed, somewhat despondently, and added, 'I think there's another problem in all this too, and I felt really awkward about it at Mr Abbott's. Surely Jacob should be involved, rather than us. He is her son, after all. Isn't he the right person to look after Bea's affairs, whatever Mr Abbott says?'

'Good point,' replied Chloe, 'he does seem to have been side-lined by both Bea and Mr Abbott, from what we've heard, but presumably Mrs Jeavons must have some level of contact with him, or at least have his contact details.'

Tony and Chloe sat in silence for several minutes, sipping their whiskies, each immersed in thought. Tony had moved on from the practicalities which were exercising Chloe's mind, though, important as he knew they were. He was intrigued by what they had heard about Bea's wealthy relative, George, and his unconventional second wife, Anastasia. The seemingly straight-laced Mr Abbott had clearly felt uncomfortable while alluding to an ostensibly scandalous part of their family history to Tony and Chloe.

How times have changed, thought Tony, with some amusement. He was roused from his musings by Chloe's voice.

'Well,' he heard, 'have you come up with any solutions yet?'

Four

Neither Luke nor Tilda had heard anything more from Seb since his strange text. They were tacitly colluding, hoping that he would just turn up soon and say that it had only been a joke. Tilda mentioned nothing of all this to her parents, who were due back from their cruise the following day. She was already dreading their return and all the questions that would accompany it.

Although she knew that the situation was in no way her fault, Tilda also knew that her parents would manage to make her feel guilty and hold her responsible for Seb's disappearance. She was angry with herself for not standing up to them, but it seemed impossible to break the habit of a lifetime. To make matters worse, the house looked a mess, and she had totally neglected the garden recently. She realised with a sinking heart that those pernicious weeds, which she had begun to conquer, were once again romping through the rose beds and her mother's prized herbaceous border. It would certainly not go unremarked.

Luke had been very supportive. He had taken it for granted that he should stay around to keep Tilda company. She was grateful for his sympathetic presence and relieved that he hadn't simply disappeared back to London at the first opportunity. She had been wondering how best to broach the subject of Helena, so she was surprised and pleased when Luke started talking about her over a hastily prepared snack.

'At first I felt guilty for mentioning her without Seb's agreement,' he said, 'but now I think it's important that we share all our information, to see if we can work out between us what's going on.'

He proceeded to describe an attractive and sophisticated foreign student, who had been hanging around with Seb, on and off, for several months.

'It was hard to work out exactly what their relationship was at first,' said Luke, 'but after a while it seemed clear they were involved in a passionate affair. That may have had something to do with Seb failing his exams... as well as all the sailing, that is. With all that going on, his mind was definitely not on his studies.' He laughed ruefully.

'At first, we were all rather envious of him being seen with such a good-looking girl, but after a while we could see that she was quite hard and calculating. We suspected she was just using Seb as a convenient escort, and I almost felt sorry for him. But then, after all the girls he's dumped in his time, perhaps he had it coming to him.'

'He had a call from her the night he disappeared,' said Tilda, 'I couldn't help overhearing.' She blushed, as Luke gave her a questioning look. 'Well, perhaps I did hang around a bit longer than I needed to,' she admitted. 'Anyway, it sounded like she was keen to see him, but he was stalling and saying that he couldn't manage it. Then, when he saw me, he got very angry and stormed out of the door... and that's the last time I saw him,' she concluded.

'Well,' said Luke slowly, 'that's interesting, because we all thought she'd gone back home, wherever that is, at the end of term and wouldn't be around anymore. I wonder what made her change her mind.'

But their musings were interrupted by Tilda's phone ringing. 'Oh hell,' said Tilda, 'it's Mum.'

'Just try and sound normal,' whispered Luke.

So Tilda answered the phone with a casual 'Hi Mum', but Luke noticed that she looked increasingly worried by whatever her mum was saying. When the call ended, Luke came and put his arm round Tilda's shoulder and asked what the problem was.

'Well,' she explained, 'Dad's had some sort of mishap, and they can't come home tomorrow. He's in hospital having tests. Mum didn't really say much, and then she suddenly ended the call. She sounded ever so worried, though. What the hell's happening to this family? And I didn't dare let on that Seb's gone AWOL.'

'Well,' said Luke, 'all we can do is wait for your mum to call again. I'm sure she'll get back to you soon. In the meantime, we ought to try and sort out the Seb situation. Should we tell the police? But what would we tell them? All we can say is that your brother stormed off to his girlfriend because he was mad with you… hardly an offence is it? And we can't reason with him because his phone is permanently turned off. He could be anywhere, doing anything. If only I could remember something about Helena's friends… but she never seemed to be with any.'

Tilda seemed lost in a world of her own, but she suddenly jumped when Luke's phone pinged. It only sounded once, which unnerved Tilda even more. Her thoughts were jumbled, and all sorts of conspiracy theories were vying for her brain's attention. She couldn't face any more stress and just burst into tears. Luke came across to her, put his arms around her and gently kissed her on the mouth.

He drew back almost immediately, looking embarrassed.

'Sorry…' he stuttered, 'I shouldn't have done that… it was wrong of me…'

Tilda just stood there, looking wan and silently shaking her head. The awkwardness seemed to last an age, until Luke's phone pinged again. This time a text from Seb's phone. Luke read it to Tilda.

"Send George's details. No questions. Urgent." Tilda and Luke both looked bewildered.

'Who the hell's George?' they asked simultaneously.

'And why does Seb want to contact him?' asked Luke.

'Haven't a clue what this is all about,' said Tilda, a hint of relief in her voice, 'but at least we know he's OK.'

Luke decided not to say that they didn't actually know who had sent the text from Seb's phone.

Several mugs of coffee and chocolate bars later, Luke and Tilda were still sitting at the kitchen table trying to come up with a possible George. Luke had gone through all the members of the sailing club, other university friends whom Seb might have known, and he hadn't remembered a single George. Tilda had tried to remember Seb's school friends, anyone he had ever brought home for any reason, their wider family, their parents' friends, and she couldn't identify any Georges either.

'Could it be a Georgina?' wondered Luke. But that name rang no bells either.

'Come on,' said Luke decisively, 'I know this is important, but we deserve a break. And Zeus certainly does too. He's been looking at you plaintively for ages, asking in his doggie way for a walk.' Zeus heard that word and immediately got up, wagging his tail.

'Good idea,' said Tilda, pleased that the tension between her and Luke had lifted, but secretly wishing that he would kiss her again.

They were wandering through the nearby wood when Tilda suddenly exclaimed, 'My grandmother had a brother George. I didn't ever know him, 'cos he died of some ghastly disease when he was in his twenties, I think. I don't suppose that helps at all though, do you?'

'Doesn't really sound like there's any connection, does it?' Luke replied. 'Come on, this walk was meant to relax us… forget George for now.'

* * *

When they arrived home, with mud-spattered Zeus trailing slowly behind, Luke announced that he would cook another of his speciality pasta dishes. He set about rummaging in the fridge. After cleaning Zeus's muddy paws, Tilda was walking through the hall when she noticed the answerphone light flashing. She pressed the button to listen to the message. At first, she thought that someone had dialled a wrong number, as the voice of a young foreign woman started speaking. Then Tilda realised that the call was indeed meant for her, as the heavily accented words began to make some sort of sense.

'This is not a game, you know. You should do as your brother tells you and send him details of George with no more delay. Don't be foolish and talk to anyone about this… *just do it*.' A click, and the message ended.

'That sounded like Helena to me.' Tilda swung around with a start. She hadn't realised that Luke had come into the hall and was listening right behind her.

'Helena,' she echoed, 'but why would she call me instead of Seb? And who on earth is this George?'

Luke looked grim.

'I've no idea,' he said, 'but Seb seems to have got sucked into something unpleasant, and I guess that he's out of his depth. If you have a George in your family, then I think we ought to find out everything we can about him. Then maybe we'll fathom out why he's of so much interest to Helena. She clearly isn't all she seemed to be at uni, and for some reason she deliberately targeted Seb. It looks like she set out to charm her way into his life, and she certainly succeeded… big-time,' he concluded wryly.

'I can't take much more,' whimpered Tilda, 'everything's out of control…' She went into the kitchen, sat on a rug next to sleeping Zeus and sobbed. Luke looked at her, unsure what to do or say. He was completely at a loss about the Seb situation and how to identify George, but he wanted to be protective of Tilda. *The only way to do that,* he thought, *is to appear to be in control.*

'Why don't you go and have a shower while I get the meal ready… it might make you feel better,' suggested Luke hesitantly.

To his relief, Tilda eventually nodded and set off upstairs. Luke watched her go, knowing that his motives were questionable. He was wrestling slightly with his conscience. He got some beers out of the fridge and opened one.

* * *

A short while later Luke quietly took two more beers up the stairs.

'You OK?' he called through the bathroom door. He noticed that the door was ajar and gently pushed it open. Tilda moved the shower curtain aside and coyly beckoned Luke to join her in the shower. Within seconds he had pulled off his clothes, and their naked, wet bodies enveloped each other. Their mouths met again, this time in a passionate kiss.

* * *

When Tilda awoke in her bed, a couple of hours later, she noticed that dusk was beginning to fall. She turned and saw Luke still sleeping, his naked body only inches from hers. She sighed contentedly. But then she was startled by the sound of a key in the front door and someone entering the house.

'Luke,' she whispered urgently, 'we're being burgled, wake up!'

Luke woke up with a start, initially unsure where he was. By this time, they could hear the intruder on the stairs, but before they could reach for a phone or get out of bed, the bedroom door was pushed open and a man was standing in the doorway.

'Well, well,' he said, 'my goody-goody sister in bed with my friend Luke… I didn't expect that, I must say! And you must 've been in a hurry, judging by the clothes lying around out here!' There was a sneer on Seb's face.

'Where the hell have you been?' demanded Luke, 'have you any idea of all the trouble you've been causing with your stupid texts? Tilda's been at the end of her tether because of you…'

'Well,' retorted Seb, 'looks like you've found a way of consoling her, doesn't it?'

There was an acid atmosphere building in the room.

But, as if he'd suddenly realised what Luke had said, Seb shouted, 'What stupid texts? Why would I want to send you any texts? What are you on about? Anyway, I lost my phone days ago and haven't got a new one yet. My bank cards went missing at the same time.'

Luke and Tilda cast bemused glances at each other, neither knowing what to believe. Luke decided to take control.

'Go downstairs and have a beer, Seb. We'll get dressed and come down too. There's a lot of sorting out to do.'

The thought of a beer was enough to lure Seb down to the kitchen, but halfway down the stairs he turned and called out to his sister, 'Where's Mum and Dad? Aren't they back from the cruise yet?'

Tilda hastily threw on a bathrobe and followed Seb down the stairs. She decided that communication was vital, and far more important than any childish arguments. She quickly caught up with him and immediately outlined what had been going on in his absence, including the abruptly curtailed call from their mother.

'I'm desperately worried that something has happened to them. They should have been home by now, and this is so unlike them,' she concluded. Seb frowned as he tried to digest everything Tilda had told him.

'It's all very strange,' he agreed. 'I can't imagine what could have held them up and prevented them from calling. How on earth do we set about finding where they are? They could be almost anywhere. And what was it you were saying about a text from me? And I need to listen to that answerphone message you were talking about.'

Tilda went to the machine and pressed the playback button, watching Seb's face as the heavily accented voice delivered its menacing message. His expression darkened, and she could tell that he recognised the speaker. So Luke had been right, and it was Helena.

* * *

By now Luke had joined them. He stood beside Tilda with a protective arm around her shoulder.

'Seb, we've been really worried about you, not to mention the strange things that have been going on. And now you say you've lost your phone and your credit cards? How did that happen?'

'I'm actually not too sure,' replied Seb. 'I'd had quite a heavy night at the pub and decided to stay at a friend's place in the village… you know Andy, don't you, sis?'

He looked at Tilda, who replied slowly, 'You mean your old friend from the football club?' Seb nodded.

'Well, in the morning I realised that my pockets had been gone through, but I have no idea when it happened, it could 've been in the pub, or somebody might 've done it while I was asleep. But I'm positive it wasn't Andy, he's a good mate, and he was as shocked as I was, when I discovered everything was missing. Anyway, I've stopped the cards, so no harm done there, but I'm bloody angry about the phone… it was an expensive one, and I've lost a lot of important info with it. I've managed to get new cards from the bank, and I'm going to buy a new phone, but it's all a bit weird to say the least.'

Seb didn't sound at all like his usual arrogant and aggressive self. He was also clearly taken aback at finding Tilda and Luke in bed together.

Neither of them had raised the subject of Helena with Seb, but suddenly he seemed keen to talk about her.

'I guess you've been wondering who the girl on the phone was, well, at least I know that. I recognised her voice at once… it's Helena… you remember her, don't you Luke?'

Seb looked at Luke, who smiled grimly and agreed that he certainly did remember her well.

'The thing is,' continued Seb, 'she's turned out to be a bit of a troublemaker and a problem. Once the first glow of our romance had worn off, I started to realise that she wasn't being exactly straight with me… to put it mildly,' he added. 'She was very curious about our family, and always asking questions about where my relatives were from and who they were, far more than the passing interest you'd expect from a girlfriend. Then she started on about this George, and she still seems to be obsessed with him. I mean, what could she possibly want to know about him for? I just kept quiet about him. All that was ages ago, and in any case, it was all swept under the carpet, so I hardly know what it was all about, and I had nothing to tell her.'

'All what was ages ago? and was swept under the carpet?' asked Tilda sharply. 'This is complete news to me, and I haven't a clue what you're talking about. The first I've heard of a "George" is from the message that was supposed to come from you. So would you please tell me exactly what you know, and perhaps we can start working out what the hell all this is about.'

Seb stared at her. 'You mean Mum and Dad never told you about our jailbird ancestor? Well, well, they *were* being careful to preserve your innocence.'

Tilda winced at the return of the familiar, sneering tone, and her plans for vengeance resurfaced in her mind. But she stood her ground.

'I'm sure they did what they thought was best at the time, but I think it would be better if you simply told me all about this George, and whatever it is he's supposed to have done.'

But Seb's arrogant bravado proved to be just that… bravado. He had to concede that he knew little more about their ancestor, George, than that he had been imprisoned in a foreign jail several decades ago.

'Well,' declared Tilda, 'we'll just have to do some digging around, won't we? Then perhaps, we can get this wretched woman out of our lives.'

Five

'Hi Maddie,' said Tony, very relieved that she had at last answered her phone, 'it's Tony Montgomery, Bea Elsworth's nephew. My wife Chloe has had a brilliant idea, which we hope you might like too, so I'll hand the phone to her to explain.'

'Well, I…' began Maddie hesitantly, but Chloe was already in full flow. Ten minutes later the call ended, and Chloe beamed with satisfaction.

'I take it my clever wife has got it all sorted then?' asked Tony.

'Yes,' said Chloe, 'Maddie has agreed to come and look after Bea here during the day, while we go to work. She knows it's only until we can find a new care home for Bea, but, in the meantime, Bea is looked after by people she knows, and Maddie will have a paid job. So, everyone's a winner! She'll be here early tomorrow morning to help me get the spare room ready for Bea.'

'You're an absolute gem,' said Tony, 'not every wife would do this for her husband's aunt,' and he kissed her lovingly on the cheek.

Chloe suddenly remembered, 'Oh yes, Maddie told us not to forget to collect Bea's jewellery box which she thinks is kept in the safe in Mrs Jeavons' office. Maddie only knew about it because Bea always wore the key on an unusual chain round her neck, she said. But I don't remember seeing that, do you?'

'No, not at all,' replied Tony. 'But while you were talking to Maddie, I've been making plans too. I shall go to The Willows first thing tomorrow on the pretext of collecting some bits and pieces which Bea needs. While I'm in her room, I plan to make a quick inventory of her main personal belongings and take photos of as many as I can. I shall only bring away a few things like toiletries and clothes, and I'll show the staff what I've taken. Can't be too careful, you know! But I shall make no mention yet of the jewellery box. And I also shan't tell them that Bea will be coming here tomorrow, doctors permitting. Then I shall hotfoot it to Mr Abbott's office and give him the full story and the photos and inventory. Any obvious flaws in those plans?' asked Tony.

'All sounds great to me,' replied Chloe, 'but I'm not convinced that Jacob or Mrs Jeavons would agree, if they knew about all this.'

Tony and Chloe both laughed, relieved that some problems were being solved, even if others were being created.

* * *

Maddie arrived the following morning and cheerfully set about preparing the ground floor spare room for Bea. It was not ideal, but Maddie voiced determination to make Bea as comfortable as possible during her temporary stay there. She cast a practised eye over the room and, with Chloe's agreement, rearranged the furniture to make the best use of space. She placed an armchair by the window, so Bea would be able to look out at the garden.

'You know, not many people would offer to take in their old aunt the way you have,' said Maddie. 'I know it's only for the time being, but I think she's going to be so pleased to have a break from life in a home, and especially the hospital now.'

'Well, we're both very fond of her, you know,' replied Chloe, 'and we couldn't let her go back to The Willows after everything that's happened between us and Mrs Jeavons. We just can't trust her anymore.'

'Yeah, well, I could tell you a thing or two about how she runs that place, not to mention the way corners are cut there, but I'm not sure I ought to talk about it,' said Maddie nervously.

Chloe frowned.

'Of course not, if it worries you… it takes a lot of courage to be a whistle-blower, and I can understand you being afraid you won't find another job, if it gets around that you're a troublemaker. But I promise you, anything you say to me will be in the strictest confidence, and of course Tony and I will back you every inch of the way.'

Maddie looked a little uncertain but seemed about to say more, when the sound of a car arriving in the drive put an end to the conversation. It was Tony arriving back from Minchford, eager to report on his meeting with Bea's lawyer.

'He was a star, everything's going to be fine,' Tony told Chloe, who had run out to meet him and drawn him into the conservatory, where Maddie wouldn't be able to overhear them.

'Not that I don't trust her, but we don't want to risk things getting around.'

Tony nodded and began to outline his meeting with Charles Abbott.

'He says it's perfectly fine for us to take Bea in temporarily, if that's what Bea wants, and neither Jacob, should he miraculously appear, nor Sally Jeavons has any right to stop us.'

'Wonderful,' said Chloe, 'that's such a relief. You'll be impressed with how clever Maddie has been in adapting the room for Bea. It looks so comfortable and welcoming… I can't wait to get her installed.'

Tony laughed.

'I can't believe how enthusiastic you are about this… you really are a wife in a million!'

'I know,' replied Chloe modestly, then added with a smile, 'just don't forget it!'

'As if…' was Tony's rueful reply.

* * *

Bea didn't seem at all surprised when Tony told her that she was to have a holiday with him and Chloe, instead of going back to The Willows. She smiled happily, and Tony decided not to mention the decision to find a different care home for her.

Best keep it simple for now, he thought. The doctor also approved of the plan. Bea would be discharged the following day, as the test results indicated no long-term causes for concern.

'She just needs to rest,' he had said.

Well, thought Tony, as he drove away from the hospital, *it's all going well so far, but I'm not sure the visit to The Willows will be quite so easy.*

And he proved to be right.

* * *

By the time he arrived at The Willows the following morning Mrs Jeavons was aware of Bea's imminent discharge from the hospital.

'I can't agree with your high-handed actions,' exploded Mrs Jeavons, 'Bea should be coming back here, to the home she knows, and be looked after by the people she knows. Older people benefit from a regular routine, and surroundings which are familiar to them.'

Hmm… thought Tony, *and where they are able to wander out into a cold garden in a nightdress?*

'And has Bea's son agreed to her staying with you?' Mrs Jeavons was continuing.

Tony pricked up his ears at this.

'I understand your thoughts, Mrs Jeavons,' he said, 'but I'm in a hurry, and I just need to collect a few things from Bea's room. So, if you'll excuse me,' and he set off down the corridor towards her room. Mrs Jeavons pushed past him, blocking his way.

'We're in the process of sprucing the room up ready for her return,' said Mrs Jeavons, appearing flustered, 'so just tell me what you want to collect, and I'll fetch everything for you.'

But Tony was not going to be deterred, especially as he was now wondering why Mrs Jeavons clearly did not want him to go to Bea's room.

A vehemently protesting Mrs Jeavons was walking unsteadily backwards, as Tony carefully manoeuvred himself towards Bea's room. The door was wide open, and many of Bea's personal possessions were strewn across her bed. Drawers were open and shelves had been cleared.

'Well,' exclaimed Tony, 'this is a very thorough bit of sprucing up! I wonder what Bea would think of it all!'

Mrs Jeavons' irritation was clear to see, and her face was reddening. But she tried to say calmly, 'Yes, we want it all to be clean and orderly for Bea's return.'

Tony was inwardly fuming, as this was to all intents and purposes a search of the room, but why? *Who had the right to go through all of Bea's belongings like this?*

Tony abandoned all plans of surreptitiously taking photos of Bea's possessions. He brazenly took out his phone and recorded the whole scene, plus close-ups of the items all over the bed.

It could have been the scene of a burglary, he thought, as he took care to ensure that Mrs Jeavons was visible in several pictures.

'I'm sure that Bea will be really pleased that her room is being so thoroughly cleaned,' he said. 'So, I'll just find the things she needs, and you can see exactly what I take. Better still, we'll make a list and both sign it.'

Mrs Jeavons appeared stunned by Tony's actions and words, and she was unsure how to respond.

While she struggled to regain her composure, Tony asked, 'I can't see the chain Bea always wore, with a key on it… any idea where that's gone?' He was looking Mrs Jeavons intently in the eyes. 'It's just that her lawyer was asking me about it yesterday,' continued Tony, in wonderment at his ability to tell untruths, 'oh yes… he mentioned the items in your office safe too.'

Mrs Jeavons was desperate to regain the initiative but could find no way of doing this.

Finally, she said, 'I can see that you're upset by what's happened to Mrs Elsworth, we all are, so why don't you just gather up the things she'll need for her stay with you, and we'll finish sorting out her room.'

Not wanting to alienate himself from her completely at this stage, Tony agreed, and he compiled a list which they both signed. On the way to his office he called in on Mr Abbott, leaving a message about the latest developments and a copy of all the pictures, together with the list.

He felt pleased with the morning's progress, but uneasy about what Mrs Jeavons was up to.

* * *

Tony arrived home that evening to find Aunt Bea sitting in an armchair in the kitchen, with a warm blanket covering her legs, chatting to Chloe.

'It's so lovely being here,' said Bea, contentment written all over her face. 'But I'm feeling very tired, it's been an exhausting day, so I'll have an early night, I think.'

Tony kissed her gently on the cheek, and Chloe took Bea to her room and helped her get ready for bed. Tony poured himself a glass of wine and thought about recent events.

And all this was set in train because Aunt Bea mentioned Anastasia to me! he said to himself. *Suddenly our lives aren't our own anymore.* But Tony wasn't resentful in any way, and he felt increasingly protective towards his elderly aunt. He also wanted to discover the secrets surrounding the enigmatic Anastasia, and why Bea had asked him to find out more. And what was Mrs Jeavons up to? And how much contact did she have with Bea's son, Jacob?

By the time Chloe reappeared in the kitchen, Tony was even more confused about what was going on.

* * *

It soon became clear that Bea was flourishing in Maddie's care. Not only was her physical strength improving, but she had fewer dizzy spells, and her self-confidence was growing. She seemed to have forgotten The Willows.

One evening, after Maddie had gone home, she turned to Chloe and asked, 'Do you remember the chain I've always worn round my neck, the one with the key on it? Do you know where it is?'

Chloe couldn't bear to upset Bea by telling her the truth, that the key had not been among her possessions at The Willows. And she certainly wasn't going to disclose Tony's description of Bea's thoroughly searched room.

'I expect the key was put in Mrs Jeavons' office for safe keeping,' Chloe replied, playing for time. 'We'll ask her about it, so please don't worry. It must feel strange not having it, when you've been used to wearing it for so long. Was it something your late husband gave you?'

'Oh no, my dear, it was given to me by Anastasia before she disappeared. She asked me to take care of it and not to let it out of my sight. She was going away, and I wasn't to give it to anyone else until she returned. But she never did.' Bea was beginning to get agitated and looked imploringly at Chloe. 'I need to know what happened to her, and now I've let her down by losing her key. Oh dear, I don't know what I'm going to do, will it be alright do you think? I mean, what would George say, if he knew? Such an impatient man, you know, and never one to be trusted with money either. The things I could tell you. Now, where was I? I'm beginning to feel a little tired, you know… it must be all that dancing last night. But wasn't it fun? All those glittering lights and handsome young men! I did so enjoy it all…' and Bea's mind was off in a world of its own.

Chloe thought this was the perfect moment to suggest a hot bedtime drink, thereby averting any more discussion about the key.

Six

Next morning Tony and Chloe headed off early to The Willows, leaving Maddie in charge of a well-rested Bea. The key, for now at least, was forgotten.

They had arranged to meet Charles Abbott at the home, hoping that his presence would give them the confidence to confront Sally Jeavons. They were to meet him in a secluded area of the car park for a private talk before going in.

On their arrival, they noticed several vehicles parked close to the entrance. Mrs Jeavons opened the door just slightly, saying firmly that she could not speak with them today. One of the residents had died during the night, and she had many formalities to attend to. With that she closed the door, and the three visitors had no alternative but to leave.

As they were walking away, Tony muttered to Chloe, 'Well, I hope the poor old soul wasn't in her nightdress out in the garden.'

Mr Abbott also heard Tony's remark and gave him a disapproving look.

'Sorry,' said Tony, realising his indiscretion, 'but I really do wonder what goes on behind that closed door.'

In response, Mr Abbott gave him a more sympathetic look. When they reached their cars, it was beginning to rain, so they hurriedly made another arrangement to visit The Willows and left.

* * *

Late that evening Tony and Chloe were half-asleep, when the phone on the bedside table rang. Tony answered it, and at first he thought the call was not for him.

A male voice, seemingly much the worse for drink, was blurting out, 'What the hell are you doing, kidnapping my old ma? You've no right to… I'll fucking get you for this.'

By now Tony was wide awake. The caller's tone was threatening, and he was snarling as he spoke.

'Who is this?' asked Tony, trying to sound calm.

'It's your long-lost cousin, mate, who the hell d' you think it is?' responded the caller. 'Just get my ma back to The Willows, or you'll have all hell to pay…', and with that he ended the call.

By now Chloe was alert too.

'What on earth was that all about?' she asked.

'That,' replied Tony, 'was my charming cousin Jacob, I assume, complaining that we have kidnapped Bea and telling us, on pain of who knows what, to take Bea back to The Willows.'

'So how did he get our number?' wondered Chloe.

'Well,' said Tony, 'the obvious answer is from Sally Jeavons. But one other, less palatable, possibility occurs to me, and that is from Maddie. Have we been taken in by her? Was her sacking just a ploy, and we fell for the whole thing hook, line and sinker?'

Chloe was dumbfounded.

'What on earth are we going to do?' she eventually asked in a feeble voice, but Tony was looking bewildered too.

After a few moments, he said, 'We'll have to ring Mr Abbott in the morning and ask his advice', knowing that neither he nor Chloe would sleep much that night.

* * *

The following morning Chloe and Tony both found it difficult to welcome Maddie in their usual friendly way. Doubts, perhaps completely unfounded, had sprung up in their minds, and they were unable to discount them entirely. Maddie, however, cheerfully set about preparing Bea's breakfast and showed no sign of noticing their reserve.

It was a wet and unpleasant morning, and neither Chloe nor Tony felt any enthusiasm for going to work. They both knew, though, that they had taken too much time off work recently. They agreed to talk more in the evening, once their desks had been cleared of the most pressing tasks. They were also concerned that Maddie might think it odd if they lingered any longer, so they left her to give Bea her breakfast as usual and hurried out of the front door.

'I'll speak to that Jeavons woman from work,' he promised, 'and I'll let you know what she says. I don't want her trying to put us off again, so I'll tell her that Charles Abbott will be with us, and that he has one or two legal questions for her. That might worry her!'

'What about Jacob?' asked Chloe. 'Are you going to confront her about that?'

'No, I'll leave that until we're speaking face to face. I want to see her reactions, especially at knowing that we can legitimately take care of Bea's affairs.'

Tony gave Chloe a kiss, and promised to text her when he had something to report.

* * *

Eventually, after some initial reluctance from Sally Jeavons, a late afternoon meeting was arranged. Charles Abbott willingly extended his working hours, and they all met up again in the car park, before going to the front door. Tony outlined Jacob's drunken rant on the phone, and the solicitor's eyes narrowed as he listened.

'I think we'll have to tread carefully with that young man, but you really have nothing to worry about,' he said. 'Jacob hasn't been near Bea, nor shown the slightest concern for his mother for a very long time, to my knowledge, and you are entitled to handle her affairs… at her request. I don't think he can do much about the situation other than make life a bit unpleasant for you. We can always apply for a court order, if circumstances warrant that in future.'

'Let's hope it doesn't come to that,' said Chloe. 'I don't want anything to upset Bea. She seems so content being with us, that I think we should allow the present arrangement to continue for the time being.'

She didn't mention their paranoid suspicions about Maddie. In the clear light of day, they did seem rather unlikely. Maddie's concern and affection for Bea were obvious, and somehow the idea of her being in league with Jacob and Sally Jeavons didn't quite add up. Still, it would be wise to bear the possibility in mind. But they would have to leave Maddie alone with Bea for hours at a time, so without installing CCTV – an unthinkable intrusion – it would be impossible to know exactly what was going on at home.

They walked up the ramp towards the heavy front door. Chloe was several steps ahead of Tony and Mr Abbott, when a dark-coloured, low car swept past them from the direction of the staff car park at the rear of the building and turned out into the road. Both men glanced at it, and Mr Abbott said quietly to Tony, 'Well, well, I'm sure I remember Jacob Elsworth having a car something like that…'

Tony gave him a surprised look.

Chloe had reached the door and pressed the bell. A smiley young care worker showed them along to Sally Jeavons' office and knocked on the door. She pushed it open and gestured that they should go in. She excused herself and immediately went to respond to a resident's buzzer. Chloe went into the office first, closely followed by Charles Abbott and Tony, who closed the door behind him. He wanted this conversation to be private.

Chloe gasped in horror at the scene which greeted them. Sally Jeavons sat slumped in her chair behind her desk. She stared at Chloe with a contorted expression on her face. Except that those startled, staring eyes saw nothing at all. It didn't take a doctor to know that she was dead, but Chloe instinctively put out her hand to try and find a pulse in the lifeless wrist. There was nothing.

It was Charles Abbott who took control of the situation and warned them not to touch anything, while he took out his mobile to call the emergency services.

Even in death Mrs Jeavons manages to look ill-tempered and unfriendly, thought Tony. He suggested to Chloe that she go and sit in the foyer, by the front door, so that she could let the police in.

Chloe was relieved to be spared the horrendous image of Mrs Jeavons' body any longer.

* * *

Although they didn't speak to each other, it was clear to both Charles Abbott and Tony that somebody had been searching the room before or after attacking the unfortunate woman. Papers had been scattered, shelves ransacked, and the safe door was wide open. The drawers of Mrs Jeavons' desk were open and their contents scattered across the floor. Mr Abbott's phone rang. He went and stood by the window, speaking softly to the caller.

Tony was suddenly more alert. He pulled out his phone and took pictures of the inside of the safe and its remaining contents. He stopped as soon as he realised that Mr Abbott was ending his call. They both then left the office and went to sit with Chloe in the foyer, having firmly closed the office door.

They waited in an uneasy silence.

* * *

It was not long before the police arrived. Detective Sergeant Baz Underwood introduced himself and Detective Constable Rita Hussein. He quickly assessed the situation and took control. Shortly afterwards they were joined by crime scene technicians and two uniformed officers.

'Our priority at this stage,' DS Underwood explained to Chloe, Tony and Mr Abbott is to secure the crime scene and ensure that any forensic evidence is preserved.'

Chloe was ashen-faced and clearly in shock. She couldn't believe that any of this was really happening. Tony tried to be solicitous, but he felt shaken up too. Mr Abbott was putting on a professional front, but he appeared tense beneath an unconvincing exterior.

No one spoke.

A few minutes later, DC Hussein came to take their contact details. She suggested that they now leave, requesting, in an official way, that they did not discuss the "incident" with anyone.

Still bewildered, the three walked back to their cars, and Mr Abbott drove off.

Tony and Chloe sat in their car for several minutes, neither speaking. Tony took his phone out of his pocket and started scrolling through some pictures.

'What on earth are you doing?' asked Chloe, thinking that this was a highly inappropriate time to be looking at photos. Tony gently explained that he had taken some pictures in Sally Jeavons' office, while Mr Abbott was taking a call.

Chloe screeched in horror, 'What the hell were you thinking of? The poor woman was dead!'

Tony quietly explained to her. 'It suddenly occurred to me that we have no idea what Bea's jewellery box looks like. We've been assuming, or at least I have, that all this business is linked to Bea, but we don't actually know that, do we? If Bea looks at the photos and spots her own belongings still in the safe, we'd know we're barking up the wrong tree, wouldn't we? Or perhaps I'm just hoping that this murder has got nothing to do with any of us. Anyway, we must get back, as Maddie should be going home by now. And we mustn't mention the "incident", as DC Hussein said. So put on your bravest face.'

Before starting the car, though, Tony looked across at Chloe and said hesitantly, 'There's just one other thing you should know. You remember the car leaving just as we arrived? Well, Mr Abbott thought he recalled Jacob having one just like it.'

The following day DC Hussein took statements from Tony and Chloe at Tony's office, as neither wanted the police coming to their home and being seen by either Bea or Maddie. The interviews were as they expected, until DC Hussein started asking questions about the shoes they had been wearing yesterday. One important piece of evidence had been found in Mrs Jeavons' office, she explained, namely a shoe-print besmirched with blood.

Seven

Seb, Tilda and Luke were sitting round the kitchen table drinking coffee and munching buttered muffins. Nothing more had been said between them about 'George', but all of them had been thinking about him.

Tilda could now wait no longer and said, 'Come on then, Seb, have you remembered any more about jailbird George? It all sounds decidedly far-fetched to me. Are you having us on?' Tilda's heart sank as her phone then rang, and the opportunity to get Seb to open up seemed lost.

'Oh hi, Mum,' she said, 'what's happening with you and Dad? When are you coming home?' While she was talking, she slipped out of the kitchen and shut the door behind her.

Several minutes later she returned and was met with expectant looks from Seb and Luke.

'Well?' they asked in unison.

Tilda was not going to be rushed, though. She sat down and sipped some coffee.

'There are so many odd things going on,' she began. 'Life in this family used to be so straightforward and boring, but now it's full of confusion, or that's how it feels to me.'

She buttered another muffin and took a bite.

'Anyway, Dad apparently fell, twisted his ankle quite badly

and hit his head on the edge of a low wall, as they were going down a long flight of wide steps. They'd been on a visit to an opera house on an evening shore trip, according to Mum. They were going down all these steps, along with dozens of other people, to get back to their ship. When they were part way down, Dad suddenly fell diagonally forwards. He swears blind that he was pushed deliberately from behind. There were apparently masses of people going up and down the steps, and Mum is adamant that it was all just an unfortunate accident, and Dad simply missed his footing in the general pushing and shoving. But I'm not so sure. Dad's not someone to make up something like that. I'm getting quite freaked out by all these strange events in our family.'

Luke leaned across the table and took her hand. 'So, when are they coming home?' he asked.

'They hope that the doctors will allow him to fly home in the next two or three days,' replied Tilda, 'but they're being extra cautious as it was a hefty knock to his head, and he has a nasty gash apparently. Mum will ring again before they leave.'

Seb didn't respond to what Tilda had been saying.

So Luke said brightly, 'Well, at least we know now what's happened and when they're coming home, so that's progress, isn't it?'

Tilda smiled, well aware that Luke was only trying to cheer her up.

* * *

Seb quietly got up from his chair, pushed aside his half-drunk coffee, and called to Zeus to go for a walk. Zeus eagerly went and sat by the back door, tail wagging, so Seb grabbed a jacket and the two of them went out.

He wandered aimlessly in the nearby woods, occasionally tossing a stick for Zeus to fetch. But his mind was racing, and he admitted to himself that recent events had unnerved him. *Had he really misjudged Helena so completely? Who was she?* He had been so proud of being seen with her, aware that several of his friends were jealous of their relationship. So he had just overlooked her strange questions about his family, excusing them on the grounds of their coming from different cultures.

But threads were beginning to unravel in his mind suddenly. And the more he thought about her behaviour with him, the more phoney the relationship felt. Seb was feeling stupid, angry at how naïve he had been, furious at how he had been totally duped by Helena, and yet still sad that their relationship was over. He had had such high hopes and fantasy-driven plans, but they were now all shattered. He had flunked his exams because of the priority he had given to Helena, so perhaps his future in the family business might be in jeopardy too. He hadn't yet told his dad that he had to go back to university to retake his final exams.

Seb was beginning to think of himself as a complete failure, and he was slipping into self-pity. He sat on a fallen tree trunk, feeling very sorry for himself. Zeus trotted over and put his head in Seb's lap.

'Well, at least I have one faithful friend,' he told the dog, and rubbed Zeus's head affectionately. A few minutes later Seb suddenly recalled what Tilda had said about their dad's fall, and his thoughts changed tack. Like Tilda, he didn't believe that his dad would have imagined a deliberate shove in the back. His dad was well built and fit, not a man who could easily be pushed over, even when going down steps. Seb wasn't prone to conspiracy theories, but he was now wondering if he had been targeted for some reason by Helena. *But surely it wasn't something spreading through his family like a pernicious disease, was it? And what was it all about anyway?*

Seb decided that he would swallow his pride and have an honest talk with Tilda, and probably Luke too. So he called Zeus, and they set off back home.

* * *

The scene which greeted Seb, as he walked into the kitchen, was one of purposeful activity.

'You OK?' asked Tilda. Seb just nodded and took Zeus back out into the porch to clean his muddy paws.

Tilda called out through the open door, 'Luke and I thought we ought to make a start on making the house look more presentable. I don't think Mum would be very impressed with its state at the moment.'

No response from Seb, but he soon appeared again and said, 'How can I help?'

Tilda swallowed her amazement and avoided catching Luke's eye.

'Well, if you don't mind loading the dishwasher, that would be great... thanks, Seb,' and she gave her brother a genuine smile, the first in a long time.

By late afternoon the whole house looked fairly respectable, so they all went and sat in the deckchairs on the lawn, each with a glass of beer in hand.

* * *

'I reckon that was pretty good teamwork,' said Luke, fearing a tricky silence, and the other two nodded in agreement.

Seb decided that this was the right moment to tackle a difficult conversation.

'While I was out with Zeus this morning,' he began, 'I did a lot of thinking. I know that I've behaved abysmally towards both of you for quite a long time, and I'm very sorry.'

Tilda could hardly believe her ears, but she let Seb continue uninterrupted.

'For ages I was besotted with that deceitful bitch Helena, and my life was totally consumed by her demands. I was completely taken in by her, and I actually thought we loved each other. But looking back on it all, and thinking about things that have happened since, I realise that her only interest was in this character called George, who I know virtually nothing about. I don't know why she's obsessed with him, whoever he is, but now it all feels horribly sinister. What's worse is that other members of this family are being dragged into it all. I really don't know what to do.'

'Perhaps,' ventured Luke, 'we should all put our cards on the table and say everything we know about the Helena and George situations, so that we all look at things from the same starting point. What do you reckon?'

So Tilda, Luke and Seb all voiced their different thoughts and speculation. Although they were no closer to establishing the reason for Helena's interest in the family, or one (presumably deceased) member of it, nevertheless a feeling of trust was building between them and a wish to support each other. 'George' remained an enigma, but Luke, Seb and Tilda started competing in concocting ever more improbable versions of his history. So, with all of them now feeling relaxed, they decided to go to the pub for an evening snack, rather than mess up the clean kitchen.

After the meal, they were wandering back home, when Luke announced that he would be leaving the following day.

'But you can't,' whimpered Tilda, 'I need you here.'

'Don't worry,' said Luke, 'I'll keep in touch and see you again soon. But I don't think your parents would take very kindly to knowing how close we are, or that I've been staying here while Seb wasn't around.'

Tilda knew that Luke was right, but she didn't like the idea. Only one more night with Luke sleeping next to her in her bed.

* * *

The following day Luke set off back to London, leaving a distraught Tilda behind. Seb was less bothered by Luke's departure, but he tried to cheer his sister up by offering to prepare their lunch.

Another first, thought Tilda, wondering how long her brother would maintain this new persona.

Their mother had rung earlier that morning to say that they would be returning tomorrow, as Dad was making good progress and now had the doctor's permission to fly.

So over lunch Tilda asked Seb what they should tell their parents about the Helena and George situation, and all the texts. As there had been no further texts, and Seb had heard nothing more from Helena, he was adamant that they need not tell their parents anything of the whole saga. So it was agreed to give the impression that all was well and that nothing out of the ordinary had happened in their parents' absence. They would focus on the cruise and Dad's accident.

* * *

That afternoon Tilda was pulling the most noticeable weeds out of the herbaceous border, feeling guilty that she'd done little gardening recently, and Seb was lounging in a deckchair, purportedly preparing for his studies next term. Tilda was sceptical about this, but something else was at the forefront of her mind.

'How well did you know Luke at uni?' she called across to Seb.

'Not very,' replied her brother.

'Odd that he remembered your address and just turned up here then, wasn't it?' Tilda continued.

'Hmm... suppose so,' said Seb.

They each returned to the task in hand. By now Tilda's brain was in overdrive.

But her thoughts were interrupted by Seb saying, 'You seem to be looking for conspiracy theories, so here's another that hasn't been mentioned... my first date with Helena was actually set up by Luke and his mate, Josh. I thought then that it was strange that neither of them wanted to go out with her, because everyone could see she was gorgeous, but they both had girlfriends, I suppose. Whoops, sorry sis, but you ought to hear the truth. It was Luke's girlfriend who actually knew Helena. But I'm sure I heard that Luke had dumped Mishka ages ago,' he added quickly.

Both Seb and Tilda were reddening in the face now. Tilda dropped the garden fork and ran into the house, while Seb watched her, shame-faced. She picked up her phone and tried to call Luke, but there was no connection.

Eight

By now Sally Jeavons' lifeless body had been removed from The Willows. Not surprisingly the murder had had far-reaching consequences for the home. Several of the staff had immediately resigned, and some of the residents had been moved elsewhere by their relatives. When they realised this, Tony and Chloe quickly went back to The Willows to collect all of Bea's belongings. They packed everything in her room into boxes and bags.

'I'm just going to see if Bea had any secret hiding places for things she treasured,' said Chloe, 'not that there can be many in this small room... but it's worth a try.' And she was right.

In the bathroom there were three new toilet rolls on a low shelf. Chloe carefully looked at each of them and noticed that one had something pushed down its cardboard centre. She extracted a beautiful gold ring, set with an emerald and two diamonds, wrapped in tissue paper.

'Wow,' exclaimed Chloe, 'let's look further!' But the bathroom revealed no more secrets.

'OK,' said Chloe, 'let's look under the mattress and any other possible nooks and crannies.'

After several minutes of fruitless searching Tony suddenly yelled, 'Eureka! bull's eye!'

On the window sill there were several indoor plants in pots, all looking in need of water. The pots were sitting on colourful deep saucers. Under one pot, in the curve of the saucer, Tony found a small flat package neatly wrapped in plastic, which turned out to contain Bea's missing chain and key.

'Well, isn't she the clever one!' exclaimed Tony, smiling broadly. 'Well done, Bea, you fooled everyone!'

'So,' said Chloe, also feeling pleased with their finds, 'all we need now is Bea's jewellery box.'

They both felt apprehensive about going into Sally Jeavons' office again, so they decided to put all the bags and boxes into their car first.

'You do realise, don't you,' began Chloe, 'that we still don't know exactly what we're looking for? Bea didn't recognise anything in your photos of the safe.'

Tony didn't reply, but he put his arm around Chloe's shoulder and ushered her towards the front door again. It soon became clear, though, that Mrs Jeavons' office remained off limits to everyone. The police 'crime scene' tape still hung from the door handle. So Tony and Chloe decided to retreat and ask Charles Abbott to deal with the retrieval of Bea's jewellery box. They could now at least compare Tony's photos with all the items from Bea's room and perhaps discover if anything else had gone missing.

* * *

On the journey home Tony and Chloe agreed to ask Bea and Maddie to sort out the contents of the boxes and bags. They decided, though, to keep quiet about having found the key. They were still unsure who had disclosed their phone number to Jacob, so they agreed to say nothing about the key to either Maddie or Charles Abbott. Bea hadn't mentioned the key recently, so perhaps she had forgotten about it for now.

The most worrying issue for Tony and Chloe was Jacob, and where he fitted into all this. Perhaps he knew their address and could turn up on the doorstep at any time. Both Tony and Chloe found this prospect alarming. And there was the safety of Bea and Maddie to consider too.

'I feel as though I'm in a quicksand,' said Chloe despondently. 'Apart from you and Bea, I don't know who I can trust, or what on earth is going on. Life used to be so much simpler.' She gave a deep, heartfelt sigh.

'Right,' said Tony after a moment's thought, 'what we need is a treat. So at the weekend we'll take Bea for a day at the coast, have a good blow in the sea air, eat fish and chips on the promenade, in true English fashion, and just enjoy ourselves… how about that?'

'Sounds brilliant,' replied Chloe with a laugh, her spirits momentarily lifted by the thought.

* * *

The next weekend everything went according to Tony's plan. Nothing further was heard from the police, nor from Jacob. Mr Abbott had agreed to retrieve Bea's jewellery box from The Willows, but there had been no word from him either. Bea was thriving in Maddie's care, and she made no mention of her former home, nor the key and chain, nor of Anastasia. Chloe, in particular, was grateful for a return to calm in their daily lives.

Long may this last, she thought.

But the murder at The Willows had inevitably hit the local news media.

Chloe was dozing in front of the television, after a fraught day at work, when her attention was abruptly caught by an announcement of the arrest of a suspect in the case of the recent murder in Minchford, and there, before Chloe's eyes, was a picture of The Willows. The suspect was not named.

Thankfully Bea was in bed, and Maddie had gone home. But Chloe wished that Tony was there with her, as the sudden reminder of Sally Jeavons' violent death and her staring, unseeing eyes, sent shivers down her spine.

She got up and went to check that both the front and back doors were locked. She wasn't sure what time Tony would be home. He had rung to say that he unexpectedly had to attend an evening meeting, but he would try not to be too late. 'So, don't wait for me… you go ahead and have your supper,' he had suggested.

Chloe was about to follow Tony's advice, when she heard Bea's little bell ringing insistently from across the hallway. She found Bea sitting up in bed looking anxious.

'I'm so sorry to bother you, my dear, but I'm really thirsty. Could you possibly make me a cup of tea? I don't remember whether Maddie gave me one before she left.'

Chloe smiled reassuringly. 'Yes, of course, I'll bring you one straightaway, and what's more I wouldn't mind a cup myself.'

Chloe was grateful for some company at the moment, albeit company that wasn't always on the ball. But Bea proved to be having one of her more lucid phases.

Sitting comfortably in her bed, sipping tea, Bea suddenly said, 'I've been thinking a lot lately about Anna and her key.'

Chloe nearly dropped her cup in surprise, murmured a non-committal reply and looked enquiringly at Bea.

'Yes,' continued Bea, 'she told me that all the family's wealth was in a bank vault in Oslo, I think it was. She said it was valuable jewellery, and it must never fall into the wrong hands. Now I've let her down by losing the key… I shall never forgive myself. What can I do?'

Chloe did some quick thinking. She must somehow reassure Bea, but it might be risky to explain that they now had the key, in case she let this slip to Maddie. Chloe later admitted to Tony that she felt badly about the deceit, but she had thought it would put Bea's mind at rest to believe that the key was in safe keeping with her lawyer.

However, this ploy did not have the intended effect. Bea became quite agitated, saying, 'Oh, but my dear, I wouldn't be too sure about Charles. He's been giving me some very strange advice recently, and he even wanted me to cut Jacob out of my will. I know he's been a wild boy, and he certainly hasn't been the best of sons to me in my old age, but I couldn't possibly disinherit him, could I? Charles was trying to get me to sign a new will… something about leaving everything in trust to The Willows, because I was already in debt to them and have little money left. Well, that didn't sound quite right to me, and I said I would have to think about it. Then he started asking me about Anna, and had I remembered anything more about her strange disappearance? He was quite persistent, so you see, my dear, I don't think he is at all the right person to be looking after the key. No, no… not at all the right person.'

Her voice trailed off, and the fog descended again. Frustratingly, Bea had become sleepy and confused, so Chloe reluctantly settled her once more for the night and quietly left the room.

* * *

Tony was tired and hungry when he arrived home, and he eagerly ate the chicken casserole which Chloe now shared with him. The meal over and coffee made, Chloe judged that the strained look had left Tony's face, and now was the time to tell him about her conversation with Bea.

'But how on earth do we find out which bank in Oslo, or whether a second key is needed to open this mysterious box?' she concluded her story with a question.

'The point is too,' added Tony, 'are we the ones entitled to open it, and who on earth do we trust to give us advice on this?'

Chloe thought for a moment, then said, 'Suppose we act as if we have complete confidence in Charles Abbott and play along with his advice that you have charge of Bea's affairs. Of course, you would never cut Jacob totally out of the picture, but Abbott doesn't know that, and he may even think he has you in his pocket. Then we could make some enquiries about Norwegian banks and maybe take a mini-break to Oslo to do a recce. In fact,' Chloe was warming to her idea, 'I really fancy a trip away. I think we could trust Maddie to look after Bea for a couple of days and nights, and we need never say where we're going.'

A smile spread over Tony's face. 'What a devious woman I married,' he laughed, 'who would have thought it?'

'But you do think it's a good idea, don't you?' persisted Chloe.

'Brilliant,' agreed Tony.

A thought suddenly struck Chloe. 'I quite forgot… they said on the News tonight that they have arrested a suspect for Sally Jeavons' murder. With everything else it quite slipped my mind. But they didn't say who it was.'

'Well,' said Tony, 'I think we need to find out as soon as we can, as it might put a different complexion on the whole business. After all, I can't think of many possible suspects, unless of course it's somebody completely unconnected with Bea, and it's all just a horrible coincidence.'

'I'm not sure I believe in coincidences,' said Chloe. 'I think it has to be connected in some way, and if it isn't Jacob, then it must be Charles Abbott.'

'Or, at a stretch, it could just be Maddie… ' suggested Tony.

* * *

In the end, it was none of these. Next morning Maddie arrived as usual for her caring duties, full of the news she had picked up on social media.

'Have you heard?' she was bursting to share it with Chloe and Tony, 'they've arrested a man on suspicion of old Mrs Jeavons' murder. He's not from around here though… they say his name is Sebastian Dean.'

Nine

Luke sat at the table in his tiny London flat wrestling with his conscience. He knew that he had treated Tilda shabbily, and he regretted this. He thought that she would probably be trying to contact him, and understandably so, but he had resolved to remain incommunicado until he had sorted out his thoughts. Luke didn't feel particularly guilty about the sex with Tilda, although she was several years younger than he was, as he knew that there was a strong mutual attraction, and they genuinely enjoyed each other's company.

It was the deceit that bothered his conscience more. The story about his aunt's funeral had been complete fabrication. He hadn't remembered where Seb's home was. They hadn't been close friends at uni, so why would he know that? The past had caught up with him in a very different way.

A few weeks previously, out of the blue, Luke had received a text message which simply said, "Get me the details or M will pay". Luke had hoped that Helena's menacing demands would cease once they had all left university for the summer vacation. He had never fathomed what they were all about anyway. Something to do with Seb's family, it seemed. *So why did he, Luke, have to be involved?* His only explanation was that Helena, having herself got no useful information out of Seb, thought that he would be more cooperative, especially if told that Mishka would suffer, if he did not provide the "details" she wanted.

So, during the final weeks of term Luke had received similar messages. He had steered clear of places where he thought he might meet Helena, and he had texted non-committal replies. But Luke was disturbed not only by Helena's emotional blackmail. He was also struggling with his conscience about how he had treated Mishka. *She, like Tilda, had deserved better from him… or had she?*

Luke got up from the table and made himself a coffee. Perhaps some caffeine would help clarify his thoughts. He went and half-lay on the narrow sofa bed, propped up by some drab cushions. *His room at uni had been more comfortable than this,* he thought, but London prices would allow him no luxury, and hopefully he could not easily be found.

A few mouthfuls of strong, black coffee and Luke was back contemplating his relationship with beguiling Mishka. He had never met anyone like her before. She was a stunning-looking young woman, but it was also her heavily accented voice, her infectious laugh and her seductive manner which had immediately attracted Luke. He had been drinking a beer alone in the students' bar, waiting for his friend Josh, when Mishka sat on the bar stool next to him and ordered a glass of champagne. This caught Luke's attention. Not many students could afford champagne, and the bartender was also surprised.

'Why don't I buy one for you too…' she asked an astonished Luke, 'and then we can toast a new friendship perhaps?'

At the time Luke could hardly believe his luck but, with hindsight, he wished that he had not allowed himself to be hooked so easily. Even now he could not understand how she had been able to change his life so completely, so quickly. Looking back on it, he realised that their relationship had always been on her terms, when and where they met, all was dictated by her. But at the time, Luke now accepted, he had felt flattered, and sex with her was just mind-blowing.

Another gulp of coffee and Luke came to acknowledge that all this was precisely mirrored by Seb's relationship with Helena, and Luke had been positively scornful of that. The biggest difference was that Seb and Helena were open about their being together, whereas Mishka, apart from her first approach to Luke in the students' bar, imposed a discreetness which meant they were almost always alone. She disclosed very little about her family, if she had any, nor anything about her past life. But initially Luke didn't worry about this… he was simply swept ecstatically along, and her company was all he craved.

Very soon, though, Mishka started asking him questions about Sebastian Dean, whom she knew was also in the sailing club. She seemed to assume that Luke and Seb were good friends, even though Luke told her that he and Seb barely knew each other. A pattern also emerged of Mishka not understanding Luke's questions whenever he queried why she wanted to know things.

Luke drank the dregs of his coffee and wandered round the small room.

He felt uneasy as Seb and Tilda suddenly came to the forefront of his mind again. He thought back to the drama of returning to the Deans' house and telling Tilda about the first mysterious text, purportedly from Seb. Luke had been severely shaken by receiving the text, and the subsequent ones, but he had also been deceitful in not revealing his knowledge of some history to all this. He had gone along with events in the present, playing the part of a bewildered innocent. He now admitted to himself that he hadn't really cared what happened to Seb, the arrogant, self-centred bastard. Luke was by then more interested in Seb's sister. He now feared, though, that he had completely undermined any further friendship with her. *And who could blame her?* he asked himself.

Luke stood looking out of the window at an uninspiring scene of parked cars and the occasional dog-walker, a fresh cup of coffee in his hand. His thoughts returned to Mishka, damn her. He didn't seem to own his mind. Random, unwelcome memories swirled about in uncontrollable confusion.

Suddenly a picture of Helena emerged with her condescendingly smiling face and alluring manner. *And she was the reason,* Luke now acknowledged, *that Mishka had given a convincing impression of being interested in him.* He had been lured into becoming an intermediary between two manipulative, callous young women and his fellow student, Seb. As far as Luke could work out, the only connection had been the sailing club, which felt to him like a very tenuous link. But the upshot had been that Luke had fixed up a date between Seb and Helena. Once that was achieved, Luke was of no further interest to Mishka, and she glided almost imperceptibly out of his life. Obviously, Luke gave the impression that he had dumped Mishka, but in reality his pride was very hurt. And somehow she had left him feeling that he was the guilty one.

There was one more twist of the knife to come, though.

Luke recalled how he had cycled to the cinema on the far side of town, not long after last seeing Mishka. He had arranged to meet his friend Josh at a cheap restaurant near the cinema before going to see a film. He was waiting under the awning overhanging the restaurant's entrance, when he noticed someone standing about fifty meters away on the opposite pavement.

It was the coat which caught his eye first. He sidled back against the wall, partially hidden by an advertising board. He looked across at the woman again but couldn't see her face clearly. The coat was unmistakable. Mishka's clothes were invariably flamboyant and idiosyncratic. But the colour and style of this woman's hair were nothing like Mishka's. This young woman had short, straight auburn hair in a geometric style, whereas Mishka had shoulder-length light brown curls. And this woman was wearing spectacles. Luke wondered if he was imagining things, but he decided to take a closer look, if he could, without being spotted. The woman was clearly waiting for a lift, as she peered at every passing car.

There was no sign of Josh yet, so Luke pulled up his hood and strolled casually along the pavement. When he was some distance past her, he crossed the road and walked slowly back towards her, keeping his eyes fixed on the pavement. He stepped back into a doorway, pretending to tie his shoelaces. From there he looked at the woman again, by now certain that it was indeed a transformed Mishka. Just then an expensive-looking car drew up, a short distance from Mishka and the crouching Luke. A man, seemingly several years older, got out and came round to open the passenger door for her. They hugged briefly and spoke a few words to each other. Luke could hardly believe his ears. Mishka, or her double, was speaking in faultless English, with no hint of her usual foreign accent and gravelly tones.

Luke quickly got out his phone and took some pictures of the man and Mishka about to get into the car. He feared that at any moment they might notice what he was doing, but luckily they were absorbed in each other and soon drove off. Luke decided that he would enlarge the pictures on his laptop, just to be certain that it was indeed Mishka. He felt totally bewildered. *What on earth was she up to? Why had she changed her appearance, apart from her coat, so dramatically? And what explained the perfect English and complete lack of a foreign accent?*

Just then Luke received a text from Josh. He was sorry, but he couldn't get to the restaurant as arranged. Luke felt relieved and decided not to go to the film. He had a lot to think about, especially when the pictures later confirmed that the auburn-haired woman was definitely Mishka.

Recalling these memories now, in his claustrophobic London flat, was an emotional rollercoaster for Luke. Suddenly a metaphorical light bulb flashed in his mind.

Hang on a minute, he thought aloud, *this all started with me bashing myself up for treating Mishka badly… that's absolute rubbish. I'm the one who has been taken for a complete ride! It was all a set-up and she just used me. It's obvious that she's never cared about me! And now Helena is still trying to embroil me in some murky business that I know nothing about… and she's using Mishka as a bargaining chip, thinking she can stir up my old feelings. Well, it ain't going to work!*

At that moment Luke felt a surge of determination. *No more feeling that things were always his fault, no more finding plausible excuses for Mishka's deviousness, no more regrets that their relationship had ended, and, perhaps most importantly, no more involvement in whatever Helena and Mishka were doing. He would take immediate, decisive action, and firstly he would ditch his phone. He would buy another and be very careful who he let access the number. He felt confident that no one knew his London address, which was a relief.*

Ironically, his phone then pinged. Luke shoved it under a cushion, grabbed his jacket and went out to fulfil his first objective, to buy a new phone.

As he was getting on the bus, Luke suddenly thought, *I wonder if that was Tilda trying to contact me?* It came back to him, with a jolt, that he really wanted to rescue that relationship somehow, if he possibly could.

But first things first, a new phone must be bought.

Ten

Tilda was feeling utterly miserable. Nothing was going right. Luke's phone was always turned off, and she was having to come to terms with the end of her first real relationship. And her wretched brother had reverted to his old ways, just when she thought that she and Seb were beginning to get on better and her plans for exacting vengeance were gradually receding. He had not been home for the past two nights, and she had no idea where he was. Her parents didn't seem bothered, going off to work each day, still chatting cheerfully about their cruise. Her dad's fall seemed to have been forgotten. Tilda felt lonely.

Suddenly a text came through on her phone, and she didn't recognise the number.

'Black Horse noon today. Don't call back. S.'

Tilda's heart sank. *Not more mysterious texts,* she thought with a sigh, *I can't take much more of this. But I'll have to go, in case it really is Seb and he's in trouble.*

The Black Horse was only a couple of miles away, so Tilda cycled there, arriving a few minutes before noon. As she was locking her bike, Seb emerged from the wooded area adjoining the pub's garden looking dishevelled and pale-faced.

'Thanks for coming, sis,' he said quietly and gave her a fleeting hug.

Tilda was very surprised. It was clear that Seb was in a bad way, so she took control of the situation.

'Go and sit at that table under the trees, and I'll get you some food and a drink,' said Tilda, hoping that she had enough money to cover this. Luckily she did, as long as Seb would be satisfied with egg and chips. She carried their drinks out into the garden.

Seb clearly hadn't shaved, brushed his hair or changed his clothes for the last couple of days. He looked drawn and almost pitiable. Tilda let him take his time.

He suddenly broke the silence and blurted out, 'I was arrested, sis, I was questioned at a police station, I was in a cell…' He appeared to be on the verge of tears. Tilda couldn't believe what she was hearing, but she sensed that Seb meant every word.

'What on earth was that all about?' she asked, flabbergasted.

'Some murder at an old folks' home apparently, miles away from here in Minchford,' responded Seb, trying to hold his emotions together. 'I kept asking why they thought I had anything to do with it, but they never gave me straight answers. They just said that they had reason to believe that I could assist with their enquiries. They made me feel totally guilty, even though I didn't know what the hell they were on about. They said they'd had an anonymous tip-off which had put my name in the frame, and they were following this up. It's all completely crazy… I don't know what to do…'

The barman was coming across the garden with Seb's food, so the conversation ceased.

Seb had clearly not eaten for a while, and it didn't take him long to clear the plate.

'Have we got enough money between us for a couple of coffees?' asked Tilda hopefully. Seb emptied his pockets and pushed the coins towards his sister.

'I need this,' said Tilda a few minutes later, clutching a large mug of strong coffee.

'Me too,' replied Seb, 'I'm sick of police station tea.'

'Well,' said Tilda, 'tell me more. Have they finished interrogating you, or have you got to go back sometime?'

'They just said that they would contact me again if their enquiries indicate they need to. Not really very reassuring, is it?'

Tilda's mind was beginning to clear, now that the initial shock was past.

'And were there no clues, in what they said to you, about where this anonymous tip-off had come from?' she asked. 'Why did they think you had a connection with an old folks' home? You haven't had truck with the police before, which I don't know about, have you?'

'Hey, hang on, sis,' interrupted Seb, 'whose side are you on? No, of course I haven't been in trouble with the police, and no, I've never been questioned like that before. They were doing a good cop, bad cop routine, and kept trying to throw me off balance in what I was saying. And I was getting so tired, but they just kept banging on. They didn't give anything away, though. Every now and again they'd slip something in which seemed totally irrelevant.'

'Like what?' asked Tilda.

'Well, at one point they suddenly said, "tell us about the Milstroms", and I had no idea what they were talking about,' said Seb.

'Hmm,' replied Tilda after a few moments' thought, 'I could be wrong, but wasn't Grandma Lisbet's maiden name Milstrom?'

Seb looked completely taken aback and disheartened. Perhaps there was a connection with him after all.

'Come on, sis, let's go home. I need to get clean before Mum and Dad arrive back from work, and then we can talk some more. But can we agree not to tell them about all this just yet?'

Tilda nodded uncertainly, feeling that their parents were bound to hear the saga at some stage.

* * *

They arrived home to find that their father was already back from work, sitting in the garden with his newspaper, enjoying the late afternoon sun. He smiled in greeting, but his eyes narrowed slightly as he took in Seb's unkempt appearance. He said nothing, though, as Seb disappeared into the house with a muttered excuse, and simply gestured to Tilda, inviting her to sit in the deckchair beside him. He folded his paper and looked inquiringly at Tilda.

'So, tell me what you and Sebastian have been getting up to while your mother and I were gallivanting around the Baltic.'

Tilda started guiltily, but she quickly recovered her composure and said, 'Not a lot really, just enjoying country life, walking Zeus, gardening, going to the pub with friends… you know the sort of thing.'

'That sounds rather dull for two sociable young people. I'm glad you found things to keep you amused anyway, and I meant to say before, that your mother and I are really grateful to you for looking after the house and garden so well… we half expected to come back and find you'd been enjoying wild parties in our absence. No, don't worry, I'm only joking,' he hastily added, as Tilda tried to look indignant. 'That wretched accident was a real nuisance, and we felt very bad about leaving you in the lurch for so long like that.'

'Please don't worry about it, Dad, I'm just glad it wasn't anything worse, and that you've recovered so quickly. It could have turned out very differently. Somebody must have been very impatient to have jostled you like that, mustn't they?' Tilda tried to sound casual, hoping that her father would tell her more about it.

However, he didn't take the bait and merely replied, 'That whole trip was very badly managed. There were too many people trying to get back to the boat at once, and it should never have been allowed. In fact, I've written a letter of complaint to the tour operators, but they'll probably try to wriggle out of it. After all, they won't want to admit any kind of liability in case I decide to claim compensation… a lot of people would.'

Tilda thought for a moment and then, taking a deep breath, tried a more direct approach. 'Mum said you thought somebody deliberately pushed you… is that right?'

'Oh, did she indeed?' Her father looked annoyed. 'I thought we'd agreed that I probably imagined the whole thing after having that bump on the head… can't think why she decided to tell you that.'

'Well, she hasn't said anything since you got home.' Tilda was anxious to downplay her mother's part in this. 'She told me about it when she phoned just after the accident, so she was probably still feeling very shocked. Do you really think you imagined a hard shove?'

Her father sighed. 'To be honest, Tilda, I don't know. It's all rather hazy now, so I really can't be sure. I only know that, at the time, I thought that someone shoved me hard deliberately, but the more I think about it the less sure I am.'

There was silence for a few moments, while Tilda and her father were each lost in their own thoughts. Suddenly Martin asked his daughter a question which took her completely unawares.

'Tilda, do you know anything about a place called Minchford?'

Tilda couldn't hide her shock. For the second time today she'd heard the name of this place. And the first time had concerned her brother being questioned about a murder. Tilda tried to camouflage her confusion, pretending that she'd just been stung on the neck by an insect. Martin was not fooled, but he let the moment pass. At some point Tilda would probably let the truth, whatever it was, slip out.

'It's just,' continued Martin, 'that shortly before your mum and I left for the cruise, I had a letter, completely out of the blue, from a solicitor in Minchford. He was asking all sorts of strange questions about the Montgomery side of my family, and particularly about a chap called George. I knew that a George had existed, but I never met him or had anything to do with that part of the family. I would guess that he died a long time ago. Strange, isn't it? I meant to write back to this solicitor chap, but, what with one thing and another, I put his letter to one side and all but forgot about it until now. But I suppose I really ought to contact him… Abbott, I think his name was… and find out more about what he wants. What do you think, Tilda?'

By now Tilda was feeling thoroughly confused. *None of this seemed to make any sense nor to have any connection with what had been going on with her, Seb and Luke. And yet the name George kept cropping up, and somebody seemed very determined to get hold of information about him.* It all felt uncomfortably coincidental and ominous to Tilda.

She nodded distractedly in response to her father's question, but she was suddenly startled out of her thoughts by her father saying, 'So what's been going on with Sebastian while we've been away? He looks like a young man with the cares of the world on his shoulders. I don't suppose he's in any kind of trouble, is he?'

Tilda felt her face beginning to colour, but mercifully she was saved from answering by the arrival of Zeus, who launched himself at her, slobbering all over her. Never had she felt so pleased to see him, as she made great play of being annoyed.

'Now look what you've done, you daft dog… you've put dirty paws all over my T-shirt, and I shall have to go and wash my face now, you repulsive animal.' She leapt thankfully to her feet and, with an apologetic shrug at her father, headed for the house.

Martin watched his daughter's retreating figure thoughtfully. He hadn't been deceived by her little charade. He was now convinced that his children were concealing something significant from him. For some reason, he felt a sense of foreboding.

Eleven

Tony needed time to think. He left work earlier than usual and took himself to Minchford library. He wanted to do some internet searching. He had no experience of bank vaults or safe deposit boxes and wanted to research them before his next conversation with Chloe. Whilst he had not discouraged her enthusiasm for a trip to Oslo, he was not convinced that it would achieve anything. They needed to know what they were looking for.

His searches gave Tony more concerns. He was left wondering whether the box was still in existence, as apparently such boxes are used infrequently nowadays. And who had been paying any rental fees or insurance for the goods in storage, whatever they were? Tony calculated that the box must have been there for many decades, or possibly the best part of a century, if Bea's aunt, Anastasia, was the original owner. He had no documents relating to the box and no proof of a legitimate interest in it, just a key, which might, or might not, fit the lock. It all seemed like a hopeless case to him.

And on top of this, Chloe was suggesting that they should be wary of Charles Abbott, as they had no way of knowing, at present, how he fitted into the whole situation. Tony was also unsure how reliable poor old Aunt Bea's memory was. He was beginning to despair.

But there were other matters on Tony's mind too. He was becoming concerned about how long the current arrangements could continue. Chloe, Bea and Maddie all assumed that Bea would simply remain in their home, as she was obviously content there and Maddie cared for her so well. Whilst Tony was pleased to give his aunt a home for the time being, two things in particular bothered him.

Firstly, Charles Abbott had talked about his having responsibility for Bea's affairs, but Tony had no access to her finances. *Was she really in debt to The Willows, as Bea thought Mr Abbott had said? Who actually had control of her money now?* These thoughts worried Tony, as he and Chloe could not afford to keep paying Maddie's wages indefinitely without a financial contribution from Bea.

His second concern was Jacob. He had not forgotten his threatening phone call. *How had Jacob located him, if the call genuinely was from him?*

On top of these worries, Tony still had occasional flashbacks to the horrific scene in Sally Jeavons' office, when they had discovered her body.

But he forced his mind back into the present, glanced around his surroundings in the library, and tried to focus on finding solutions to the problems facing him. His mental turmoil continued, though. He glanced at his watch and decided to go home, but to keep quiet about how he had spent the last hour. He needed more time to think it all through.

* * *

Chloe opened the front door as soon as she heard his car.

'Where on earth have you been?' she asked, exasperation in her voice, 'I've been trying to get hold of you for ages, but no one knew where you were!'

Before Tony could apologise, Chloe continued, almost in tears, 'Jacob's been here, and he's saying he's found somewhere else for Bea to live! He wanted to take her straightaway, but she didn't want to go with him. He scared me, Tony, and he kept saying we have no right to keep her here, and he knew exactly what we're up to… but I haven't a clue what he was talking about. He said he'll come and fetch her in a few days.' Chloe was visibly shaking as she spoke, and she burst into tears.

Tony gently ushered his wife into the conservatory, feeling very uneasy himself.

'Is Maddie with Bea now?' he asked, wondering how both of them had dealt with the situation.

'No,' replied Chloe, 'Maddie had to leave early today, because she had a dentist's appointment, so I was here with Bea alone. She's having a rest in her room now. I think Jacob's visit probably exhausted her.'

Tony quietly went and checked that Bea was alright and saw her sleeping in her chair.

'Come on then, Chlo, tell me all about it,' he said gently.

So Chloe told the story, sobbing at times. 'A strange man appeared on our doorstep,' she began, 'saying he was Bea's son, and he'd found a new home for her, much nearer to him, and he was going to move her there. Bea heard his voice and called out to him, so he pushed past me and went to find his mother. He told her his plans, and her face went white.

"But I'm happy here," she had said timidly, "I don't want to go anywhere else." But Jacob told Bea that she couldn't stay here, and nor could she go back to a place where people are murdered, so he'd found a new place for her. At the word "murdered" Bea looked scared.

"I'll come and fetch you in a few days," Jacob had said, and with that he left the house.'

Tony had been listening carefully to Chloe. Not for the first time today, he felt bewildered. He hadn't reckoned on this turn of events.

* * *

Later, while Chloe was preparing supper and Bea was still in her room, Tony asked quietly, 'Did you see Jacob's car?'

'He arrived in a taxi, which waited out in the road and then took him off again,' replied Chloe, 'so I suppose he hadn't thought he'd be here long.'

Well, thought Tony, *that's one possibility.*

'I think we should all have supper,' he said, 'and you and I should just wait and see what Bea says about the visit… just follow her lead. If we don't bring the topic up, we might gauge what impact it had on her, and we can take any discussion from there. I'm really pleased, though, that Maddie hasn't said anything to Bea about Mrs Jeavons' murder. It seems that Maddie has stuck to our agreement about that, so that's reassuring, isn't it?'

Chloe nodded half-heartedly in agreement. It was clear to Tony, though, that his wife was still in shock following the afternoon's events.

The ensuing silence was suddenly broken by the ringing of Bea's little bell. She gave Tony a contented smile as he went into her room and said, 'I've had such a lovely sleep, but I'm feeling a bit peckish now. Is it nearly supper time?'

Twelve

The morning briefing was a painful experience for everyone.

DC Rita Hussein had wanted to crawl under the nearest proverbial stone. She felt worn out and demotivated.

All those involved in the Jeavons murder investigation had been roundly criticised and sworn at by DI Gordon Buchan. What the hell were they all playing at? Why was there no progress on the care home murder? The Chief Constable was breathing down the DI's neck, and he had no signs of progress to report. Didn't they realise how incompetent this made the team look? The media were constantly saying how useless the police are. The DI was having to fend off probing questions at press conferences and make 'no progress' sound like 'good progress is being made.' Relatives of the home's residents were bombarding the police switchboard with demands to know if they should move their loved ones... were they safe there? For heavens' sake, was this a burglary that went wrong, or a targeted killing? And so the DI's rant had gone on.

Rita and Baz had both left the meeting feeling battered and with fleeting thoughts of immediate resignation.

Baz went straight outside to have a calming cigarette. He couldn't cope with that sort of tirade without a supportive intake of nicotine.

Rita meanwhile went to the coffee machine for her temporary solution, a double espresso. It was the injustice of the DI's verbal abuse which riled her most. *Weren't they in the business of seeking justice? Or was that just leftover idealism from her pre-training days?* Her spirits were sinking ever lower.

Baz came into the office clutching a bag of mints. He offered them to Rita, put one in his own mouth and sat down.

'Right,' he said after a few moments, 'sod all of that.'

Baz shifted in his chair and looked at the chart on the wall showing the names of potential suspects and the various links between them.

'We've worked bloody hard on this case, and I don't care who's putting pressure on our beloved boss, we *will* crack it eventually. So, we'll review it all again. Perhaps we've missed something obvious.'

Rita groaned. She felt mentally exhausted. But the coffee was beginning to take effect, and she knew that Baz was right, so she nodded and tried to focus on the task in hand.

'First,' began Baz, 'the facts. What have we got?'

Rita put a clean chart on the wall, covering the previous one. Writing on it as she spoke, Rita started. 'Murder of fifty-nine-year old woman, Sally Jeavons, in care home where she was manager. Wound to neck, but perhaps not sole cause of death. Awaiting autopsy results. No weapon found at scene nor in environs. SJ disliked by staff generally and had recently dismissed a carer, Maddie Smith. SJ divorced and no children. Been manager for decade or more.'

Rita paused.

'Hmm,' said Baz quietly, 'strange, isn't it… nothing unusual ever happens in Minchford, and then suddenly there's a murder that fires up the imagination of the press, and everyone is gunning for us. But back to the important stuff. So, the motive is not known. She was obviously not liked, but that applies to us at the moment too…'

'Too bloody true!' laughed Rita.

Generally, she got on well with Baz. She was grateful that he had not passed the buck downwards, as the DI had done. But he was always supportive of her when work was hard-going.

'Yep,' continued Rita, 'no murder weapon, no clear motive, no unidentified fingerprints at the scene, just a shoe-print in blood which some idiot of an officer slipped in and ruined. I'm beginning to see the boss's point!' She laughed again, and Baz joined in. The impact of the DI's drubbing was fading.

'Right then,' said Baz, 'witnesses and suspects?'

'Jeavons is thought to have been dead for some hours when she was found in her office in the late afternoon by three visitors, namely Tony Montgomery, nephew of one of the residents, and his wife Chloe. With them was Charles Abbott, a long-established solicitor in Minchford. Bit of a dozy old codger, isn't he?'

Baz raised his eyebrows at Rita and said, 'Just the facts, eh?'

'Sorry boss,' she said, and continued, 'there were eight carers on duty, plus three kitchen and cleaning staff. All have been spoken to, and none saw or heard anything out of the ordinary. None of them had any reason to go to Jeavons' office that afternoon. All their reactions seemed genuine, mainly shock and fear. Not much in the way of sadness at her death. No theories expressed about why she was murdered.'

'And they've all been interviewed, haven't they?' asked Baz.

'Correct,' replied Rita.

'And there were no other visitors to the home on that day? No doctors, or vicars, or relatives?'

'Correct,' repeated Rita.

'And all the cars in the car park have been checked out?'

'Correct again,' said Rita.

'So, we have a completely unwitnessed, violent murder, possibly in the context of a burglary, and no one heard or saw anything or anybody suspicious, and no one has come forward with any potential motives. Just one anonymous tip-off which led us nowhere. Great!' said Baz sarcastically.

Rita felt it was her turn to be upbeat now and to keep her boss on track.

'Fancy a coffee or tea,' she asked, 'and I could get some sandwiches from the canteen, if you like?'

Baz recognised Rita's way of trying to keep the momentum going. He'd seen it many times before and liked her for it.

'Good thinking,' he said and grinned. 'Why not get some large lumps of calorie-filled cake too? I reckon we're going to be here for a while yet.'

Rita nodded and went off to the canteen.

* * *

Baz wandered over to the window, looked briefly at the grey, rain-laden clouds, and returned to his thoughts. He felt very fortunate to have Rita Hussein as his DC on this case. She was intelligent, determined, and good fun too. It didn't matter that she was religious and teetotal, and that she rarely joined in any social activities organised by her colleagues. Her ability was highly respected, and perhaps envied by some. She never pushed her personal beliefs at other people or commented on unacceptable behaviour from colleagues.

So it was quite unlike her to describe the solicitor as 'a bit of a dozy old codger', he thought, *I wonder what... ,* but his speculation was interrupted by Rita coming into the room with an overflowing tray.

'Well,' said Baz, looking pleased, 'this lot should improve our thought processes. Thanks, Rita.' He took a cheese and pickle sandwich. 'Right then, what are our key loose ends at the moment?' asked Baz, his mouth full of sandwich.

'Well,' replied Rita, 'I'd be interested in knowing more about why Tony Montgomery and his wife were visiting the home with

Mr Abbott. I got the impression that they were both completely honest with us, so I'm not suggesting that they are implicated in Jeavons' murder. It's just that the circumstances are a bit strange. Tony's aunt, Beatrice Elsworth, was a resident at The Willows, until she had a fall in the garden there very early one morning and was taken to hospital. The poor woman was only in a thin nightdress at the time, and how and why she was in the garden is a mystery to Tony. Anyway, she is now staying with the Montgomerys, and the carer Jeavons sacked is looking after her in their home. The story goes that Tony and Chloe Montgomery went back to The Willows to get his aunt's jewellery box out of the safe in Jeavons' office, as they had no intention of letting Mrs Elsworth go back to the home. They wanted the solicitor to be with them, as he had worked for Mrs Elsworth for many years. I think Tony felt that Jeavons might be difficult about the whole thing. And then the three of them found her dead.'

Baz had been thinking the whole scenario through, while Rita was reminding him of the details. 'So, they had no opportunity to retrieve the jewellery box, and no one knows if it was stolen in the apparent burglary… hmm… might be significant or it might not. Worth a bit more digging around though, eh?' asked Baz.

Rita made a note of this.

'And the sacked carer,' continued Baz, 'let's talk to her again.'

Another note for Rita.

Baz stood up and went over to the window again. Rita knew this habit well. Something was bothering Baz which he couldn't quite pinpoint, and it was best to leave him to think. Sooner or later he would tell her.

Rita helped herself to a couple of biscuits and sat down, relieved to have a short break. She was finding it stressful working on her first murder investigation, but it would be good for her career if she and Baz could make a successful job of it. But, unfortunately, that wasn't how the hierarchy seemed to view their work at present. She was stirred from her thoughts by Baz returning to his seat.

'One big stumbling block for me at the moment,' he said, 'is who put that young man, Sebastian Dean, in the frame, and why. The tech team has only been able to suggest that the anonymous call was made from a cheap mobile phone which was bought for that specific call and then ditched. Place and date of purchase not yet established. Thanks, chaps, very helpful! But what about Dean himself, if we start from a 'no smoke without fire' point of view?'

'Well,' admitted Rita, 'I don't think that was our finest hour, if I'm honest about it. I have an uncomfortable feeling that we jumped too quickly on that one. After all, he's a university student from a good home, who's never been in trouble with the police, and in hindsight I think he was given an unjustifiably hard time. He clearly had no detailed knowledge of Minchford, nor The Willows, and no connection with Jeavons. There's no way he was a paid hit man. As to why someone put his name in the frame, that remains unknown. Perhaps someone was being vindictive for reasons which have nothing to do with the murder. I think we put the frighteners on him, but I doubt if he'll figure in the investigation again,' concluded Rita.

'We'll keep his name on the board, though,' advised Baz, 'perhaps he's not as squeaky clean as we think. A bit more background digging around perhaps?'

Another note in Rita's book.

Thirteen

Martin Dean continued to wonder what Seb and Tilda were hiding from him and their mother. He felt sure that they had something troubling them, which they were not prepared to share. *And why had Tilda tried to press him on the details of his fall? Usually she would have asked a casual question, just to show a bit of interest, and left it at that. But she had latched onto whether or not the push had been deliberate. She had seemed disquieted by the mention of Minchford too.*

Hmm… he continued to ponder, *I really wonder what this is all about…* He decided not to share his concerns with his wife at present. The cruise had been intended as a relaxing time, but it had ended very differently. *Ros doesn't need any more worries,* he thought, *so I'll just get to the root of it all with Seb and Tilda for now.*

* * *

Meanwhile Seb was racking his brains, trying to work out the best way of telling his parents that he would soon be returning to university to retake his final year, and he would therefore not be available for the junior management position which his dad had lined up for him. He knew that his father had arranged, and paid upfront for, a prestigious management course for him. This would involve two days per week studying, with the remaining time spent working in the family business. Seb dreaded telling his parents that he had completely messed up at university. He viewed with even more horror the prospect of divulging that he had been questioned by the police in connection with a murder. And he wasn't yet sure if the police intended to question him again.

Alone in his bedroom, Seb felt angry with himself for succumbing to the wiles and manipulation of bloody Helena. *How could I have done this?* he kept asking himself, but he could come up with no better answer than, *Because I was a stupid idiot and believed all her flattery.*

* * *

Tilda was in torment too. She was wandering in the woods with faithful Zeus, occasionally throwing a stick for him to retrieve. *At least he's happy,* she thought ruefully. Tilda wondered constantly why her relationship with Luke had come to such an abrupt end. *And why wouldn't he respond to her calls?* She felt devastated. This had been her first sexual relationship, and yet… She just didn't understand, but there was no one she could talk to about it. She didn't dare tell either of her parents. And Seb might revert to being his former sneering self. So, it all churned round and round in her mind.

Contact with Luke was the only solution, she thought, *but how could she achieve this?*

* * *

That evening Martin suggested that the whole family should go to the Black Horse for dinner. 'It'll save Mum having to cook, and we can have a few drinks and a good chat. How about it?'

Seb's and Tilda's hearts sank at the suggestion, each remembering when they were last at that pub. But there was nothing to be done other than to appear pleased.

During the meal one of the staff was passing the Deans' table and noticed Seb.

'Well,' he said cheerfully, 'you look a lot better than last time I saw you… you were in a helluva state then, weren't you?', and he carried on walking towards the kitchens. Seb's face was turning scarlet with embarrassment, so Tilda tried to rescue the situation.

'Oh,' she laughed, hoping it sounded genuine, 'that must have been the evening you came here with your friend and got totally plastered… I don't suppose you remember much about that, do you? You made an awful racket trying to find the stairs when you finally got home, and you ended up sleeping on the hall floor!'

Seb nodded half-heartedly, inwardly grateful to his sister. His dad, though, was not fooled by his daughter, but he said nothing.

Other than that diversion the evening was pleasant enough, with Tilda ensuring that the conversation was mainly about her parents' cruise. Neither she nor Seb really wanted to hear the details of their fellow passengers, the beautiful cities they had visited and the shortcomings of the tour operator's management of the cruise, but Tilda thought these were the safest topics.

Eventually Martin stood up and said, 'I'm going to walk home… I've got some thinking to do. So I'll leave the car with you. I keep remembering that I ought to respond to that solicitor's letter, as it's quite a while since he sent it. All a bit intriguing really. I don't suppose either of you two has needed a solicitor recently, have you? And not paid the bill?' Martin chuckled as he said this, but Seb's reddening face did not escape him.

Once Martin had left, Ros ordered coffees. She looked intently at Seb and Tilda.

'I know that children tend to think that their parents are idiots,' she started, 'and don't have a clue about the next generation, but it's not always true, you know. Your dad and I have both picked up that there's something you're not telling us, and it seems to be something serious. If you can honestly tell me that it's not, and that we are completely wrong, then we won't press you any further. But do credit us with a bit of perception… we are always here to help you, no matter what the problem.'

'Thanks, Mum,' whispered Tilda, trying to hold back some tears. Seb just nodded slowly, his eyes fixed firmly on the tablecloth.

No more was said on that subject.

* * *

A couple of days later Martin mentioned to Tilda that he had rung the solicitor in Minchford.

'He gave me very little information over the phone,' he said, 'but he is trying to trace relatives of a George Montgomery, the same name as some ancient relation of mine.'

'Wow,' exclaimed Tilda, 'perhaps he's left an enormous fortune, and you're the one to inherit! That would be brilliant!'

'Hold your horses,' laughed her father, 'don't start planning how you're going to spend this mythical money! I didn't get the impression that there are heaps of gold bullion coming our way. But you can hope, if you like. I couldn't give Mr Abbott any useful information, so I doubt if we'll hear any more about the whole thing. Sorry!'

'Oooh,' replied Tilda, 'I must tell Seb about this, he'll think it's a real hoot!'

Tilda rushed off to find her brother, while their father wondered, *or will he meet the explanation of the letter with a huge amount of relief?*

* * *

Tilda found Seb in his room playing computer games. 'Come on,' she said, 'we need to go out for a walk. We've got to have a talk, but not here, in case the walls have ears. Let's go down to the river, and Zeus can have a paddle. Dad's been telling me about the solicitor chap, but on top of that I've had an absolute brainwave!'

'Oh well,' grunted Seb, 'if I must.'

He grabbed a sweater, whistled for Zeus, and Tilda shouted to her dad that she and Seb were taking Zeus for a walk. It was a sunny early evening as they walked along the tow path. Now and again Zeus leapt into the shallows, apparently pretending to be a brown bear pouncing on unsuspecting salmon. Zeus was less adept at catching anything, though, much to Tilda's relief. She laughed at his antics.

'Well,' asked Seb eventually, 'how far do we have to walk before you divulge your stroke of genius?'

Tilda's first reaction was to flinch at feeling mocked by her brother, as had happened so often in the past, but the expression on his face was a genuinely amused one. She told Seb what their dad had said about the solicitor and how she had pretended to believe he must be an heir-hunter.

'I know it's a helluva coincidence that this chap is in Minchford, which neither of us knew anything about before the police took you there. But there was absolutely nothing to connect you with his letter or the phone call. I'm sure if Dad thought there was a link, he would've mentioned it somehow.'

Seb looked around for Zeus, who seemed to have wandered off. Seb whistled, and a bedraggled, dripping dog emerged from the rushes growing in the river's shallows. He came over to Seb and shook himself enthusiastically, showering Seb with dirty water.

'Thanks, mate,' laughed Seb, and Zeus shook himself again. Seb and Tilda set off along the tow path, hoping that Zeus would now prefer terra firma.

'But,' began Seb, 'you said that the solicitor mentioned Dad's old relative, whose name just happened to be George. Do you honestly think that was a coincidence too? There've been far too many Georges around lately, for my liking.'

'Yes,' said Tilda thoughtfully, 'but it is a fairly common name, well, particularly in previous generations. Think how many kings have been called George, for instance.'

'OK,' replied her brother, 'point taken. Now, about this intriguing brainwave…'

Tilda spotted a bench by the water's edge and motioned to Seb to sit down there. A swan paddled regally by, with five grey cygnets following in formation.

'That's how I feel sometimes now that Mum and Dad are back,' said Tilda, 'furiously paddling beneath the water while maintaining a serene appearance above it.'

'In your dreams,' retorted her brother with a laugh, 'who do you think you're kidding?'

'Well, anyway,' continued Tilda, 'I have most definitely had a brilliant idea, which might solve a few things for us. I know you're dreading telling Mum and Dad that you've had lousy exam results and have to return to uni for retakes. It scuppers all Dad's plans for you and leaves him short of a member of staff. And he'll have wasted all that money he's paid out for your posh management course. So…'

'Thanks for reminding me, sis,' interrupted Seb, 'don't you think I feel bad enough already?'

'Well,' she said, 'why don't we suggest to Dad, once he's over his initial disappointment and anger…'

'Thanks again, sis, you really are cheering me up no end,' interjected Seb.

'As I was trying to say, Seb,' persisted Tilda, 'why don't we see if Luke would like a one-year locum-type job and get a free management course out of it too? Perhaps it would soften the blow for Dad, and it would keep the job for you at the end of the year. Don't you think that's a stroke of genius?'

Tilda beamed expectantly, awaiting Seb's reaction.

There was a long silence until Seb said, 'Just a few immediate thoughts… how do we get hold of Luke to put this hare-brained scheme to him? I thought we had no idea where he is, or do you know something I don't? Next, how does this help with the subject of my arrest, which won't stay a secret for ever? And lastly for now, do you honestly think it's a good idea to lure Luke back into your life after all that's happened?'

Tilda was thoroughly crestfallen. She burst into tears and set off along the tow path away from her ungrateful brother. Seb was taken aback by Tilda's reaction. He quickly realised that she was his only ally and that he had been stupid to dismiss her ideas. After all, he hadn't come up with any better ones.

'Tilda,' he shouted after his sister, 'I'm sorry,' but she carried on walking away from him. Seb decided not to pursue her but to go home with Zeus. He would think carefully how to patch things up with Tilda.

His father was tying back an unruly climbing rose when Seb arrived home with bedraggled Zeus.

'Just had a phone call for you, Seb,' said his father. 'She wouldn't leave her name or a message. She had a very obviously foreign accent… does that mean anything to you? Oh yes, she also asked if Luke was here with us. I couldn't for the life of me remember you mentioning a Luke, so I couldn't help her there. Anyway, she said she'd ring back sometime… "no rush", she said.'

'Thanks, Dad,' replied Seb, in as calm a voice as he could muster, and he went on into the house, deep in thought.

Fourteen

'Right, Rita,' said her boss, 'I've been thinking… we'll review it all again from square one.'

'But guv… ' Rita began.

'Yeah, I know, we formulated our plan yesterday, but we need to go back a step or two,' interrupted Baz, 'so today we'll speak again with all the staff who are on duty at The Willows… individually. No prior warning. We'll just turn up when the residents are having their afternoon nap. I gather there's a locum manager there now, a Paula Trelawney, so let's hope she's cooperative.'

'And what exactly are we after?' asked Rita, unsuccessfully trying to hide her exasperation.

'It's as much soft intelligence as facts,' said Baz, 'I want them to talk about Beatrice Elsworth being found in the garden in her nightdress, about the sacking of the carer Maddie, and about the murder. It's been a while now, and they may be prepared to say more. It's not all so raw now.'

Baz was allowing no room for discussion, and Rita wondered if DI Buchan had been bending Baz's ear again.

* * *

A few hours later Rita wearily trudged up the police station's steps and made straight for the coffee machine. *Please, oh please, no more weak tea,* she muttered to herself.

Baz was on the phone when she entered his office. She soon deduced that it was the DI on the other end.

'Yes, sir,' said Baz deferentially, 'we interviewed all the staff on duty this afternoon. We're about to collate our findings now. Yes, sir, we'll report to the morning briefing tomorrow.' Baz put the phone down and shrugged his shoulders.

'No peace for us then, Rita,' he groaned, 'put a new chart on the wall, please. So, what have we got?'

'A whole lot of scarcely concealed hostility, to Sally Jeavons, to Maddie, to us, to each other, but little in the way of useful or verifiable information,' replied Rita, sounding tired and irritated. She felt that the whole exercise that afternoon had been pointless and unproductive, but she knew she ought to be careful how she expressed that to her boss.

'OK, guv,' she summarised, 'the new angles are these. Paula Trelawney, interim manager, wants to cooperate with us and get the murder solved in order to build up the business again. At the moment The Willows has suffered reputational damage and is running at a significant loss. But she's not involved in any way in the murder, is my assessment. She doesn't seem to have formed useful relationships yet with any of the staff, so I think we can sideline her in the enquiry. But I think she's astute and engaged enough to let us know if she hears or sees anything relevant.'

Baz nodded in agreement.

'Petra Tradovic, a carer, on the other hand,' continued Rita, 'left me with quite a lot of question marks. She came over as surly and a bit condescending, and she made it clear that she thinks we're incompetent. But I couldn't put my finger on what her problem with us is. She said a couple of times, though, that we should be concentrating on visitors to The Willows, not on the staff.'

Rita paused, and again Baz nodded his agreement. He went over to the wall chart and noted down the key words for each of the interviewees so far.

'Then there was Lucy Kingdon, another carer,' said Rita, gradually warming to the task in hand. Perhaps some useful leads would come out of the interviews after all. 'She was initially quite tentative but also very pro-Maddie Smith. She felt that Maddie had been abominably treated, firstly by her colleagues (not identified) who snitched on her talking to Bea Elsworth's relatives, and secondly by Sally Jeavons, who had sacked her. Lucy also hinted that Jeavons was "up to no good", but then she suddenly clammed up again. I thought, guv, that we might get more from her, if we time it right.'

Another nod of agreement from her boss.

The debrief was suddenly interrupted by Baz's phone ringing. For a while Baz just listened and made a few written notes. 'Is the identity known?' he asked. More listening, and then, 'We're on our way, sir,' before the call was ended.

'Right Rita,' he said, 'we're off to the woods just beyond Little Fordington. A dog-walker has found a body, a female slumped against a tree trunk with her wrists slashed. Identity not yet known. A dog was sitting whimpering next to the body.'

Fifteen

Luke was at a loose end and feeling sorry for himself. His underlying determination to sort his life out was undiminished, but he had underestimated the difficulties he would face. He was short of money, and so far all attempts at finding an interesting job had been thwarted. He had naively thought that, with a good university degree to his name, he would easily find a well-paid job in London. But no such luck. He seemed to have no problem being offered interviews, but then his lack of work experience always counted against him. He couldn't continue paying a London rent without a regular income.

And then he thought about Tilda and realised what an idiot he had been. He gradually convinced himself that he had nothing to lose by phoning her, only to remember that her number was in his old phone which now lay at the bottom of the nearby canal.

Perhaps that's an omen, he thought dejectedly. And then he recalled that he had noted down her parents' home phone number. *That's my only option,* he said to himself.

Luke was very relieved when Tilda herself answered the Deans' phone. They quickly arranged to meet the following morning at the bus station café, within cycling distance of Tilda's home. Luke would come by train and then walk to the bus station. It was a brief conversation, but each of them was pleased that contact had been re-established.

'I know I treated you badly,' began Luke, when they were sitting in a quiet corner of the café, each with a cup of coffee. 'I'm so, so sorry,' he continued, 'you deserved much better from me.'

'Hmm,' replied Tilda, 'I think you're right. But we can't change the past, only look to the future. So, what made you ring me?'

Luke hesitantly put his hand over Tilda's and smiled when she didn't withdraw it.

'I've… I've missed you so much,' he stuttered, 'but I wasn't sure if you'd want me to contact you.'

'What about all the texts I sent you… didn't that give you some sort of clue?' retorted Tilda, more pointedly than she had intended.

There was an uneasy silence.

Luke drank some coffee and then asked, 'How's things at home then? Do your folks know that Seb's returning to uni yet? Has he had any more calls from Helena?'

Tilda gave Luke the general picture, but she wasn't yet ready to mention the solution she had come up with. She also didn't tell Luke about Seb being arrested in connection with a murder. She wondered why she was not prepared to confide fully in Luke. *Perhaps he would have to win her trust again, and how long might that take?*

'So how have things been with you?' asked Tilda.

Luke was more forthcoming, describing to Tilda some of the unsuccessful job interviews he'd had and trying to make them amusing. They were both beginning to relax.

'Come on,' suggested Luke, 'let's go for a walk. I've had enough of this place.'

Tilda nodded enthusiastically, wishing they could go somewhere rather more private than the local park.

Eventually Tilda could contain herself no longer and blurted out, 'Seb was arrested on suspicion of murder, it was horrendous.'

Luke drew back, trying to work out if Tilda really meant what she had said. She clearly did.

'What on earth are you talking about?' he asked.

A garbled version of Seb's story spilled out of Tilda among intermittent sobs. Luke didn't interrupt but just looked at Tilda with increasing astonishment.

'Why the hell did they think that Seb was connected with this murder? It's just crazy,' said Luke.

'Apparently they had an anonymous tip-off, which must have sounded credible enough to warrant them questioning him. There was one other weird thing too,' Tilda continued, 'they asked him if he knew anything about people called Milstrom. He said he didn't, but that's actually the name of someone in our family a couple of generations back.'

'Oh, come on, Tilda,' replied Luke rather dismissively, 'that's a bit far-fetched, there must be masses of people called Milstrom, especially in Scandinavia!'

This reaction was enough to stop Tilda completing the story, and a tense silence ensued.

Luke was the first to break it, saying, 'Sorry, Tilda, I didn't mean that I don't believe you. It all sounds horrific, especially for Seb. It must have really shaken him up, poor guy.'

Tilda nodded dejectedly. They walked along hand in hand, each deep in thought, ignoring the activity around them in the park.

Suddenly Tilda asked, 'Why did you change your phone, Luke? Was it to avoid me contacting you?'

Luke stopped abruptly, turned Tilda towards him and put his arms around her. He was thoroughly taken aback by her questions.

'Are you mad?' he asked, horrified. 'Of course not! I wanted to break with the past, that's true, I just couldn't take any more hassle from bloody Helena. I wish I'd never met her or bloody Mishka.' Luke's face had drained of its colour at Tilda's questions, and he looked bemused. 'Did you honestly think that I had given up on you?' he asked quietly.

'Well, yes, I suppose so,' replied Tilda, 'it seemed the obvious thing to think, can't you see that?'

Luke nodded despondently. They walked along for a while, neither speaking, each trying to make sense of incoherent thoughts.

Eventually Tilda broke the silence, asking as casually as she could, 'So what are you going to do about a job then?'

Luke was feeling like a failure in all aspects of his life and wasn't sure what to say to Tilda.

'Well, there's nothing in the pipeline at the moment. If I don't find something soon, I'll have to move out of London, but there's nowhere else I particularly want to go. And, of course, I've got to start paying off my student debts eventually. So altogether you're looking at a man with a bleak future,' he said.

Tilda may have been prone to self-pity herself occasionally, but she wasn't very tolerant of it in others.

'Stop feeling sorry for yourself,' she said brusquely, 'that won't get you anywhere.'

Luke was shocked by her tone, but he knew she was right. The meeting with Tilda was not going as he had hoped.

Tilda was determined not to apologise for what she had said, nor how she had said it. She seemed to be surrounded by men with problems, who insisted on using her as a sounding-board. And yet she was the youngest, and not long ago she had been regarded as the least worldly-wise.

Suddenly she said, 'Shall I call Seb and see if he wants to come over and join us?' She wasn't sure why she asked this, but there was so much friction in the air that she thought something had to change.

Disappointed, Luke agreed.

Sixteen

Chloe was beginning to panic. Maddie hadn't turned up for work yet. She should have been there half an hour ago. It was the first morning she had been late. Tony had already left for work, and Chloe was due in an important meeting in just over an hour. Bea was getting agitated too, as her routine seemed to be awry. Chloe had tried ringing Maddie's phone, but it appeared to be turned off. *This isn't like Maddie at all,* she thought.

Another twenty minutes went by, and there was still no sign of Maddie. Chloe was really panicking now. She grabbed her phone and went into the kitchen, out of earshot of Bea. Amid profuse apologies she explained the situation to her colleague, Kate, and briefed her on the key points of the imminent meeting. Kate was her usual unflappable and cooperative self, so Chloe was able to stay at home with Bea. She was determined, though, to read the riot act to Maddie when she eventually turned up, as this must never happen again.

Chloe tried to calm herself down while she was preparing Bea's breakfast, when the threatening image of Jacob came into her mind. She hadn't given him a thought yet this morning, but now his recent visit came back to her vividly, and her hands shook. *Would he return to collect Bea in the next day or two? Had he really found somewhere else for her to live? He hadn't shown any interest in Bea until now, so what was he up to?*

Tony and Chloe had talked about the situation, from every angle, until late into the night, but they kept returning to the same sad conclusion. If Jacob really had found a new home for Bea, there was little they could do to stop him taking her. They could try reasoning with him, but that seemed unlikely to have any impact on Jacob. Tony thought that they should have a word with Mr Abbott and get some advice from him, but Chloe still had reservations about Charles Abbott, although she couldn't pinpoint the reason for this.

So, no solutions had been found, and Chloe was feeling very vulnerable now. *How could she protect Bea?* she asked herself.

* * *

Meanwhile, on his way to work, Tony happened to spot Charles Abbott walking towards his office. He was still inclined to seek advice from Mr Abbott, but he knew that Chloe was against this, so he resisted the temptation to follow the lawyer to his office. He had only just sat down at his desk when the phone rang, and Chloe, sounding distraught, was telling him that Maddie had not arrived yet. It was clear to Tony, though, that her greater concern was the possibility of Jacob appearing on their doorstep again. All he could do was to remind Chloe to keep all the downstairs doors and windows locked, and to call the police if Jacob behaved in a threatening way.

'Don't let him into the house,' Tony urged her, 'just talk to him through the letterbox.'

He wished he could go home to be with Chloe and Bea, but work pressures wouldn't allow this. He decided to ring Chloe in a couple of hours, by which time Maddie would hopefully have arrived, with a good explanation.

Seventeen

'One more and we can call it an epidemic,' said Rita ruefully. Baz gave her a disapproving look. They were driving back to Minchford from the gruesome scene in the woods. It was virtually dark by now. There had been a thunderstorm earlier, and they had been drenched by sudden torrential rain. The car heater was on maximum in an attempt to dry their clothes, and the windows kept misting over. They had hardly spoken at the crime scene. It was a sickening sight, and Rita had felt very queasy. Such a waste of a young life.

The body had been slumped against the broad trunk of a tall tree, whose canopy had sheltered it from the heaviest rain. Her jacket's hood had slipped forwards, largely concealing her face. The body was well hidden from the nearby track, a favourite with local dog-walkers. The nearest car park was about a minute's walk away. Apart from two police cars, the only other car belonged to the woman who had found the body. She was very distressed, and a police constable took her home. Her son would collect the car tomorrow.

It had been a long day for Rita and Baz, but they decided to debrief at the station immediately. Rita had some dry clothes in her locker, so she went off to get changed.

* * *

'As the witness said,' began Rita, 'if the victim had been local, she would probably have recognised the dog, if not the woman. Dog-walkers tend to be sociable apparently and talk about their dogs, if not about themselves. So possibly she wasn't from the local area.'

'Well,' replied Baz, 'that sounds reasonable enough. But if she wasn't local, how did she get there? It's quite a remote spot. And if you were about to commit suicide, would you take your dog with you?'

'So are you saying, guv, that we definitely rule out suicide? That someone unknown slashed the victim's wrists to make it look like a self-inflicted death? And left the knife in her hand?' asked Rita.

Baz nodded thoughtfully.

'That would be my hypothesis at the moment,' he replied slowly, 'but we'll have to wait and hear what forensics have to say.'

Rita's heart sank. She was tired and despondent, and now they had a second suspicious death to resolve. DI Buchan was already critical of their work on the first case.

Baz sensed Rita's reaction.

'Right, let's make this debrief quick, and then tomorrow is another day!'

A message came up on Baz's computer screen.

'Tony Montgomery has reported Maddie Smith as missing. Didn't turn up for work today, and he's heard nothing from her. It's out of character, and he's concerned,' he told Rita.

'Any connection, do you reckon?' he asked.

Eighteen

The next day Rita Hussein was due to start work at noon, so in the morning she drove to the local swimming pool hoping that some strenuous exercise might take her mind off yesterday's events. During the night she had woken with a start several times, as grisly images punctuated her dreams. By chance, Rita's friend, Angie, was also at the pool, so after an energetic swim they went to the café for a coffee. They chatted about the new fashion website which Angie had used, and about a film they both wanted to see.

On her way home from the pool Rita found herself wondering why she hadn't chosen a carefree lifestyle, like Angie, rather than the stress of her current job. She knew deep down, though, that she wouldn't want to swap.

At noon she walked into Baz's office and immediately saw the graphic images of the body propped up against the tree. There were several images pinned on a board, including one close-up of the victim's left forearm and the right hand clutching the bloodied serrated knife. Above the images was written the believed identity of the victim, Madeleine Smith, together with a reminder that her name had not yet been confirmed nor released to the press. Baz had also been creating a new chart of possible suspects and key words in relation to potential motives.

'You've been busy, guv,' said Rita, trying to sound up-beat.

'Well,' replied Baz, 'you can guess whose office I was summoned to an hour ago…'

Rita studied the new chart for a while and then asked, in a surprised voice, 'Is Tony Montgomery really a suspect?'

'Think it through, Rita, and remember that we need evidence to rule people out as well as in,' replied Baz. Rita accepted the reminder with a nod. 'So?' he asked.

'Well,' said Rita hesitantly, 'Tony was one of the first three witnesses at the scene of the Jeavons murder, the evidence tells us that. Now he seems to have a link with the second murder victim, if it proves to be Smith.'

'Bit of an unlucky coincidence for him, don't you think?' added Baz, trying to restore a more relaxed tone between them.

Rita attempted a smile and said, 'Guess so.'

'Something else to remember,' said Baz, 'is that occasionally the least likely person turns out to be the offender. How many times have we seen relatives of victims in tears at televised press conferences, pleading for witnesses to come forward and help the police, and then proving to have committed the crime themselves?'

Rita gave Baz an acknowledging nod.

'Guilty people usually trip themselves up eventually,' he added.

* * *

In the early evening an unmarked police car pulled up outside the Montgomerys' house. Tony was clearly surprised, but he ushered the two officers into the dining room.

'So, have you managed to find your aunt's jewellery box yet?' asked Baz casually.

Tony was even more surprised now.

'Oh, er… ' he replied uncertainly, 'no, we've had other things to think about recently. It's just slipped our minds, I suppose, but you're right, we ought to go back to The Willows and find it.'

'Right,' continued Baz, 'you don't want to forget about that, do you?'

Tony shook his head slightly, feeling confused.

'Are you off on holiday?' asked Rita cheerfully.

'What do you mean?' stuttered Tony nervously, wondering where this conversation was going.

'Oh,' said Rita with a little laugh, 'it's just that I noticed the map of Norway on the table.'

'Right then,' said Baz, 'tell us about Madeleine Smith going missing.'

Tony struggled to regain his composure and take command of his thoughts. He felt there was something odd about the way the police officers were talking to him. *So, think carefully,* he told himself.

Tony explained that the day before yesterday Maddie had left early to go to the dentist, and then yesterday and today she hadn't turned up to look after Bea. She was always reliable, and Tony couldn't understand why she hadn't let them know, if there was a problem. His wife had tried phoning Maddie several times, but the phone seemed to be turned off all the time. Tony explained that he had contacted the police because it all seemed completely out of character for Maddie.

'I hope I did the right thing,' said Tony.

Rita noted down more details about Maddie, and they then left. In the car on the way back to the station, Baz and Rita discussed the visit.

'Well,' began Rita, 'he was certainly nonplussed by questions about the jewellery box and the map, and it took him a while to re-group.'

'True,' agreed Baz, 'you did well to pick up on the map of Norway… it quite threw him, didn't it?'

'And in all probability it was perfectly innocent,' suggested Rita.

'On the other hand,' continued Baz, 'if he is responsible for the body in the woods, he would be nervous having the police on his doorstep. We must keep an open mind about that one. Does he seem to you to be a double-killer?'

Rita made no reply. *Focus on evidence and facts,* she reminded herself.

Nineteen

Both Tony and Chloe felt unsettled by the visit from the police. For Tony the most disturbing aspect was that he was unclear why they had visited them at all. He felt sure it was nothing to do with Bea's jewellery box, nor anything to do with their possible holiday plans. The murder of Sally Jeavons wasn't mentioned, which only left Maddie's disappearance. But he had nothing new to tell them about Maddie. He had told the police everything he knew by phone.

Uppermost in Chloe's mind were the difficulties in looking after Bea, if Maddie wasn't intending to come back to them. She was still perplexed by Maddie's behaviour. She had always seemed reliable and trustworthy, and she had certainly cared for Bea very well. Chloe was reluctantly thinking about how to find a suitable new carer for Tony's aunt. Bea was simply one of their family now.

But then the spectre of Jacob flashed across Chloe's mind again. They had heard no more from him. *But*, she thought, *it's only a matter of time.*

Later that evening, when Bea was sleeping peacefully in her bed, Tony and Chloe sat together to watch the television news programme. 'Why can't they sometimes report good news?' asked Chloe in a tired voice.

But her thoughts were interrupted abruptly by a grainy photograph of a young woman appearing on the screen. Chloe grabbed Tony's arm and shrieked, 'That's Maddie... look!'

Tony sat bolt upright, and the colour drained from his face. The newsreader was saying, "Police report that the body found in Little Fordington woods has been identified as that of twenty-four-year old Madeleine Phoebe Smith who lived locally. The cause of death is not yet established. Police investigations are continuing."

And then, as if that news had been of little consequence, the newsreader moved on to the weather forecast for the coming days.

Tony and Chloe both felt numb, and neither spoke for several minutes. Eventually Chloe switched off the television. They sat in stunned silence, until Chloe started sobbing quietly.

'I can't take much more of all this,' she said in a soft, trembling voice. Tony held her hand, nodding but saying nothing. After a while he went into the kitchen and poured a whisky for each of them, which they sipped in continuing silence.

Gradually, as the news of Maddie's death began to sink in, Tony thought back to the visit from the police earlier in the evening. He grew angry as he convinced himself that they must have known all along that Maddie was dead. They were playing with him, trying to trip him up, to entrap him. These feelings rapidly turned to fear. *Had he said anything that the police could construe as implicating him in Maddie's death?* Random, irrational thoughts raced around in Tony's mind. He told himself that he had nothing to fear, that the police could have no evidence against him, but he couldn't dispel some nagging uncertainties.

By now Chloe was overwhelmed with sadness. *Maddie had always been so kind to Bea,* she thought. *She was so young, and her death at that age was totally undeserved. Who could have treated her so brutally?*

It dawned on Chloe that she knew very little about Maddie's family or friends. Their conversations had usually been about

Bea and her care, and there had been scarcely any social chit-chat between them. Chloe now regretted this.

Amid the sadness her thoughts gradually turned to practicalities. *How should they break the news to Bea? She would be distraught at what had happened to Maddie, whom she relied on and liked so much. But they had to tell Bea a version of the truth, in case she heard about Maddie's death from another, less sensitive source.*

An image of Jacob came into Chloe's mind, and she shuddered.

The silence was broken by Tony suddenly saying, 'I wonder if Bea is in danger.'

Chloe gave him a horrified look.

'Well, think about it, Chlo,' he continued, 'as far as we know, this whole sequence of events started with Bea being out in The Willows' garden in the early morning in her nightdress and having a nasty fall. Then Sally Jeavons was killed in her office, and not long afterwards Maddie is found dead. We have no idea why someone wanted rid of Jeavons or Maddie, so we can't know if Bea might be on their list too.'

'Oh, for heavens' sake, Tony,' shrieked Chloe, 'listen to yourself! You're letting your imagination run away with you completely! No, I can't explain any of this, but why on earth would anyone want to harm Bea? We'll go mad if we start thinking like that! Yes, we need to protect Bea, but only because she's your elderly aunt, not because there's some madman after her!' Chloe was surprised by her own vehemence, but she was determined not to retract anything she had said.

Tony thought it better not to respond and probably argue with Chloe. So they sat in silence again.

Sometime soon, though, thought Tony, *we're going to have to discuss the worrying subject of Jacob.*

Twenty

Martin Dean leaned back in his office chair, hands clasped behind his head. Luke had just left his office.

Initially Martin had been furious at being told by Seb that he had failed nearly all his exams and would have to repeat his final year at university.

'What the hell were you doing there all that time?' Martin had shouted at his son. 'How could you be so bloody irresponsible?'

Seb had stood there, shame-faced, shaking his head in a forlorn way. It had taken Martin a couple of hours to emerge from his anger and frustration. And then, back at home, Tilda had suggested a possible solution to the whole damned mess. Why not use Luke as a stop-gap in the business? Martin's first reaction was to dismiss the whole scheme as ridiculous, but gradually, with persuasion from Tilda, he'd begun to see some merit in her suggestion.

So, Martin had had a lengthy telephone conversation with Luke and then invited him for a formal interview.

Now Martin was in his office assessing whether employing Luke really would be a viable option. The whole idea seemed fraught with complications, and Martin was concerned that he still knew little about Luke. He certainly appeared to have suitable potential for working in Martin's business, and he had shown enthusiasm at the prospect of undertaking a management course. But he had disclosed very little about himself beyond the context of the job.

But I know one person who would be overjoyed if I took him on, chuckled Martin to himself, *and that's my daughter! I wonder what that's all about.*

* * *

Luke decided to go straight back to London after the interview. He desperately wanted to talk to Tilda, but it suddenly felt as if an invisible barrier was rising between them. *After all,* he thought, *if he was offered the job, she would be his boss's daughter, which might prove to be a tricky dynamic.*

Luke was walking from the underground station to his flat, deep in thought. He turned the corner into his street and caught sight of a woman with short auburn hair standing on the pavement looking up at his flat. Luke stopped abruptly and then walked a few paces backwards around the corner, in the hope of still being able to watch the woman without being seen. She rang the doorbell of Luke's flat, waited a short while, and then stood on the pavement still looking at the building. She then crossed the street and walked along the pavement on the opposite side, away from Luke. There was a man waiting for her, but Luke couldn't see him fully. There were cars parked in his line of vision. He heard the car doors slam, the engine was revved, and they drove off.

Luke was trembling. *How could Mishka possibly have found out this address?* he asked himself.

He turned and walked quickly back towards the underground station. The public library was not far past the station, so Luke decided to go in there and calm down. He took the lift to the upper floor and snatched a book randomly from the nearest shelf. He found a seat by a window from which he could watch the entrance to the library. He looked around the room surreptitiously and heaved a sigh of relief when he did not recognise anyone. His heartbeat had been racing, but slowly he began to relax. He looked at the book in his hands and was amused to see that it was a guide to breastfeeding for first-time mothers! He placed it open in his lap whilst he carefully scanned the street-scene outside.

Luke had planned to spend the rest of the day weighing up whether he would accept the job with Seb's father, if offered it. It would certainly be a tempting opportunity, especially with a free management course thrown in, and it would be a financial life-line for him. But he would have to find somewhere new to live, and there was the added complication of his relationship with Tilda. Uppermost in Luke's mind, though, was something Martin Dean had said to him after the formal interview had concluded.

'By the way, Luke,' he had said casually, 'Seb had a phone call from a woman with a strong foreign accent, which I happened to answer. When I said that Seb wasn't in, she asked if someone called Luke was there. A bit odd, wasn't it?'

Luke had tried to give the impression that he had no idea what the caller could have meant. Now, though, in the light of the events which had caused him to take refuge in the library, Luke's anxiety levels rose again.

* * *

An hour later Luke was still sitting in his window seat, with the book open at the same page. He now felt certain that neither Mishka nor her companion had seen him watching them outside his flat. He felt safe for the moment. *But would he feel safe if he went back to his flat?* Luke decided that he had no alternative. *And why should he be harassed out of his own home, such as it was?*

Luke tried to look at the situation objectively, without much success. *He had been lured into something which was essentially Seb's problem,* he concluded, *which he couldn't fathom out, and now he, Luke, felt under a threat of some kind. So why can't bloody Seb sort it out and get the message to bloody Helena and Mishka that it's all got nothing to do with me?*

At that moment it all seemed so simple.

Suddenly Luke remembered that Seb had been questioned by the police about a murder. He shuddered involuntarily as long-suppressed memories came into his mind. He forced his thoughts back to the present.

Seb's a total disaster area, he concluded, *and I'm caught up in his mess.*

Deep down, though, Luke knew that he could not rely on Seb to extricate him from the mess. Luke would have to do it alone. He regretted that Tilda would probably be the sacrificial lamb in the plan which was slowly forming in his mind. *A complete break with the Dean family was the only solution,* Luke decided. *Tilda will get over it quite soon,* he rationalised, *she's young and attractive, and another chap will sweep her off her feet before long.*

Luke knew he was being callous, but from now on his own best interests would come first.

As far as Seb was concerned, Luke hadn't liked him much at university, and he'd only occasionally liked him since. Seb was essentially self-centred, and Luke had no sympathy for him, half-hoping that Martin Dean would give the job to Tilda instead, improbable as that was. Debating all angles, Luke tentatively started to map out a different future for himself.

The first step, he decided, *was to phone Martin Dean. He would tell him that he had given the matter much thought and had come to the conclusion that he no longer wished to be considered for the job.*

In the evening he took that first step, much to the bewilderment of Martin. Luke had assured him that no additional financial incentives, if offered, would persuade him to change his mind.

Luke sat in his depressing little flat, feeling a mixture of elation and apprehension, and wondered how Tilda had taken the news.

He turned off his phone.

Twenty-One

Seb and Tilda were sitting in The Black Horse, both feeling despondent. Their father had told them that Luke no longer wished to be considered for the job. Neither of them could understand Luke's decision, and their father had not been able to explain his change of heart.

'What on earth has caused his about-turn?' wailed Tilda. 'He sounded quite keen on the idea when we suggested it.'

Seb shook his head.

'No idea,' he said, 'I can't make any sense of it. And it'll only increase Dad's anger towards me. Why didn't Luke say something to one of us first?'

Tilda picked up her phone to call Luke. His phone was turned off. She suspected, miserably, that it would probably stay that way.

Seb's thoughts, however, had moved on to what his father had said about a woman with a foreign accent phoning the house, and the fact that she had mentioned Luke. That scared him far more than his dad's anger. *Why the hell was Helena still trying to contact him? She surely realised by now that he knew nothing about 'George', whoever he was.*

When they arrived home from the pub, Seb's father called out to him from the sitting room, where he was watching television.

'Seb, your foreign friend phoned earlier. I forgot to tell you. Said to remind you about your mutual friend... you'd know who she meant, she said. Then she asked again if Luke was here. She said she'd lost his phone number, so did I have it? Obviously, he gave it to me prior to the interview, so I gave it to her. Hope that was OK?'

Seb's stomach lurched, and he felt sick. He managed to say, 'Thanks, Dad', before heading to the bathroom to throw up.

Twenty-Two

Tony Montgomery left the offices of Brownlow and Noggs in a state of confusion. He had asked to speak to Charles Abbott. Tony wanted answers to questions about Bea's situation. But now he was wandering towards the centre of Minchford wondering why he had bothered. Chloe had been against the plan and had decided not to go with him. She still had an uneasy feeling about the solicitor.

Tony walked on into the market square. It was market day, so the square was a hive of activity with some stallholders selling fresh fruit and vegetables, whilst others displayed everything from batik scarves to second-hand books and ancient vinyl records. Tony wished he could stay and browse some of the stalls, but he knew he had to get control of his thoughts before reaching his office.

As well as being confused, Tony was frustrated. He had asked unambiguous questions, but Charles Abbott seemed unwilling to give him straight answers. Meanwhile Tony was totting up how much this unproductive appointment was costing him. For convoluted reasons, unfathomable to Tony, Mr Abbott had not yet retrieved Bea's jewellery box from The Willows. There were difficulties about "evidence from a crime-scene" and "change of management", all of which struck Tony as mere obfuscation.

Mr Abbott was equally unforthcoming about how the police investigation was progressing, *but perhaps,* thought Tony, *he really doesn't know.* But whatever subject Tony had tried to pursue, whether Bea's finances, any news about Maddie's death, whether he'd had any contact with Jacob, Tony felt as if he was talking to a brick wall. Mr Abbott had a practised facility for hiding behind "ethical and confidentiality issues", so he was very sorry, but he could not disclose certain matters to Tony. So Tony had given up the unequal struggle, thanked Charles Abbott through gritted teeth and left the solicitor's office.

Sod it! he muttered to himself.

He walked from the market through the picturesque back streets, reluctantly on his way to his office. His phone rang.

'Hi, darling,' said Chloe's cheerful voice, 'how did it go?'

Tony stepped into an office doorway, out of the way of other pedestrians.

'Hmm… ' he replied, 'a total waste of time. You were right all along. I couldn't get anything out of the damned man. He should write a book on how to avoid answering questions, but oh, so pleasantly.'

'So, did you actually get anything useful out of him?' asked Chloe, feeling smug but also disappointed.

'Sod all,' conceded Tony, 'I wish we could kick him into the long grass, but we can't. He still has control of Bea's purse strings, and we need her money to care for her properly. Anyway, can we discuss all this later? I really ought to get to my office.'

With that they ended the call.

* * *

When Tony arrived home some hours later, Bea was in a state of distress, and Chloe was also upset but trying to calm Bea. On hearing Tony close the front door, Chloe came out of Bea's room and signalled to Tony to go into the kitchen.

'Another phone call from Jacob,' she whispered, 'he insisted on speaking to Bea, and now her mind's all over the place. Anyway, you should go and see what she says to you.'

This is all I need right now, thought Tony, but he put a smile on his face and went into Bea's room. She was sitting in her armchair by the window with a tartan blanket over her legs.

'I've been watching the birds on the birdfeeder,' she said, as if nothing else were on her mind, 'they're greedy little things, aren't they? And then the starlings come along and squabble over all the bits the smaller birds drop. I love watching them!'

Tony and Chloe gave each other a bemused look. Whatever had been distressing Bea seemed to have been forgotten.

* * *

Later that evening, when Bea was settled in bed, Chloe could contain herself no longer.

'It was awful, Tony, it really was,' she said. 'I put the phone on All-hear, so I could hear what Jacob was saying to Bea.'

'That's my clever wife,' interrupted Tony, trying to sound supportive.

'It made me cringe,' continued Chloe, ignoring the interruption, 'the way he talked to Bea, as though he's always been really concerned about her, and no one but him should look after her now. I couldn't tell if Bea was swallowing all his deceitful rubbish. She seemed OK at the time, but then she got almost hysterical after the call and soon after that you came home, thank heavens!'

'So what did Jacob say about the new place which he has found for Bea? Or when he thinks he'll move her?' asked Tony.

'Well,' replied Chloe, 'that's the strange part. He gave her absolutely no clue about either. I think we should change our phone number, don't you?'

The sound of Bea's little handbell came from her bedroom. Chloe went to find out what her problem was, fearing that she might be feeling disturbed again by Jacob's phone call, but no, it was a request for a hot milky drink.

Twenty-Three

Paula Trelawney liked to be orderly in the way she worked, especially when it came to record-keeping and financial matters. Since the murder of her predecessor it had been difficult to attract new residents to The Willows, but slowly Paula was beginning to make an impact, as she made links with social workers.

It was taking longer, though, to fathom out Sally Jeavons' so-called systems when it came to records. *To call them idiosyncratic would be generous,* thought Paula. But she was determined to have everything shipshape for the regulators' inspection, due in a few months. Equally worrying were the meetings she had been summoned to by The Willows' owners. She had learned that they were entirely profit-focussed, so if there was no profit, there would be no home. They would cut their losses and invest elsewhere.

Paula was also dealing with low morale among the staff at The Willows. She wished the police would hurry up and charge someone with Sally Jeavons' murder, as this would surely allay the fear and suspicion which still surfaced occasionally. And this had been compounded by Maddie Smith being found dead in unexplained circumstances. Paula foresaw that if jobs arose at other elderly people's homes in Minchford, some of her staff would be relieved to leave The Willows. But Paula was a determined woman. She would do all in her power to transform the home.

One small but significant change had been to rearrange her newly painted office, making it more colourful and welcoming to visitors.

There was a knock on her office door, which was ajar. Paula gestured to a hesitant Lucy Kingdon to come in and close the door.

'Well, Lucy,' asked Paula in a soft voice, 'how can I help you?'

Paula came out from behind her desk, and she and Lucy sat either side of the low coffee table.

'I'll be quick,' said Lucy, 'you never know who's watching you. It's just that I heard someone say something that's been worrying me.'

'So what did you hear, Lucy?' asked Paula.

After some gentle coaxing, Lucy told her boss that she'd overheard another carer, Petra Tradovic, talking on her phone. Petra was behaving quite furtively and changed tack immediately on spotting Lucy a few feet away. But Lucy had heard Petra saying what a lot of idiots the police who had interviewed her had been, and that they had no idea who had killed Mrs Jeavons.

Paula Trelawney nodded thoughtfully.

'You were absolutely right to come and tell me, thank you, Lucy,' she said. 'Let me know if you hear anything else that worries you. And don't mention our conversation to any of the others, please.'

Lucy gave a slight nod and quickly left the office.

Paula pondered on what Lucy had told her. She had picked up that Petra was not liked by her colleagues and that she could come across as surly. Lucy, on the other hand, was a quiet, conscientious worker, kind to the residents and always willing to lend a hand. It would be unlike Lucy to be malicious or spread rumours.

On balance, Paula thought that she should take Lucy's report seriously, but what action did it warrant?

* * *

It was DC Rita Hussein who answered the phone.

'I hope I'm not wasting your time,' said Paula several times, 'I really wasn't sure whether or not to ring you.'

But DC Hussein encouraged Paula to tell her precisely what Lucy had said about Petra's phone call. Eventually Paula was thanked and assured that she could now leave the matter to the police.

Paula leaned back in her chair and contemplated her conversation with DC Hussein. She still wasn't sure whether it had been appropriate to contact the police. *There was very little substance in what Lucy had reported to her,* she thought, *and Petra was working in a foreign country, with English as her second language. Perhaps Lucy had misheard what Petra had said.* The more she thought about it, the more confused Paula became. She decided to take no immediate action, other than to keep a close eye on Petra.

Paula returned to the paperwork on her desk with a groan. Her priority was to review Sally Jeavons' inventory of the residents' possessions stored in the office safe. A local solicitor, Mr Abbott, had called a couple of times about jewellery boxes, savings books, and other valuables which belonged to residents who had subsequently died. *He seems to be dealing with the affairs of quite a few residents,* she noted. Paula was getting frustrated, though, with all the unfiled papers. Some just had lists of figures on them, and others had names and addresses but no indication of which resident they related to. And Paula could find no record of what had been stored in the safe prior to the murder and ransacking of the office.

Paula heard the clink of crockery as the tea-trolley was being wheeled from room to room. She decided to go and chat to some of the residents and forget the paperwork for ten minutes. As she left her office, she locked the door.

As it happened, Petra Tradovic was in the residents' lounge assisting an elderly man drink his tea from a plastic mug. Petra could be brusque, but now she was carrying out her caring tasks with a smile. Paula made a mental note to look at Petra's staff file, just out of interest.

Twenty-Four

'Guv,' said Rita, 'I've been going back through my notes of interviews at The Willows.'

'Hmm…' replied her boss, without looking away from his computer screen. He'd been engrossed in figures on the screen for hours, or so it seemed to Rita.

'I'd like to go and talk to one of the carers, Petra Tradovic, again. She made a comment about us needing to look at visitors to the home, not at the staff. We didn't follow it up at the time, but I think we should. Is that OK, guv?' Baz had only been half listening, but suddenly he was switched onto the murders again.

'Right,' said Baz, straightening his back and swivelling his chair round, 'let's see what the charts tell us about that idea.' He paused. 'Actually, it seemed to me that there were depressingly few visitors to the poor old dears, if the visitors' book is at all accurate,' he said, 'a handful of relatives now and again, the solicitor who'd been at the murder scene, the local vicar for a service once a week, a doctor or two, occasional visits from a chap at the local library, and that was about it. So what's your plan, Rita?'

She explained that it was really just a gut feeling that Petra Tradovic's throwaway comment needed to be followed up. Baz welcomed Rita's initiative. He was very conscious that the investigation was progressing slowly.

So Rita went to The Willows, deliberately not forewarning Petra. On arriving there, she was told that Petra was not on duty today. Rita was cursing her luck, when a voice called out, and Paula Trelawney came along the corridor towards her.

'Do come in,' she said, 'this is actually good timing, if you've got a few minutes.'

Thinking back to Paula's phone call the previous day, Rita's interest was aroused, and she followed Paula into the office.

Paula explained that she had been looking at the personal file relating to Petra Tradovic, who had been working at The Willows for about a year. It was Sally Jeavons who had given her the job. But her personal file contained very little information. There were no references from previous employers nor copies of documentation confirming that she could work in this country. Paula knew that she would have to rectify the situation, and she had qualms about mentioning all this to the police, but in the circumstances, she felt she had to.

Rita's brain was not focussing on poor management, though, but rather on finding out more about Petra, in view of her reported comments about the police and the murder. Her date of birth would be a good start, and after scanning some papers, Paula found it. No confirmation of her country of origin, though.

***

Back at the office Rita found Baz with his eyes still fixed on the screen.

'Time for a coffee, then?' he asked. 'Some positive news would be good too.'

Rita returned from the canteen with some doughnuts and two large cups of coffee. *These should cheer him up,* she thought, *even if I haven't got much news.* Baz was relieved to have a diversion from the tedious figures. He listened closely to Rita's report of her visit to The Willows.

'Well,' said Baz, when Rita had finished, 'another development is that forensics rang while you were out. They've found that both Sally Jeavons and Maddie Smith died due to an injection of a drug, whose name I can't recall offhand, which effectively stopped their hearts. All the slashes on Smith's arms were inflicted while she was dying, and the same goes for Jeavons' wounds. So definitely both murders.'

Rita nodded, careful not to say that they had already deduced that. She wondered, though, who would have access to potentially lethal drugs.

The conversation returned to the subject of Petra. Rita was still keen to interview her, and also to run her scant details through the police database. She wanted to get hold of Petra's phone too. And find out who her friends and family were. After a few minutes of this, Baz had to rein in Rita's plans, as they were at risk of becoming fanciful… understandable, but questionable in terms of ethical policing.

Paula had told Rita when Petra would next be on duty. In the meantime, Rita would run some background checks on her.

'You know, guv,' said Rita, 'perhaps we haven't paid enough attention to Mrs Elsworth and her family. After all,' she continued, 'she might be quite central to all the events. She had that unexplained fall in the garden, then the manager of the home gets murdered, and then the carer who was sacked went and looked after Mrs Elsworth at her relative's home, and now she's been murdered. Have we missed something blindingly obvious?'

Baz's focus was suddenly on the nephew, Tony Montgomery, again.

Twenty-Five

Martin Dean was usually decisive in matters concerning his business. He had spent many years investing his energy and money in the company, and thus far his sound decision-making had paid off. The business was prospering, even though it had had to weather occasional lean times. Martin had always wanted to hand over to Seb, when he reached retirement age, or sooner. He had promised Ros that they would go on a long luxurious cruise soon after he had handed over the reins.

Now, though, his irresponsible son had thrown a proverbial spanner in the works. Martin thought a temporary solution had been found, but Luke had inexplicably not wanted the job. For a couple of days Martin had been looking at the situation from all angles. He had to be decisive. Seb would soon return to university, at a hefty cost to his father. Could Martin be sure that Seb wouldn't fritter his time away again?

After much deliberation, and a late-night discussion with his wife, Martin had come to the conclusion that an ultimatum was due. It might be uncomfortable for everyone, but Seb had to learn that actions have consequences.

* * *

As the family was finishing dinner that evening, Martin announced, in an uncharacteristically authoritative way, that there was to be a family meeting immediately the table had been cleared. Ros looked apprehensive, while Seb and Tilda exchanged surprised glances. Martin ignored their expressions and drank the final few drops of wine. The dishwasher was loaded, and they all returned to their places at the dining table.

Martin cleared his throat, as if about to make a momentous announcement. Tilda stifled a giggle, and Martin glared at his daughter.

'There's nothing amusing about what I'm going to say,' he began. 'You all know that my plans for the company have been undermined, and you also know how bloody disappointed I am about that.'

Seb's face reddened and he shifted slightly in his seat, while Ros looked aghast at her husband's unaccustomed language.

'It's not only that, though,' Martin continued, 'there are other things rumbling around, which you both, Seb and Tilda, need to come clean about. Stop playing your mother and me for imbeciles… we're not! In case you pretend not to know what I'm talking about, let me list a few things. There's Luke for a start, there's something you're not telling us about him.'

Tilda's face turned scarlet, and she feigned a minor coughing fit to cover it. This did not fool her parents, but they ignored it.

'Then there's some nameless foreign woman who rings here. Seb, it's obvious you don't want to tell us about her either, whoever she is. And I'm pretty sure that something happened, while we were away, that you're keeping from us. And what was so distracting at university that you failed exams which you should have waltzed through? Need I spell out any more?'

Tilda wished the ground would open up and swallow her. *Could she really tell her parents that she had slept with Luke? Was it actually legal at her age?* She felt scared.

Seb was mentally sifting through his father's list and wondering how little he could successfully disclose. He thought that damage-limitation was the only way. *He was certainly not going to say that he had spent a night in a police cell, at least not for the time being. He hoped fervently that Tilda would not be so daft as to mention it.*

But Tilda had her own nagging secret, and she was silently begging Seb not to say anything about that.

There was a long uncomfortable silence as neither Seb nor Tilda said anything. Eventually Seb swallowed his pride and mumbled an apology for having wasted his last year at university. This clearly did not placate his father, who glared at his son.

'Well, go on,' he said sharply.

An excruciating time followed for Seb. He confessed that he had spent most of his time at the sailing club. But Martin was not impressed by Seb's achievements in the world of sailing. He told his parents that he had spent too much time with a particular girlfriend and had fallen under her spell. Martin just made a snorting sound.

He was becoming increasingly fractious. Ros, the peacemaker in the family, tried to stem her husband's outbursts of annoyance, although she did have some sympathy with him. Seb and Tilda continued to be unforthcoming.

Martin finally lost all patience with his children.

'Right,' he declared loudly, 'if you two won't cooperate, I have no alternative but to give you an ultimatum. You've both got to learn how to behave responsibly. So, this is my decision. You, Seb, will not return to university, where you will probably waste another year. I refuse to pay another penny for your education until you have proved to your mother and me that you can be trusted.'

Seb and Tilda exchanged horrified glances. Martin hesitated briefly, allowing his children to digest this.

'You, Seb, will immediately start work in the company and believe me, I mean *work*! The management course will be put on hold for a year, and you can do it when you've proved your worth.'

There was a pause.

'And as far as you're concerned, young lady,' continued Martin, looking at Tilda, 'I expect you to knuckle down and get excellent results at the end of your final year at college, and to ignore your brother's appalling example. And maybe sometime soon you'll come clean about why you quizzed me so much about my fall. I'm not daft… you clearly had some interest in the whole scenario beyond touching daughterly love. Think about that, Tilda. Oh, and it's a pity that Luke isn't joining us, as you were scheming. But you'll get over it.'

Tilda was taken aback. She had obviously underestimated her dad.

Twenty-Six

'Well, how about this, guv,' said Rita, 'we've had a call to a burglary. And guess whose house it is.'

But Baz was not in the mood for guessing games.

'Just tell me,' he snapped at Rita.

'Sorry, guv,' she said sheepishly, 'I just thought it might be another piece of the jigsaw. There's been a break-in at the Montgomerys' house. Sad part is that old Mrs Elsworth has apparently been assaulted, and she's on her way to hospital again. Poor old soul. It was Mrs Montgomery who found Mrs Elsworth on the floor with her hands tied behind her back.'

'Right,' said Baz, 'let's get there.'

* * *

A police officer answered the door to Rita and Baz. He briefed them on what had been found so far. Another officer was trying to calm Chloe, who looked pale and dazed.

Baz and Rita were told that Chloe Montgomery had been looking after Bea Elsworth, but was called to an emergency at her office. Chloe had asked her neighbour, Ailsa Rudd, to call in a couple of times while she was out, just to check that Bea was alright. Chloe had left a spare front door key under the flower pot in the porch. Ailsa had been round once, made Bea a cup of tea, and planned to return in an hour if there was no sign of Chloe's car by then. A police officer was talking to Ailsa Rudd at her home now.

When Chloe came home, though, she found Bea lying on the floor in her bedroom with her hands bound behind her back with one of her silk scarves and another scarf acting as a gag in her mouth. The contents of drawers and cupboards were strewn all over the floor. One of the windows was wide open and the curtain was flapping in the breeze. Chloe was too shocked to say yet whether anything had been taken. Her priority had been to get Bea seen by a doctor. She had rung her husband, and he took Bea to the hospital, while she waited for the police.

* * *

Leaving the forensics team to do their work, Baz and Rita were returning to the station. On their way, Rita was thinking aloud about old Mrs Elsworth. First a mysterious fall, then a murder in a place where people should feel safe, then her carer is killed, and now a burglary and assault in her nephew's home.

'What is there about her which attracts all this bad luck?' she asked Baz.

But Baz's mind was elsewhere, and Rita noticed that they were not taking the quickest route to the police station.

'Where're we going, guv?' she asked. There was no reply from Baz, but a few minutes later he was pulling into the parking area in front of The Willows.

'Just a hunch,' he muttered softly.

He rang the bell, and the door was answered by Lucy Kingdon. She smiled on recognising Baz and Rita, and asked them in. Meanwhile Paula Trelawney had seen the car arrive and came out of her office to greet them.

'We won't take up much of your time,' began Baz, 'but would you mind giving us a copy of the staff duty roster for today? You're not under any obligation to, but there are one or two things we want to check. Would that be OK?'

Paula wanted to ask questions about the reason for the request, but something in Baz's manner suggested that it would be best not to.

'Of course,' she replied, 'no problem at all.'

Five minutes later Baz and Rita were on their way back to the police station, with the roster.

* * *

'What was all that about?' asked Rita eventually. Baz was sitting in his swivel chair studying the photocopied papers which Paula Trelawney had given him.

'It may be nothing,' he said enigmatically.

Rita continued to wait. She went over to the window and looked out, just in time to see several officers running out of the station, jump into their marked cars, and screech their way out of the police compound, sirens blaring. She wondered idly what incident had caused the sudden exodus. She thought back to her time as a uniformed officer, based in her home town in the north. She had enjoyed it, but becoming a detective had been a really good move for her. It had involved a major change of lifestyle, but she was pleased that she'd taken the opportunity, not least because she had a good boss and mentor in Baz.

Her musings were interrupted.

'Come and take a look at these,' said Baz, 'and tell me if you see anything relevant in them.'

Rita examined the roster. It took a while to cross-reference the codes which Paula Trelawney used for each member of staff with the staggered shift patterns.

'Well,' she eventually said, with a tone of uncertainty in her voice, 'the carer who is of most interest to us is Petra Tradovic, and, as far as I can work this out, she went on duty today at twelve noon and her shift ends at eight o'clock this evening. So, if she turned up for work today, she wasn't involved in the Montgomery burglary. Is that what you're getting at, guv?'

Before Baz could reply, his phone rang. It was Paula Trelawney. She had been thinking about the roster he was given. It had been such an unexpected request that she now realised, on reflection, that there was more information she could give the police about it. She told Baz that two carers on the roster had not worked their full shifts today. Firstly, Hayley French had rung in sick early this morning and hoped to be at work tomorrow. Secondly, Petra Tradovic had left in the early afternoon to attend a hospital appointment. She had shown Paula a reminder text from the hospital to confirm the appointment. Petra hoped to return to work at about 5pm.

'Well, well,' said Baz after the call had ended.

He relayed the new information to Rita. 'At least that story will be easy enough to check out. Get onto the local hospital, will you, and see if Ms Tradovic really had an appointment, and if she turned up.'

Rita nodded.

Twenty-Seven

Luke had been taught as a child to be prudent with money. But his meagre savings were now perilously low, and he had turned down his only potential job since leaving university. He looked around his poky London flat. All his possessions were packed into a couple of zipped bags, a cardboard box secured with sticky tape and two large plastic bags. He was waiting for a cab to take him and his belongings to his next home. He was worried about the extravagance of calling a cab, but he decided there was no realistic alternative. He didn't want to make several journeys back and forth, as he would have to do on a bus or train. *That would also increase his chances of being seen,* he reasoned.

Since seeing Mishka outside his flat, he had left it as infrequently as possible, usually only venturing out after dark. Having searched the internet and after making dozens of phone calls, Luke had eventually found a temporary place to live, well away from his current flat.

His new home was to be in a village pub, which was being renovated and extended by its new owners. The deal was that Luke would have a room and facilities rent-free, in return for working on the renovation, plus a small wage.

The owners, Mick and Debbie, knew that Luke had no experience of building work, but Mick had cheerfully told him,

"Don't worry, anyone can shift rubble into a skip or sand down doors."

Luke was apprehensive about doing hard manual work. Quietly he hoped that he might do some bar work once he knew Mick better.

When the cab arrived, Luke looked up and down the street as he transferred his belongings from the hallway into the cab. There was no sign of Mishka, and Luke heaved a sigh of relief as he set off for his new home.

During the journey, he thought about Tilda. He wanted to phone her or even meet up with her, if he could persuade her to do that. But he knew that he was probably being unrealistic. He had treated her shamefully and then inexplicably turned down the chance to live and work near her. *What messages was all that giving the poor girl?*

* * *

When the cab finally drew up outside The Ancient Mariner, Luke was pleasantly surprised. He had expected to see a semi-derelict building which was mainly unusable. On the contrary, the façade looked newly painted and was festooned with hanging baskets of foliage and colourful flowers. It had a welcoming appearance and was a popular pub, judging by the number of cars in the parking area. Luke stacked his baggage by the entrance porch and went to look for Mick or Debbie.

This is all a bit too good to be true, thought Luke, as Mick gave him a tour of the premises.

Luke assessed Mick as in his early forties, a man who was very enthusiastic about the expansion of the pub's business. He had worked in banking previously, but he and Debbie had decided to get out of the rat race, as he viewed it, and run their own pub. They had found The Ancient Mariner just over a year ago. It was then in a dilapidated state. Gradually the regular clientele was growing, but Mick had plans to develop the restaurant potential of the pub, hence all the building work. In a couple of years Mick wanted to have established the best gastro pub in the area. Mick's enthusiasm was somehow infectious, and Luke was warming to the thought of his new job, however menial. Only half of the pub had been renovated so far. The unfinished part had been cleverly screened off, so that it didn't distract from the ambience of the bar areas.

Luke was finally shown his room by jovial Mick.

'Hardly a palace,' laughed Mick, 'but good enough, I hope.'

Luke was amazed. It was actually two rooms, a sitting room with a small galley kitchen at one end, and a double bedroom with a tiny shower room and loo. He thought back to his dingy bed-sit in London and couldn't help smiling.

'This is great, thanks Mick,' he said.

* * *

Over the next few days Luke discovered that Mick had been serious about shifting rubble into a skip, in fact into several skips. Each evening he had new blisters, aches and pains. And this wasn't just fine weather work. He found himself trudging through wet mud on some days, trying to negotiate a heavy wheelbarrow over to the skips.

But on balance Luke was pleased that he had moved there. Mick and Debbie had made him feel very welcome, and he was getting to know some of the locals too. *This would suit him in the short-term,* he thought.

His one big regret, though, was losing Tilda. *He didn't even have a picture of her.*

Mick quickly realised that Luke was struggling with the hard, manual labour. He also noticed that Luke would benefit from a sturdier pair of work boots. So he suggested to Luke that he should go to the nearby town, Broomsby, the following day and get whatever work clothing he needed. Luke was relieved to give his aching muscles a rest. He also liked the idea of seeing what leisure possibilities the town might hold.

But Luke's reconnaissance of Broomsby left him wondering what other towns might be on the bus route which passed The Ancient Mariner. *It was a pleasant enough little town, but hardly an action hotspot,* Luke concluded. There were a couple of pubs on the High Street, but they were not as inviting as The Ancient Mariner, even in its unfinished state. And Luke found no signs of potential nightlife in Broomsby. The most thriving business was the one which Mick had directed him to. Luke had bought a serviceable pair of boots there, which had cost him far more than he had hoped.

* * *

On arriving back at the pub, Debbie called across the bar to him.

'Hey, Luke,' she said, 'we had a friend of yours here earlier. Said she was a friend from uni days. She certainly turned a few heads in here, I can tell you! How did you let a girl like that slip through your net?' Debbie laughed.

Luke smiled weakly and tried not to look panic-stricken.

Debbie went on, 'She only stayed a minute or two when she knew you weren't here. Old Joe, over by the window, said a man in a posh car was waiting outside for her. I asked if she wanted to leave a message, but she just said to tell you not to try and escape again, as she'll always find you. She had a lovely laugh and such a refined way of speaking…'

As calmly as he could, Luke thanked Debbie for the message and headed upstairs to his room. He threw his new boots onto the bed and sat on the floor with his head in his hands. *How had that bloody woman found him? He had been so careful about the move. He hadn't even given his landlord a forwarding address.*

And what had Debbie said about her voice… "refined"? That certainly wasn't how Luke would have described Mishka's heavily accented English, which he had initially found so seductive. But then he thought back to the incident at uni, when he should have been meeting up with Josh. He recalled having been astounded at briefly eavesdropping on her conversation with the unknown man, when she had spoken immaculate English. He wondered if he still had access to the photos he had surreptitiously taken then.

Luke's emotions were oscillating from seething anger to white-knuckled fear and back again.

How will I ever be rid of this bloody stalker? he asked himself.

Twenty-Eight

Ros Dean was standing in the kitchen finishing off some ironing and listening to a gardening programme on the radio. The phone in the hall rang. She switched off the iron and turned the radio down.

'Hello,' she said cheerfully.

A business-like voice replied, 'Mrs Dean? I would like to speak with Sebastian Dean, please. This is DC Hussein from Minchford police.'

Ros's heart sank. *What on earth has Seb been up to,* she wondered. Trying to sound unconcerned, she said, 'My son is at work at the moment. Can I give him a message, or can you tell me what this is about?'

'What time will he be home?' the business-like voice asked. It was clear that she was going to be told nothing, so Ros meekly agreed to ask Seb to ring DC Hussein later, and she wrote down the number.

Ros returned to the kitchen, turned off the radio and thought about the call. She suddenly realised that she was shaking. It was the tone of the call which bothered her most. There was an almost officious edge to it. *Was Seb in some sort of trouble that he hadn't told his parents about? And why a call from Minchford police? That was the place the policewoman had said, wasn't it?*

Ros was on the verge of ringing her husband and telling him about the call, but she stopped herself. She knew that Martin was convinced that Seb and Tilda were keeping something significant from them, so this phone call might be an opening for Seb to explain things. So Ros made a cup of camomile tea and finished off the remaining pieces of ironing. She would tell Seb about the call when he arrived home that afternoon.

* * *

Tilda arrived home from college, grabbed one of Ros's newly baked scones as she passed through the kitchen, and went up to her room, saying 'Got an horrendous amount of work to do… call me for supper, will you?' to Ros, and the whirlwind was gone!

Martin was the next to arrive home, unusually early. He gratefully accepted a cold beer from Ros and slumped into a chair in front of the television news.

'What a day!' he sighed, but offered no more details. Ros knew better than to ask.

She was wondering, though, what Seb's entrance would be like. Little did he know that the police were expecting a call from him. Ros continued preparing supper for them all. She was making a beef mince lasagne, knowing that this was a family favourite and hoping it might help a potentially difficult evening.

Seb eventually came through the kitchen door.

'Had a good day?' asked Ros.

'Yeah,' was the reply, 'it's been quite interesting.'

Seb sat down on a kitchen chair, having got a beer from the fridge. He seemed to want to talk to his mum about his day. But Ros decided to tell Seb straightaway that he had a message from a policewoman.

'By the way, Seb,' she began, 'you had a call earlier from Minchford police. A DC Hussein. She wouldn't tell me what it was about, but she asked that you ring her as soon as possible today.'

Seb put his beer on the table, and the colour drained dramatically from his face. Ros saw that he was shocked by this news. She pulled up a chair next to her son and put her hand on his shoulder.

'Are you OK?' she asked gently.

'Yeah, Mum, I'll be fine… just surprised, that's all,' Seb replied.

Ros's maternal intuition told her otherwise, but she gave Seb the paper on which she had scribbled the policewoman's name and phone number. He could make the call when he felt ready.

Seb went up to his room and closed the door. *What the hell do the police want now?* The question was relentlessly recurring in his mind. Memories of that hellish time in Minchford police station flooded back, and he felt sick. *That revolting, claustrophobic cell, the constant banging of doors, noises of drunks throwing up, the foul-smelling interview room with its CCTV recording his every move, the revolting food, and the endless, pointless questions. Why did they think he was implicated in a murder? They had "intelligence", but what, and who the hell from?*

Seb forced his thoughts back into the present. He had to ring that woman in a few minutes. He had to be calm. *Perhaps they just wanted him to know that they had charged someone else with the murder, and he was no longer of any interest to them. Perhaps they wanted to apologise to him.* Seb was not convincing himself with these thoughts, but his pulse rate was slowing a little.

A few more swigs of beer, and he would be ready… he thought, *or, better perhaps, no more beer until later.*

Seb had earlier scrunched up the paper with the number, but now he flattened it out. He got his mobile out of his jacket pocket and, with trembling fingers, rang DC Hussein.

Twenty-Nine

Tony arrived at the hospital and took Aunt Bea into the Accident and Emergency Department. She was given a thorough examination, but thankfully she had no serious injuries. She was bruised around her wrists, where she had been tied, and also on one side of her mouth, where the gag had rubbed, but otherwise she was physically fine. The nurse voiced surprise at how well Mrs Elsworth had come through her ordeal. There was no reason for her to be admitted as an in-patient. Tony discreetly phoned Chloe and said that Bea was coming home with him soon.

During Bea's absence, the police had gathered whatever forensic evidence they could find and left, telling Chloe that she could now tidy up the room, if she wished to. They would be in contact again soon.

After Tony's call, she set about restoring order to Bea's room, trying to work out what, if anything, had been stolen. She knew that Bea liked to keep a small quantity of cash in a distinctive dark blue leather purse with a metal clasp in the form of a Maltese cross, and that seemed to be missing. The walnut sewing box, which was serving as Bea's jewellery box for the time being, was lying, upturned, on the carpet, and there was no sign of Bea's favourite, Scandinavian-looking silver brooch. Other than that, nothing seemed to have been taken.

Perhaps I disturbed them when I came home, speculated Chloe, and she shuddered at the thought. *Whoever it was had presumably made a hasty exit through the open window.*

* * *

A short while later, Tony helped a slightly unsteady Bea into the house.

'Oooh,' she exclaimed, 'something smells nice. Is that our supper? They didn't give me any supper at the hospital… they always used to!'

Tony gave his wife an amused look, and he noticed how tired Chloe looked. So he helped Bea into her usual chair in the kitchen, put a rug over her knees, and poured a glass of wine for each of them. Bea smiled contentedly.

Chloe was concerned about how Bea might react on going into her room again. But she needn't have worried. After supper Bea announced that she felt really tired. It had been an exhausting day, but so nice to go for a drive in Tony's car. Perhaps they could do it again soon? Tony and Chloe smiled at each other. There was something endearing about Bea's occasional wanderings into her own world. If they helped Bea to forget the traumas of the real world, that was a bonus.

Bea was soon sleeping peacefully in her bed.

* * *

Sleep did not come so easily to Chloe that night, though. She constantly thought about the day's events, and about how they could realistically care for Bea. She felt terribly guilty at having left Bea alone in the house for a couple of hours, even with the backup of Ailsa from next door. *Could she be accused of neglect?* That thought horrified her. *They really needed to find another person like Maddie, but where did they start looking?*

Amidst these thoughts the spectre of Jacob emerged, making Chloe shudder. Eventually, exhausted, she fell into a fitful sleep.

Tony snored rhythmically beside her.

* * *

The following morning, Chloe phoned DC Hussein to report that two items were missing from Bea's room, the dark blue purse and the silver brooch. She also confirmed that there was no indication of the burglars having been in any other rooms.

DC Hussein seemed particularly interested in the description of the missing items. She told Chloe that they did not plan to interview either Bea or her today, but they would be in touch soon. Chloe heaved a sigh of relief. She really wanted life to revert to normality.

* * *

In the early evening, just after Tony had arrived home from work, the phone rang. Tony answered it in the hall. Chloe was intrigued. Most of their social calls were made on their mobiles. But she could pick up few clues, as Tony was listening far more than speaking. The call continued for several minutes, ending with Tony saying, 'Yes, of course I'll tell her,' which aroused Chloe's curiosity even more.

'Who on earth was that?' asked Chloe.

Tony smiled enigmatically.

'Well,' replied Tony, 'that's one less thing to worry about,' and he went into the kitchen to pour some wine.

'Oh, for heavens' sake, Tony, just tell me,' said Chloe, a tad tetchily.

Tony sat at the kitchen table and motioned to Chloe to sit opposite him.

'That was DC Hussein,' began Tony, 'and they've caught our burglar! How about that?' Chloe looked astonished.

'Well, it didn't take her all that time to tell you just that… come on, I want to hear the rest. Who was it?' she asked.

Tony knew he was teasing Chloe, so he launched into the whole story.

DC Hussein had explained that the burglar, a thirteen-year-old local boy, was caught inside a house seven or eight further down the road. Someone in the house opposite just happened to be looking out of an upstairs window and noticed the boy acting suspiciously. He seemed to be fiddling with the front door lock. She knew the people who lived in the house, but she'd never seen this boy before. So she rang the police, and he was still inside when they pitched up. Apparently, they've had dealings with this lad before. He was bunking off school and looking for empty houses to steal money from.

DC Hussein said he always admits to everything straightaway, and he did this time. He emptied his pockets and Bea's purse, with her money, and the brooch were there. He apparently told the police that he didn't want to tie up "the old girl", as he referred to Bea, but she kept being a nuisance and telling him off! He was adamant that she was sitting on the side of her bed when he legged it out through the window, and not lying on the floor. The police are inclined to believe him. 'So I suppose,' concluded Tony, 'that Bea actually lost her balance and fell to the floor.'

Chloe had been listening carefully. She was very relieved that this situation had been resolved so quickly, and that Jacob wasn't involved in any way, as she had secretly feared. She found it unnerving, though, that someone, albeit an experienced young burglar, had got into the house so easily in broad daylight. But the guilt Chloe felt about leaving Bea unprotected in the house would not be easily erased from her mind.

'Wasn't there something else?' asked Chloe, 'Something you were meant to tell me?'

'Oh yes,' replied Tony. 'DC Hussein repeated that she is unlikely to need to interview Bea or you, as things stand at present. And one other thing… would you please not leave your front door key under a flower pot in future.'

Tony gave his wife a sideways look and smiled.

Thirty

'Does the name Tradovic mean anything to you?' asked DC Hussein.

She was speaking to Seb Dean, who had rung her as requested. She sensed that Seb was anxious, but she came straight to the point. Baz had advised her to do that. He knew that the police had given Seb a hard time, but Baz's intuition told him that there must be a connection between him and the Jeavons murder… and they would root it out.

Rita had phoned the local hospital earlier and learned that Petra Tradovic had genuinely had an appointment there, as she had told Paula Trelawney. Ms Tradovic had attended. So any initial suspicions that she might have been involved in the Montgomerys' burglary were unfounded. And anyway, that offence had now been cleared up.

Seb was bewildered by DC Hussein's question and hesitated before replying, 'No, it doesn't mean anything to me, why should it?'

But Rita had no intention of answering questions, just asking them. She said, 'Thank you for calling back, Mr Dean, and thank you for your assistance,' and she ended the call.

Seb was shaking. *What the hell was that all about?* he wondered.

He knew he would have to give his mother an explanation of the mysterious call from the police. He was sure that she would want to know the details. And he would certainly need to get his story straight with Tilda. He desperately hoped that his mother had not already mentioned the call to her. Tilda would immediately make the connection between today's call and his arrest. *But would she be able, or willing, to cover for Seb? And how could they be sure that their stories tallied?*

Seb's initial idea was to say honestly that the police were enquiring about whether he knew someone, and he had assured them that he didn't. Thinking this through, though, Seb foresaw that it would give rise to a barrage of questions from his mum, and worse still, from his dad. *After all, why would the police in another town contact him, unless they already knew of him? And saying that he had been interviewed by the police, while they were away, wouldn't help matters either.* The more he thought about it, the more agitated Seb became. *The most dire scenario,* he thought, *would be if his dad took it upon himself to contact Minchford police to ask for an explanation. That would be totally mortifying.*

Thirty-One

Chloe was sitting in the dining room reading a gripping novel, when there was a loud knock on the front door. Bea was in her room listening to her favourite Mozart piano concerto.

Chloe walked over to the window and looked to see who was at the door. 'Oh hell, no,' she said to herself, when she saw Jacob standing by the door.

She went into the kitchen and phoned Tony. She left a message, explaining that Jacob was at their home. She took a deep breath, quietly closed Bea's door, and walked slowly to the front door, determined not to allow Jacob in. There was another longer, louder knock.

Chloe left the safety chain on the door, opened it a few centimetres, and asked Jacob softly what he wanted. But Jacob was not in the mood for a quiet conversation.

'What do you think I sodding want?' he shouted, 'I want to talk to my ma.'

Chloe fought with herself to remain calm, in appearance at least.

'Take the bloody chain off and sodding well let me in,' bellowed Jacob.

Chloe tried to push the door closed, but Jacob had his foot wedged in the gap to stop her. This stand-off went on for several minutes, which felt like an age to Chloe. Jacob was shouting obscenities at Chloe and threatening her with violence if she didn't let him into the house.

She was very relieved to see her neighbour, Ailsa, appear at the front gate, seemingly having heard the commotion. Ailsa looked at Chloe and called out, 'Shall I call the police? Are you OK?'

Chloe called back, 'Yes, get the police,' and she saw Ailsa take her phone out of her pocket.

Jacob was panicked by this exchange, turned on his heel and charged at the gate. He pushed Ailsa violently into the hedge, ran a short distance down the road, got into a car and sped off. Ailsa disentangled herself painfully from the thorny hedge and had the presence of mind to try and read the car's registration number. But she could only see part of it. She then went back to Chloe's house.

Ailsa found Chloe sitting on the floor in the hallway, the front door now open, her back against a wall. She had her arms around her bent-up knees, and she was visibly shaking.

'Right,' said Ailsa, taking charge, 'some hot, sweet tea is what you need. Come on, we'll go into the kitchen and have a chat. Hopefully the police won't be too long.'

Ailsa closed the front door, and Chloe meekly stood up, feeling unsteady, and let Ailsa lead her into the kitchen. Ailsa was perturbed by what she had witnessed at Chloe's front door, but she thought it best to curb her curiosity. She gave Chloe a few minutes to recover, so they sat and drank their tea in silence.

Chloe gradually calmed down and was very relieved that Bea hadn't heard the altercation at the door.

'Do you want to talk about it?' asked Ailsa kindly.

'Well,' replied Chloe, 'that charming man is Bea's son.'

Ailsa looked astonished. She was eager to hear more, but she let Chloe take her time.

'I'm so glad you heard him,' said Chloe in a croaky voice, 'I was so scared… it's not the first time he's been here.'

By now tears were streaming down Chloe's face, so Ailsa took some tissues from a box she had spotted on the window sill.

'Well, thank heavens I was just getting home from the bus stop. I might not have heard him if I'd been in the house,' said Ailsa quietly, pulling her chair nearer to Chloe.

'What does he actually want?' she asked. 'He'd hardly have been in a mood to chat with Bea, by the look of things.'

'Well, that's what we can't understand,' replied Chloe, between sobs. 'Tony has always been the one to care about Bea, not Jacob. He's only recently appeared on the scene again, having taken no interest in Bea for years, as far as we can tell. And Bea has hardly ever mentioned him. But suddenly he's very angry about us making decisions with her, and he wants to take her away to some other care home, or so he says. We have no idea why. Well, you've seen him… how could he possibly look after Bea properly?'

Chloe's tone was gradually turning to anger as she told Ailsa the story. 'Obviously Jacob had to be informed about Bea's fall at The Willows, but I'm certain he didn't bother to visit her in the hospital. If he was really concerned about her, he'd have done that at least, wouldn't he?' Chloe was becoming increasingly agitated as she spoke.

'And is it just a coincidence that he turned up here, all guns blazing, just after we'd been burgled and Bea was hurt?' she added.

Ailsa was initially at a loss to know how to respond. She and Chloe had never been close friends, but just neighbours who helped each other out occasionally. She would never have guessed that such a drama was playing out next door. The Montgomerys had always been such polite, quiet neighbours. But Ailsa was essentially a practical person and would always be willing to help.

'Would you like me to stay with you until your husband gets home, or until the police arrive?' she asked. Chloe nodded, a grateful expression on her face.

'Then I'll make a cuppa for Bea, and perhaps we could go and sit with her for a while. She might be wondering why her door is closed, and we don't want her worrying, do we?' asked Ailsa.

A short time later Chloe heard a key in the front door lock, and Tony called out. She was very relieved that he was now at home with her. Ailsa put on her jacket, and Chloe thanked her profusely for being such a good friend in a crisis.

'Don't be silly,' said Ailsa in response, 'I'm sure you'd do the same for me… but I really hope you don't have to!'

She gave them a smile and a little wave as she left.

* * *

Tony sensed that Chloe needed a hug, and he kissed her gently on the cheek.

'Right,' he said quietly, 'I think a glass of wine is in order. And I fancy fish and chips from the local chippy this evening. Does that sound good to you, Bea?' Bea smiled happily at her nephew.

'Come on, Chlo, let's go and choose some wine, and you can tell me about your day. Then over supper, I want to hear what mischief you've been up to today,' he said, with a grin towards Bea.

Chloe had hardly begun recounting to Tony the horror of Jacob's visit, when the front door bell rang. She involuntarily took a step backwards, a scared look on her face. Tony motioned to her to stay in the kitchen and went to open the door. A uniformed police officer was standing on the step.

Tony invited PC Nicola Robertson into the dining room and went to find Chloe.

The fish and chips would have to wait.

Thirty-Two

Luke decided that he couldn't let the Mishka situation drift on any longer. *He'd had enough of it all.* As far as he was concerned, he had been unwittingly lured by seductive Mishka into something which he didn't understand. He now accepted that he had merely been a pawn in whatever game she was playing, and that he himself had never been of any interest to her. She had played him for an idiot, and that's exactly what he had been.

What riled Luke even more was that he was apparently not her intended ultimate target. *It was Seb Dean,* he now knew, *whom she and Helena were interested in, not him at all. He was simply a useful means to an end. But if that was the case, why was bloody Mishka still stalking him? She and Helena knew where the Deans lived, they knew the phone number, so why couldn't they concentrate on Seb instead?*

Luke could come up with no answers. But he did make one decision. And he hoped that he'd be able to stick to it. *He would not be intimidated by Mishka any longer. His paranoia must stop, right now. His life might not seem to have a particularly brilliant future at the moment, but he would take control of it. No more trying to disappear off people's radars. He would move on when and where he decided.*

Luke felt marginally better for having made this decision. He knew, though, that keeping to it would have costs. If possible, he still didn't want Tilda to be one of those costs. He really wanted to have a reconciliation with her, somehow.

Luke thought that the only way to extricate himself completely from this mess was to try and analyse the mess. He took a few sheets of paper out of his newly-acquired but ropey printer and found a pen. He smirked at his doing this... another sign of paranoia? But he felt more secure putting his thoughts on paper, just at the moment, than storing them on his laptop. His plan was to note down anything significant involving Mishka, Helena or Seb since this whole fiasco had started. *There had to be some clues as to what it was all about,* or that was Luke's hope.

The noise from the pub drifted up to Luke's room. He fancied a beer and some company for a while. But none of the regulars were around this evening, so Luke picked up his beer and returned to his flat.

He decided to think up the headlines in the conundrum facing him. Firstly, there was Mishka. Next there was Helena, and Seb. Then there were mysterious texts. At one point, Helena used blackmailing tactics. Someone called George seemed central to the saga. There were times when Mishka's appearance and even her voice seemed to change dramatically. There was an unknown man, or men, who knew Mishka.

Luke decided to end the list there for the time being. There were more than enough topics there to keep his mind busy, and probably to cause him some sleepless nights.

Perhaps I'll go and get another beer, he thought.

Thirty-Three

'I was standing at the photocopier just now,' began Rita, as she entered her boss's office, 'and Nicola Robertson came in and said she'd like a word.' Baz looked up from his computer, a puzzled expression on his face.

'Who?' he asked.

'Nicola,' repeated Rita, 'you know, guv, the PC who went for promotion a few weeks back.'

'Oh, right, so what did she want?' asked Baz, without much enthusiasm.

'To tell us about another incident at the Montgomery household,' said Rita. 'She was writing up her record of a visit she'd made, when she noticed that we'd been there recently too… well, that I had actually.'

Baz swivelled his chair round, looking much more interested now. 'So why did they call the police this time?' he asked.

Rita repeated what PC Robertson had told her. 'A neighbour had heard shouting on the Montgomerys' doorstep as she was arriving home from somewhere. She saw that Mrs Montgomery had only opened the door slightly, and she thought she was telling the man to leave her alone. He was trying to force the door open, but also to stop it being shut. According to the neighbour, Ailsa Rudd, the same one who had been calling in to look after the old lady when she was burgled, the man was using foul language to Mrs Montgomery and threatening violence against her. He was shouting and making quite a disturbance. So Mrs Rudd phoned the police. The man then ran down the path, out of the gate, pushing Mrs Rudd hard into a hedge. He ran down the road to a car and sped off. She tried to get the car's registration number, but could only see two or three digits. So Nicola has just got back from interviewing both Mrs Montgomery and Mrs Rudd. Mrs Montgomery said that the man concerned is the old lady's son, name of Jacob Elsworth. She had no address for him.'

Baz leaned back in his chair and looked at the ceiling. 'Very eventful house, that one,' he reflected.

Rita decided that she would also give feedback to Baz on her brief phone conversation with Sebastian Dean.

'Another thing, guv,' she added, 'I've been meaning to tell you that Sebastian Dean rang me back. I would gauge from his reaction that he really had no idea who I was talking about when I mentioned the name Tradovic to him. I'm convinced that there's no link between him and Petra Tradovic.'

'Had to be checked out though,' said her boss, and he returned his attention to the computer screen.

Rita wandered along the corridor and found an empty office where she could sit and think without being disturbed. She was frustrated at the slow rate of progress on the two murders. She had been so pleased to become a detective constable. *But solving crimes in the real world is quite different from in fictional worlds. And serious crimes don't happen in a neat, convenient sequence,* thought Rita, *so that one can be solved before the next investigation starts. There are so many balls to be juggled and kept in the air at the same time.*

Rita quickly decided that this train of thought was not productive. If she wanted to prove that she had the makings of a good detective, she needed results. *And how often would she have two murders to work on?* So Rita determined to banish any despondent thoughts and to try some lateral thinking.

Have Baz and I missed something obvious, she asked herself.

Thirty-Four

'There are a few things I want to come clean about,' began Seb hesitantly, 'but no questions until I've finished… OK?'

The Deans were all sitting round the dining table. Martin insisted that they all eat together in the evenings; it was a ritual his parents had instilled in him, when he was a child. Martin and Ros looked at each other, wondering what was coming, and Tilda had an apprehensive look on her face.

'OK, Seb,' said his father, 'we agree.'

Seb took a deep breath, hoping that "coming clean" was a wise move on his part. He had been weighing up how much to disclose to his parents ever since his father had announced that he would not be returning to university. With the wisdom of hindsight, Seb acknowledged to himself that he had been a selfish idiot as far as the Helena saga was concerned. He had easily succumbed to her charms and flattery, and he had unwittingly become embroiled in something he still didn't understand. But he had far more qualms about telling his parents of his detention in a police station… in connection with a murder.

The next ten minutes were very uncomfortable for Seb. The family kept to its agreement, although there were occasional astonished looks. Seb knew that he was giving his parents an abbreviated, sanitised version of his relationship with Helena, *but that was all they needed,* he thought. From his perspective, that relationship was in the past, and hopefully there would be no more phone calls from her.

But the recent call from DC Hussein in Minchford required more detailed explanation. Seb stressed, though, that he envisaged no more contact from her in future. That whole episode was also in the past, or so Seb fervently hoped.

As far as he knew, neither of his parents had had any personal dealings with the police, not even a speeding offence. So to hear that their son was "helping the police with their enquiries" came as a real shock to them. Seb glossed over the aspects which had terrified him most, and just gave a factual account of parts of the interviews. He didn't mention how long he had been held at the police station, nor the state he had been in, when he called Tilda to the garden of The Black Horse. He foresaw that his parents would, understandably, want to know why he had been 'put in the frame'. Seb still had no answer to this.

When he had disclosed all that he planned to, Seb took some sips of wine and waited for the anticipated fallout. The initial silence made him edgy.

His father was the first to speak. 'It took some guts for you to tell us all that, Seb,' began Martin, 'well done.'

Seb felt a surge of relief, but he feared that the negatives were yet to come.

'But,' continued Martin, 'I'm left with many questions. What exactly does this bizarre woman, Helena, want from you? You said something about a man called George, but who is he, and why does she think you know him? And what has he got that she is after?'

Seb looked dejected.

'Honestly, Dad, if I could answer those questions, believe me, I would!' replied Seb, 'I just want her out of my life!'

'But this business of the murder is obviously very serious,' Martin went on. 'You say the victim was the manager of a care home? In Minchford? They must surely have had some convincing information which suggested that you were involved, but what the hell was it?'

Another silence ensued.

Then Martin suddenly said, 'Minchford… I thought it rang a bell. That's where the solicitor was from who wrote to me. He was asking all sorts of strange questions about some of our Montgomery relatives. Do you remember, Ros?'

Ros shook her head and looked blank. She was completely bewildered by the evening's revelations. She had never envisaged her family being involved with the police… all this was simply outside her realms of experience. She wished it would all go away, and that they could return to peaceful family life.

But Martin had the bit between his teeth now.

'I think I talked to you about it too, Tilda,' he said. 'He was asking about George Montgomery, I seem to remember, but I couldn't really help him, as I'd never had much to do with that side of the family. The story went that there'd been a major rift in the past, but I've never known the details. It looks as though it has resurfaced for some reason, but heaven knows why it should be of interest to this woman, Helena. Is it just a coincidence that the person she wants to find happens to be called George too? What do you reckon, Seb?'

Seb didn't answer immediately. His stomach was churning, and he was feeling increasingly anxious. He also felt relieved, though, that he had opened up to his parents, and his dad was being supportive. But he knew that he had minimised parts of the story, unable to disclose the whole truth at this stage.

Tilda was feeling relieved too. In the past she would never have trusted her brother to keep quiet about any indiscretions, however minor. He would previously have revelled in seeing her squirm in front of their parents. But this evening he had neither compromised nor belittled her. Tilda was viewing her brother in a more positive light.

She suddenly recalled a conversation between Luke, Seb and herself, while her parents were on their cruise.

'Didn't you say once, Seb, that we had some relative called George, who'd been flung in jail for some reason, and that he'd died there? I'm sure you said it was abroad somewhere, ages ago. Do you remember?'

Seb was about to reply, when his father chipped in.

'That's absolutely right,' confirmed Martin. 'It's coming back to me now. That story was always repeated at family gatherings, years ago, but I'm not sure that anyone really knew how much got embellished with each telling! I suspect that the details changed each time it was told. I first heard about old George when I was a boy, so it was all quite exciting having a notorious criminal in the family, and I'm probably as guilty as anyone else of exaggerating his dastardly deeds! But that George wasn't a Montgomery. His name was George Darwin, and he was my grandmother's father. Perhaps Mr Abbott is after the wrong George. Well, I don't intend to enlighten him. Anyway, obviously I never met George Darwin, and I have no idea when or where he actually died. So why anyone should be interested in him now is quite beyond me! It seems a bit far-fetched to me that a solicitor and your ex-girlfriend would both be after information about him, if that's who they mean... all very strange.'

Ros had been fidgeting during the whole conversation. She didn't like mysteries. And she certainly tried to avoid anything which disturbed family life. This discussion had been unsettling for her in many ways.

Thirty-Five

Chloe was searching in the cupboards and drawers in Bea's room, hoping to find some warm gloves for Bea. Tony had suggested that they all go to a craft fair in the grounds of a local stately home next weekend. He planned to take Bea's wheelchair in the car. As long as the weather was fine, it would make a pleasant change for all of them. But Chloe knew that Bea's arthritic hands tended to become cold quickly, so gloves would be essential.

The search for gloves was unsuccessful. But Chloe noticed two cardboard boxes stacked neatly at the back of the lowest shelf in a cupboard. They looked like some of the boxes she and Tony had used to bring Bea's belongings to their home from The Willows. She thought that Maddie had emptied them all, but perhaps there was nothing in them which Bea needed immediately, so she had stored them out of the way. Chloe was curious about their contents, so she took them into the conservatory to have a look.

She lifted the lid of the first box. It contained a collection of old Christmas cards, dozens of them. She opened the first few. They were cards to Bea from her friends and clearly dated back several years or even decades. Beneath them in the box Chloe found two embroidered silk handkerchiefs neatly wrapped in yellowing tissue paper, with a small card between them. The card, which had pale pink roses round its edges, was inscribed "For my beloved wife Beatrice, with my love, Edgar". Tears welled up in Chloe's eyes. She felt moved by the card, but also guilty at intruding into a distant intimacy in Bea's life. She wondered whether to keep looking in the box or to return it to the cupboard. She was intrigued by what else the boxes might reveal.

She replaced everything in the first box but couldn't resist a quick look in the second one. At first glance, it seemed to contain official documents, so Chloe replaced the lid. She decided to put the boxes in her bedroom, under the bed, and consult with Tony about what they should do. Chloe was mindful that the boxes were actually Bea's personal possessions, although it seemed probable that she had forgotten about their existence.

Chloe hadn't noticed how long she had been searching in Bea's room. But when she checked, Bea was still in her chair in the kitchen, dozing peacefully.

Chloe, on the other hand, had several worries. Firstly, she was not pulling her weight with her work colleagues… she kept taking time off. In addition to that, she and Tony had been vacillating about how best to care for Bea in the future. They had not yet tried to find a replacement for Maddie. They also hadn't started looking for another home for her. Neither of them really wanted Bea to move, after all the events at The Willows. An even worse prospect, though, was that Jacob would insist on making decisions about his mother and moving her somewhere unsuitable.

Chloe wasn't at all sure that she and Tony had more rights in respect of Bea's care than Jacob had. She felt certain that it was more of a legal minefield than Charles Abbott had led them to believe.

* * *

Chloe was sitting at the kitchen table, thinking.

Bea suddenly looked up and said, 'I wonder what Anna is up to these days. Such a pretty name, Anastasia, isn't it? She was so kind to me, but she never comes to see me nowadays.'

Chloe was taken aback momentarily but then saw an unexpected opening. She encouraged Bea to tell her more.

'Can you recall when you last saw Anna?' she asked gently.

'Oh, my dear, she always looked so beautiful, so entrancing. Everyone admired her. She had an air of mystery which fascinated everyone, especially the men. She could have chosen anyone, but she and George fell head over heels in love with each other. George was such a saucy man! Poor Juliana.'

Bea's entire face had lit up, and she chuckled softly, engrossed in her memories. But for Chloe the moment had passed. She was eager to hear more, but Bea sat back in her chair with a happy expression on her face and closed her eyes.

* * *

Later that evening, after Bea had gone to bed, Chloe told Tony about the boxes. His response was unequivocal. They should look at the papers and see if they could learn anything about Jacob or even Anastasia. Tony didn't anticipate that anything useful would be revealed about Anastasia, as he assumed that she had died decades ago.

'On a more practical level,' suggested Chloe, 'we might discover something about Bea's financial situation, if there are old bank statements in the box.'

'I don't suppose there's much money to find,' laughed Tony, 'perhaps just a silver sixpence or two in an ancient envelope, but I doubt even that!'

They started to place the papers in neat rows on their bed. It was clear that no one had sorted them out for years. There was no semblance of any order, just a jumble of random papers at first glance. There were old photographs too, some dating back to Bea's childhood or even earlier, judging by the clothing being worn. Chloe was fascinated by them, especially as a few had names written in spidery handwriting on the back, presumably identifying the subjects.

'We'll have to persuade Bea to have a look at these sometime and tell us who the people are, if she can remember,' said Chloe enthusiastically, 'there's probably lots of your family history here.'

'Good idea,' agreed Tony, 'but let's go through all these papers first, eh?'

After another hour of skim-reading papers and putting them in related piles, they were both feeling disheartened.

'How on earth did someone manage to cram all these documents into one box?' sighed Chloe. 'It'll take forever to make sense of them!'

'I'm not sure about that,' said Tony, 'that pile of bank statements is growing nicely, and they might tell us something. I wonder what Mr Abbott would make of us going through all this lot!'

Chloe gave him a questioning look.

'And what would Jacob think of it?' he continued.

Chloe was silent for a while, disquieted by the potential implications of what they were doing. Then she had a sudden thought.

'I forgot to tell you,' she said, 'Bea suddenly started talking about Anastasia before you came home. She was saying how mysterious and gorgeous Anastasia was, and how she and George had fallen desperately in love with each other. But then she mentioned someone I hadn't heard of before... Juliana. Just after that Bea closed down again. She seemed to be lost in lovely memories, so I didn't disturb her. But who's this Juliana? I don't recall having heard her name before. Do you know where she fits in?'

Tony looked uncertain and slowly shook his head.

'Perhaps she's in one of the photographs,' he suggested. 'Come to think of it, perhaps Anastasia is too.'

Thirty-Six

Paula Trelawney was also battling with piles of papers. It was taking her hours to find any system in the way Sally Jeavons had dealt with paperwork. Paula couldn't understand how all this had gone unnoticed by her employers for so long. Gradually, though, Paula worked out that papers fell into two basic categories. Anything relating to the elderly person's admission to The Willows, correspondence from relatives or professionals, and a daily record of a resident's health and drug prescriptions, was filed neatly in a resident's personal file. The second category of papers, the ones perplexing Paula more, concerned financial matters, personal possessions, and some residents' wills. Paula was puzzled... *why hadn't this mess been picked up by auditors?*

Paula decided to ignore the past and focus on getting things orderly in the present. Then she could hand over clearly accountable systems to her successor.

Many of the papers seemed to relate to former residents. Paula set about identifying those first. Several people had moved out of The Willows immediately after the murder of Sally Jeavons. And two residents had since died.

Paula thought back to the death of Elsie Butterworth, just two weeks ago. Elsie had been a colourful character with an endearing sense of humour. She had been eighty-nine when she died. That afternoon she had been happily joining in a sing-song in the residents' lounge and chatting with the volunteers who came in to help. Then, that night, she had just quietly slipped away. *The saddest part,* thought Paula, *was that Elsie had no relatives to come to her funeral, so the only people there were staff from The Willows and a few members of the church which she had previously attended, when there was someone to take her.* But Paula remembered Elsie with fondness, even though she had only known her briefly.

So when Paula came across a document with Elsie's name on it, she read it carefully. It was a letter dated some time ago, from a firm of solicitors, Brownlow and Noggs. The gist of it was an invitation to Mrs Butterworth to discuss her will with them and to revise it, if she wished. Paula felt uneasy that an elderly resident would be approached in this apparently unsolicited way… and what was the letter doing in Sally Jeavons' possession? Paula looked at it more carefully. The signatory was Charles Abbott. *Now why did she know that name?* It suddenly clicked… *he had been one of the people to discover Sally Jeavons' body, hadn't he?* A shiver went down Paula's spine.

The letter to dear old Elsie spurred Paula on. She determined to separate out any documents from solicitors to individual residents, alive or dead. Paula felt protective towards them. If there were any dubious practices going on, she wanted to know about them.

Thirty-Seven

Chloe was rushing around, getting ready to go to work. She had no alternative this morning but to go to her office for a few hours. Her phone rang. Chloe cursed. She momentarily contemplated letting it go into voicemail, but then thought better of it... *it might be the police, or Jacob,* she thought.

She answered, and a woman's voice said tentatively, 'Is that Mrs Montgomery? I'm Sadie Smith, Maddie's mum.'

Chloe was taken aback. Apart from sending Mrs Smith a condolence card after her daughter's death, Chloe had had no contact with her.

'How can I help you, Mrs Smith?' Chloe asked in a kindly voice, desperately hoping it would be a short call. She really had to get to the office.

'I hope you don't mind me calling,' said Mrs Smith hesitantly, 'I don't mean to be forward or anything. It's just that Maddie was so happy when she worked for you and Bea, er, sorry, Mrs Elsworth, so I was just wondering if you'd found anyone else yet... instead of my Maddie. You see, I looked after my old mum when she had cancer, until she passed away, bless her soul. And without Maddie's wages coming into the house now, to be honest, I'm struggling a bit with all the bills.'

By now the words were tumbling out of Mrs Smith's mouth. Chloe was listening in astonishment. A woman she'd never met was apparently offering to solve her immediate problems. Taken at face value, it seemed too good to be true. Chloe waited a couple of moments before she replied.

'Oh, I shouldn't have phoned,' said Mrs Smith uncertainly, 'I'm so sorry… it was wrong of me.'

'No, no,' replied Chloe quickly, hoping that the woman wouldn't hang up, 'I'm really pleased you did. It's just been a surprise for me. Look, I'll be at home this afternoon, so why don't you come and have a cup of tea with Bea and me at about 3.30? And then we can see where we take things from there. Does that sound alright to you?'

'I'll be there, don't you worry… I won't let you down,' was the reply, and she hung up.

Chloe grabbed her coat and bag, quickly checked to see that Bea was alright, and rushed out of the front door to her car. A wave of relief washed over her. She felt sure that Maddie's mum would prove to be as caring and capable as her daughter. What a stroke of luck! She couldn't wait to tell Tony.

* * *

That afternoon Sadie Smith rang the doorbell just before 3.30. When Chloe answered the door, she looked at Maddie's mother and saw a striking resemblance to Maddie. Chloe felt somehow reassured.

'I'm so pleased you've come, Mrs Smith,' said Chloe with a smile, 'and Bea is looking forward to meeting you. But be warned, she's not always sure why Maddie doesn't come and see her anymore, so you may find her confused at times.'

Mrs Smith nodded sadly. 'It's taking me a while to get used to being without our Maddie too,' she said. 'But please call me Sadie, it's what everyone calls me, and I feel easier with that.' Chloe looked at her and smiled.

She took Sadie through into the kitchen, where Bea was sitting in her usual chair with a magazine on her lap.

'Oh, I can see that you are Maddie's mother,' said Bea cheerfully, 'you've got the same lovely smile!' Sadie beamed.

'Make yourself at home,' suggested Chloe, 'while I make us all some tea. It's always the right time for a cuppa, isn't it?'

So, while Chloe busied herself with the kettle and cups, Sadie took a chair from beside the kitchen table and placed it next to Bea. They were soon chatting like old friends. When the tea was ready, Sadie got up, put the magazine on the kitchen table, and moved the wheeled tray-table over Bea's lap. She did it all so naturally, as if she knew the routines in the house already. Chloe realised that she should be interviewing Sadie more formally, but she convinced herself that actions were speaking louder than words.

An hour passed and Sadie had talked about her husband, Mervyn, who had been made redundant recently from a warehousing job, and their son, Patrick, who was doing an apprenticeship in bricklaying. Chloe noticed that Sadie only mentioned Maddie in response to something Bea said. It was clear that her feelings were still raw when she thought of her daughter. But Chloe didn't detect any bitterness, just deep sadness.

Chloe explained that she mainly wanted a reliable person who could look after Bea's personal care, give her some snacks and lunch each day, make sure Bea took her pills at the right times, and sometimes do some laundry. Sadie looked as though she had won the lottery... she could do all that, no problem! And she felt as if she was doing it for Maddie too, she said. Maddie had really enjoyed working there. She had felt appreciated, which was certainly not the case with her previous boss. Chloe was pleased that Sadie had not mentioned either The Willows or Sally Jeavons by name.

* * *

When Tony came home that evening, Chloe was bursting with the news that Sadie was willing to be there by eight o'clock the next morning, and that they had agreed terms. Chloe felt certain that Bea would get on well with Sadie, who was chatty, but sensitive too.

'Well, thank heavens that's one problem solved,' said Tony. 'But did you say anything to Sadie about the Jacob situation? I really think she ought to know, just in case he calls or turns up on the doorstep again.'

Chloe knew that she had fudged that issue with Sadie. She had told Sadie that she needn't answer phone calls, and that she should keep the chain on the front door, if someone knocked. Chloe had given their recent burglary as the reason for this. Tony looked unconvinced. Jacob was unpredictable and could be very unpleasant. Tony said that they should be fair to Sadie and forewarn her. Chloe reluctantly agreed. She hoped that Sadie would not change her mind about working for them, if she knew that a violent bully might appear at the house demanding to take Bea away.

* * *

The following morning Sadie arrived on time. She was drenched. It was raining heavily and, during the walk from the bus stop, cars had been driving past her through puddles in the road and splashing Sadie's legs.

'Not to worry,' she told Chloe cheerfully, 'I've brought a pair of indoor shoes and my work overall, so there's no problem.' Sadie took off her wet coat and hung it over a kitchen chair by the radiator. Chloe watched her with amusement… Sadie was making herself at home right away.

Chloe then explained Bea's routines to Sadie. Together they helped Bea get up, prepared her breakfast and settled her in her chair. Chloe felt confident leaving Bea in Sadie's care and went to work, saying she would be back in the early afternoon.

* * *

When Chloe arrived home, she was greeted by a happy scene in the kitchen. Bea and Sadie were clearly at ease, playing a card game on Bea's tray-table. The kitchen looked spic and span, and Chloe felt momentarily ashamed of how she had left it.

'Shall I make you a cuppa, Mrs Montgomery?' asked Sadie, getting up from her chair.

'No, no,' replied Chloe, 'carry on with your game… it looks like you're having a good time.'

'But I think Sadie sometimes cheats,' chipped in Bea, with a mischievous smile on her face. They all laughed, and Sadie didn't appear offended at all.

Thirty-Eight

It was early evening, and Paula Trelawney was still in her office trying to make sense of Sally Jeavons' unfiled papers. The more she read, the more perplexed and uncomfortable she felt. Paula was an experienced manager. She knew how to run a care home efficiently, and Mrs Jeavons' legacy to her was a shambles in Paula's view.

Then a sudden thought struck Paula. *Was all this disorder actually deliberate? Was this a way of disguising practices which Sally Jeavons wanted to remain undiscovered?* Paula was horrified at herself for even thinking this about a woman who had died recently in such brutal circumstances. But the idea niggled away in Paula's mind while she returned her attention to the paperwork.

She decided to tackle the pile of inventories of residents' possessions which had been stored in the office safe. She immediately hit a problem. No one knew what had been stolen from the safe at the time of Mrs Jeavons' murder. She would have to check what had been removed by relatives who had found alternative homes. Everything had been in turmoil at that stage, and there were probably no reliable records. *Stop worrying,* Paula told herself, *and work with what you've got!*

A few hours later, Paula decided she'd done enough for one day. She'd been at The Willows since breakfast time and was exhausted. But she had compiled a detailed list of everything still in the safe and, where possible, which resident owned each item. She closed and locked the safe. There was still a pile of inventories with no identifying names on them, and Paula had replaced some items in the safe, not knowing which resident owned them. But some progress had been made.

Paula was about to leave her office, when the solicitor, Charles Abbott, suddenly came into her mind. *His name had cropped up a lot among the papers she had been sifting through,* she thought, *and then he had the misfortune to find Mrs Jeavons' murdered body. She had been told that he was there with Mrs Elsworth's relatives, but why were they there together?*

Oh, for heavens' sake, get a grip, she muttered to herself, *and get a life!*

She locked her office, told the staff she was leaving, and went to find her car. It was quite dark by now and the street lights were on. Paula sat in her car, trying to catch up on her personal messages before driving to the gym. She felt in need of a good workout after sitting at her desk for so many hours.

Paula was about to start the engine when she looked across the car park and noticed two people standing in the far corner. Paula was ultra-cautious about security at The Willows in view of the murder and robbery, so she sat and watched them. They were shielded from her direct view by some bushes. It seemed to be a man and a woman in animated conversation. Paula thought it was a strange place to be having a conversation. The two then parted company. The man disappeared from Paula's view, but the woman looked around before walking quickly towards the staff entrance of The Willows. She was in her uniform. It was Petra Tradovic.

Interesting, thought Paula, *I wonder who the chap was.* She started the car and set off for the gym.

Thirty-Nine

Rita Hussein had just spent a tedious hour trawling through CCTV images, helping out a colleague who had an imminent deadline. Rita had plenty of work to do on her own cases, but PC Trev Saunders had assisted Rita recently, so she owed him a favour. Relieved that she had only needed to help out for an hour, she was returning to her office when Tracey, from the traffic team, called out to Rita. She had some information which might be interesting to Rita, she said.

'Well, well,' said Rita after thanking Tracey, 'this may be a new lead… '

* * *

Rita burst into Baz's office. She knew that he was engrossed in the details of a disciplinary process against another officer. Nevertheless, she was sure he would want to hear the latest twist in their murder investigations.

'Hussein,' snapped Baz, 'this had better be good… what have you got then?'

Baz rarely addressed Rita by her family name only, and she knew this was a bad sign. She regretted barging into his office and disturbing him. She would make her feedback concise.

'Sorry, guv,' she started, 'I know you're busy. In brief, the traffic team were clamping down on speeding drivers on the Little Fordington road yesterday evening, near the dangerous bends leading out west. They stopped quite a few drivers who were well over the speed limit. Among them was one car which Tracey thought would be of interest to us. She checked it out, and it's registered to a Jacob Elsworth. But it wasn't him driving... he wasn't even in the car. The driver was a woman, who gave her name as Katya Tradovic. She admitted exceeding the speed limit and accepted that she 'll be fined. Bit of a coincidence though, isn't it, guv... there can't be many people called Tradovic in this area, and we know two of them. And one is linked to Mrs Elsworth's son somehow.'

Baz had listened attentively and looked pleased.

'Get to it then, Rita,' said Baz, 'the chart needs updating... we need more background on Jacob Elsworth, and we must be sure that there are two women called Tradovic and not just one with two first names. Right then, another meeting here at four o'clock, with some progress.' Rita nodded and left his office.

Before settling to the required tasks, Rita went to the canteen and brought a mug of coffee back to her office. She was determined to have some substantial information to give Baz later. Even better, she would like to have a watertight theory on who had killed either Sally Jeavons or Maddie Smith, or both.

Dream on, Rita told herself, *but I'll do my damnedest!*

* * *

Rita presented herself in Baz's office promptly at four o'clock.

'Right, Rita, what have you found?' he asked.

Rita cleared her throat.

'Firstly,' she began, 'I've pulled together all we know about Jacob Elsworth, after doing some more research today. He is forty-seven years old, the only child of Bea, whom we know, and Edgar

Elsworth, who died twenty-six years ago. He was brought up in Kingsdown, about thirty miles from here. It seems that Jacob was quite a tearaway when he was younger. He came to the attention of the police on at least three occasions as a juvenile, the most serious incident being a break-in at a neighbour's house. He was taken into local authority care for a year and then returned to his parents. Next, when he was in his early twenties, Elsworth was convicted of assault. Records show that he was involved in a street brawl, and his victim was an innocent bystander. He was given a community sentence which he completed without further incident. Then nothing recorded until he was in his late thirties, when he was convicted of being drunk and disorderly and he was fined. Then another gap until he received a custodial sentence for another crime of violence. I don't know the details yet. Lastly, as you know, he came to our attention recently at the Montgomerys' house, and that's still under investigation. I haven't yet found out anything about his personal circumstances, nor what sort of work he does. He doesn't claim any state benefits, but he has this flash car, so he has an income from somewhere, I assume.'

Rita was suddenly annoyed with herself. She knew that Baz disapproved of assumptions. But he continued to listen closely, without commenting.

'The car has been registered to Jacob Elsworth for two years,' Rita continued, 'at an address in Great Fordington. The house is privately owned, without a mortgage. Whether he actually lives there is not clear. As far as his relationship with his mother is concerned, I am told that he's had little contact with her over the years and apparently didn't visit her in The Willows. So why he was making a nuisance of himself at the Montgomery's front door is unclear. It's also not known what his relationship with Katya Tradovic is… but he clearly trusts her enough to drive his car.'

Rita paused, waiting to see if Baz had any questions or observations. It appeared not, so she continued.

'As far as Katya is concerned, I have more questions than answers, I'm afraid, guv. I rang Paula Trelawney at The Willows. I think she wants the murders solved as much as we do. I discovered that Petra Tradovic has no next of kin listed at The Willows. Paula has been trying to bring the records there up to scratch, as Sally Jeavons apparently left a mess. Overall Petra has given away very little information about herself and has never mentioned a sister, as far as Paula is aware. The traffic team are trying to find out more about Katya too, as she gave an address where the occupants haven't heard of her and an obsolete phone number. So she's stacking up potential offences. She claims to have a valid driver's licence, but didn't have it or any other form of identification with her. No record of a licence in that name has yet been verified. So, while she's of interest to the traffic team, I can't see any real link to us at the moment. But she seems to be a slippery character, and my gut tells me there's a link with Petra, but I've no evidence of that yet.'

Rita paused for breath.

'Hmm… ' was Baz's only contribution at this stage.

After a few moments he asked, 'What do the hospital records say about Petra's next of kin? She had a hospital appointment recently, didn't she?'

'Oh, sod it,' muttered Rita, only half under her breath, 'how did I miss that?'

Baz gave her a sympathetic grin, ignored her language, and asked, 'Perhaps that's why I'm the boss?'

Rita couldn't help but laugh… she deserved that dig.

Forty

Ros Dean was still trying to digest all the revelations from both Seb and her husband. She liked her life to be peaceful and orderly, so hearing that her son had been "helping the police with their enquiries", especially into a murder, had left her feeling shaken. She wished it would all just go away. But Martin and Seb seemed to have a joint project now, wanting to get to the root of everything. Martin had been up in the loft going through an old suitcase which had lain untouched for years.

Father and son were now engrossed in looking at a large sheet of paper which was held together by sticky tape and tattered round the edges. From a distance, it looked to Ros like a diagram, covered with crossings-out, corrections, and lines in different directions. Martin explained that it was actually a rudimentary family tree, which his grandfather Harald had started to construct about sixty years ago. When he had died, Martin's mother Lisbet had added to it. Judging by the handwriting styles and variety of inks used on the paper, other people had added information at different times.

'Wow,' exclaimed Seb, 'this is really cool. And it's been up in the loft all this time, and we've never looked at it!'

Martin was pleased. It was a long time since he and Seb had taken a mutual interest in something to do with the family.

He hoped that Ros might show some interest too, instead of withdrawing into her own world whenever the family's past was mentioned.

'Look, Dad,' continued Seb, 'these dates go back way over a hundred years, into the late nineteenth century. That's amazing. It would have helped if they'd learned to write legibly in those days, though.'

Martin laughed, enjoying his son's enthusiasm.

'At some point,' suggested Martin, 'we ought to add your generation to this family tree. My mum Lisbet has added my name, but sadly she died before you were born. You'd have loved her. She was so proud of her Scandinavian heritage and kept up lots of traditions from her childhood, even after she moved to this country. I noticed that there were lots of old photos in the suitcase up in the loft too, but that's a job for another day. We're supposed to be working out who this George is, who seems to be so interesting to other people.'

'At a quick glance I can see three or four Georges already,' began Seb, 'but I can't work out how many lines of descent are shown on here. They seem to have had really big families in those days, but I suppose they couldn't depend on all their children surviving to adulthood.'

'Hmm,' agreed Martin, 'it's not at all easy working out who belonged to which branch of the family. We need a magnifying glass really.'

A few moments later, Ros had found one for them.

'That's great,' said Seb, determined to be the first to find possible Georges. 'Look, Dad, there's a George here. Did your mum have a brother called George? Is he the one who ended up in prison?'

'Yes and no,' replied his father with a laugh. 'Mum's brother died in his twenties, I think, of some unmentionable disease. At least, it didn't get mentioned in polite society, I seem to remember.'

Seb guffawed. He bent over the family tree again. 'Going back from your mum, Lisbet, her mother seems to have been Birgit, and she was married to Harald Milstrom. Does that sound right to you, Dad?'

'Yes, it does,' confirmed Martin, 'and they also had a son called Martin, and that's who I was named after. I remember Uncle Martin coming over to England a few times to visit my parents. He was an architect, and I recall him showing me pictures of beautiful wooden houses he'd designed, typically Scandinavian. He almost persuaded me to study architecture myself, but I thought the training was too long. I wasn't the keenest of students... seems to run in the family, doesn't it?' Seb looked at him, wondering if this was a serious jibe, but it clearly wasn't.

'So Birgit and Harald were your grandparents, right, Dad?' recapped Seb, 'And we can discount their son, George, as he died quite young?' Martin nodded. 'But if we go one generation further back, bingo, another George! So, George Darwin and his wife, Juliana, were your great-grandparents. They were Birgit's mum and dad. Do you know anything about this George, Dad?'

Martin was pleased at Seb's enthusiasm.

'Now this George *was* an interesting character,' began Martin, 'he's the one I told you and Tilda about the other day. I've been trying to dredge up some more memories and family stories about him. He led a colourful life from what I remember, but I've never been sure what was fact about him, and how much the story was embellished over the years. I think we all tried to out-do each other when speculating about him!'

Tilda had come into the room just as Martin mentioned her name. She should have been studying, but she had heard laughter coming from downstairs and wanted to know what she was missing. She was very surprised by what she saw. Her dad and Seb were poring over a large sheet of paper, clearly enjoying themselves.

'What am I missing, then?' she asked.

Seb explained and told her that her timing was good, as they had just found the most interesting George so far. She pulled up a chair and joined in.

'So, Dad,' said Tilda, 'tell us all about this George then.'

'Well,' said Martin, 'we should probably take all I tell you with a large pinch of salt. I'm really not sure what is the truth and what is family history over-egged as time has passed. My mum was the main story-teller in the family, and she had a wild imagination at times.'

'OK, Dad,' interrupted Tilda impatiently, 'we get the picture, just tell us what you think you know!'

'Well,' continued Martin, looking askance at his daughter, 'his life must have spanned the end of the nineteenth and early years of the twentieth centuries, so a very different context from nowadays.'

'Oh, come on, Dad,' said Tilda, 'get to the juicy bits! I've got studying to do.'

But Martin was not going to be rushed.

'Hang on,' he retorted, 'I haven't given all this family history much thought until recently, and I need to get it as right as I can. I don't want to be perpetuating half-truths, if I can help it.'

Tilda looked suitably admonished, but she was clearly still eager for her father to hurry up.

By now Ros had also pulled up a chair, not wishing to be excluded any longer. Martin smiled at her, pleased that the whole family was involved.

'As I understand it,' he said, 'George Darwin, my great-grandfather, was an astute businessman, who often travelled abroad, building up foreign contacts and so on. Don't forget that all foreign travel was a much more hazardous affair back then than it is now, so he was quite a pioneer, in some ways.'

Tilda heaved a sigh and put her head on her arms outstretched on the table.

'OK, Tilda, point taken, so here's a juicy bit for you,' said Martin.

Tilda sat up immediately.

'It seems,' continued her father, 'that old George had more interests than just his business while he was on his foreign trips. His wife, Juliana, was at home, in charge of the household and their child, Birgit. It seems George got lonely, and the story goes that he met a beautiful, aristocratic young woman, and they had an ardent love affair over a long period of time. His business trips became more frequent after he'd met her. Then, after one trip, he didn't come home. Communications were so much more problematic then, of course, so Juliana had no idea for many months what had happened to her husband. Eventually she was officially informed that George was in jail. I don't know exactly what he was accused of. Some versions of the story say it was treason, which might have carried the death penalty, others say he master-minded a huge jewellery heist and was flung in jail. Whatever the truth of the matter, the ending is always consistent... he died in jail, however that happened, and his body never came back to England. It all took a massive toll on Juliana's health, and she died soon after she'd heard of George's death. So Birgit, my grandmother, was brought up by other relatives, as far as I know.'

'OK,' said Tilda after a few moments thought, 'I'm all for a bit of scandal in the family, but what's this got to do with the George who's been plaguing Seb's life? Are we sure it's the right George? I'm sure you said, Dad, that the solicitor chap wanted to know about another George, not George Darwin, this one. What was that George's surname?'

'You're absolutely right, Tilda,' replied her father, 'his name was George Montgomery, and he should be on this family tree somewhere.'

Seb and Tilda scrutinised the paper competitively.

'Got him!' exclaimed Tilda, much to Seb's annoyance. 'Looks like his mother was the other George's sister. Hmm… the plot thickens!'

'So that makes him your great-uncle, Dad, is that right?' asked Seb, determined not to be overshadowed by his younger sister.

'Spot on,' replied their father, 'but, at some point, there was a mighty falling-out between the Darwin and the Montgomery sides of the family, and I haven't ever really known anything about them. That's why the letter from that solicitor felt so strange. I still can't imagine what made him think that I could shed any light on George Montgomery. Not that I would have given him any information anyway, without knowing a good deal more about why. I seem to remember that you, Tilda, hoped that we were being left a vast fortune by a long-lost relative. Sorry to disappoint you!'

'I'm sure you've mentioned to me in the past,' said Ros, 'that he was rather disreputable.'

They all looked at Ros. This was her first involvement in the discussion. 'I thought he had a colourful past too, and that he had a son who followed in his father's footsteps. Or have I got that all mixed up?' she asked unsurely.

Seb and Tilda were scouring the family tree again.

'No sign of a son on here,' said Seb, 'but if the two sides of the family weren't speaking to each other, perhaps the Darwins just didn't bother with that side of the family any more,' he suggested.

'So what's the scandal about *this* George?' asked Tilda. She had been rather disappointed at the lack of salacious detail in George Darwin's story and hoped that George Montgomery's past might have been sexually murkier.

'I have a feeling, Tilda,' replied her father, 'that we're looking at criminal activities in his case and the occasional spell in prison. I can't immediately recall any scandalous sexual sagas. Sorry, Tilda, but my family is a bit of a disappointment to you! I do remember one lovely person from that side, though, and that was George's younger sister, Beatrice, but I've no idea if she's still alive. Is she on the family tree?'

Sure enough, Tilda found Beatrice Montgomery's name, but no clues as to whether or not she had ever married.

'What was so lovely about her?' asked Tilda.

Martin thought for a few moments, smiling at the memories.

'I only met her on two or three occasions,' he recalled. 'She was so sad about the huge rift between the two families and tried to effect a reconciliation, but it didn't work. She had a lovely smile, and she was such fun with children. But my mum didn't want to keep in touch with her, and I haven't heard anything about her for decades. As I say, she may be dead by now.' Martin had a wistful look on his face as he said this.

Seb had returned to the family tree.

'It looks as though George and Beatrice had a brother too, called Arthur, but again there's no indication if he married or had children,' he said, 'but possibly all three are still alive.'

Ros was beginning to think that all this investigating had gone on long enough. Tilda had homework to finish, she herself had a meal to cook, and Seb had mentioned earlier that he was planning to meet up with his friend Andy.

'Shall we call it a day with this for now?' she asked tentatively, 'and just mull over what we've found out so far? Then we can come back to it another time.'

Martin knew that a suggestion like this from Ros was really a reminder to all the family that there were more important things to do.

So he agreed, and Tilda reluctantly returned to her study, saying, 'Promise you won't talk about this anymore without me.'

Her father nodded.

Forty-One

Paula Trelawney resumed the tiresome battle with Mrs Jeavons' legacy of paperwork. She still had an uncomfortable feeling that the name of the local solicitor, Charles Abbott, cropped up too many times. She had looked in the visitors' book, and his name was not recorded there since the death of Mrs Jeavons. Going back through the book, Paula saw that he had previously visited very regularly. She wondered why the pattern had changed.

But perhaps that was an understandable reaction to being confronted, on his last visit, with the murdered body of a woman whom he knew, she thought.

It appeared, though, that he had drummed up a substantial amount of business for his firm at The Willows. She wondered if he had written any more unsolicited letters to residents recently, like the one she had found suggesting a review of Elsie Butterworth's will.

Paula put these thoughts to the back of her mind and concentrated on the monthly invoices and payments for residents' care. Each of them was addressed to a relative or another named individual, relieving the residents of that responsibility. Paula sorted them into alphabetical order, ready for filing. She was a real stickler for accuracy, and her brain had always seemed wired to spot mistakes. She was checking payments received, determined to chase up any non-payments.

Hang on a minute… she suddenly told herself, *these numbers don't tally…*

There was a knock at her door, which was ajar. She prided herself on being accessible to her staff. Lucy Kingdon had come to tell Paula that the doctor had been called to Mr Saunders, a gentle man in his late eighties, who appeared to have had a stroke. He was in his room, having felt unwell when staff had gone to help him get dressed. Lucy felt that Paula should know, as Mr Saunders' daughter needed to be contacted. Paula locked her office door and went with Lucy to Mr Saunders' room. She assured herself that he was comfortable, returned to her office and rang his daughter.

Paula thumbed through the pile of Mrs Jeavons' papers again.

Let's just have another look, she said to herself. Again she found a strange discrepancy in the account numbers for payments to The Willows. She ferreted around and found the correct number. Most invoices required payment to that account. Paula discovered three, though, which quoted a slightly different account for payment. Just one digit didn't tally.

By now, Paula was feeling out of her depth. She didn't have the expertise to deal with what she suspected might be some form of fraud. She noted the names of the three residents. Then she decided that she needed some expert advice.

Paula contemplated ringing her employers to report her suspicions. On balance, though, she decided to seek advice from the police.

DC Hussein is approachable, she thought, *and if I'm making a mountain out of a molehill, she will say so.*

Paula dialled her number and waited.

Forty-Two

Rita had a spring in her step as she entered her boss's office. She had been speaking to Paula Trelawney at The Willows. *Perhaps this new information might lead to the breakthrough they needed.* She realised that Baz had been protecting her from criticism. The DI was fuming that there was still no one firmly in the frame for the two murders.

Baz was on the phone when Rita walked in. He gestured to her to sit down and ended his call.

'Please, oh please,' he said wearily, 'give me something positive, Rita.'

'Well, guv,' she replied, trying to sound upbeat, 'we might be closing in on a motive for the Jeavons murder.'

'Give me more,' said Baz, suddenly sitting upright in his chair and looking expectantly at Rita.

'I've just had the manager of The Willows on the phone,' she explained. 'She seems to be on the ball and is finding out how badly run the home was with Sally Jeavons in charge. Paula has been reviewing various systems, particularly to do with records and finances. She believes that she may have uncovered a fraud, and she asked my advice about what she should do. As it might tie in with the murder, or even both murders, I've arranged to go and speak with her at The Willows tomorrow. I need your decision, though, about when to involve the fraud team.'

Baz leaned back in his chair, his eyes fixed on the ceiling, assessing the situation. Rita was desperately hoping that he would allow her to follow this up. It was the first glimmer of progress for a while, and she wanted to prove her ability. It seemed like an eternity until Baz responded.

Finally, he transferred his gaze to Rita and said, 'OK, Rita, you take this on initially, and I'll take the flack when it comes.'

* * *

Back at The Willows, Paula Trelawney felt relieved that she had spoken to DC Hussein and that a meeting was arranged for the next day. She wanted to continue going through the paperwork. She felt excited about doing some detective work, but she was also relieved that the responsibility might soon lie with the police.

Paula's thoughts were interrupted by her phone ringing. The hospital was calling to inform her that Mr Saunders had died peacefully, with his daughter at his bedside. Paula was jolted back into the reality of her job. She had trained to work with elderly people, not to do police work. She must now think about the most appropriate way in which to tell the residents about Mr Saunders' death. He had been a well-liked member of their community, and some of the residents would be very sad at the news. Some of the staff would too.

Paula put the detective work to one side.

Forty-Three

Luke had just finished painting the ceiling of the new restaurant area. His neck and shoulders ached, but the renovation was making good progress. Most of the heavy work was completed, much to Luke's relief. He still had to paint the walls and woodwork, but that would be easier than the ceiling. His hair was matted with white paint. But he looked up at his handiwork and felt a sense of achievement. Mick was always appreciative of Luke's efforts, even if aware that he worked more slowly than a professional would. The agreement between them seemed to be working to the benefit of both.

Luke cleaned his paintbrushes and went to change out of his work clothes in the boot room at the back of the pub. He scrubbed most of the paint off his hands and went up to his flat. He stood in the small shower, trying to wash the paint out of his hair. His thoughts turned to the time when he and Tilda had first showered together. Her parents had still been away on their cruise and Seb hadn't been around. That shower had been so sensuous, as they explored each other's bodies for the first time, standing under the gentle flow of warm water. Within minutes they had wrapped themselves in a large towel and eagerly made their way to Tilda's bed. It had not occurred to Luke that Tilda had never had sex before, that she was several years younger and much less experienced than him.

With hindsight he realised that his relationship with Mishka had been completely stage-managed by her. The sex was not spontaneous and loving, as it had been with Tilda. For Mishka, Luke now accepted, sex with him was an emotionally meaningless act. She was a cold manipulator. Thoughts of her made Luke angry with himself. Thoughts of Tilda created an ill-defined longing.

Luke had spent a couple of evenings trying to work out how finally to rid himself of Mishka's harassment. He had concluded that he needed to talk to Seb, even though the Dean family might not be keen for that contact to be renewed. *After all, he had let them down over the job offer,* he reminded himself. And Luke pushed to the back of his mind that he might be acting out of ulterior motives. He tried to convince himself that this was not about Tilda.

Luke no longer had Tilda's phone number. It was in his previous phone, which he had impulsively ditched in the canal. He decided to summon up the courage to visit the Deans' home next weekend. Not for the first time, he wished that he owned a car, but his finances wouldn't stretch to that. Luke worked out that he could reach their home by a combination of two buses and a train. *All the hassle would be worth it,* he thought.

* * *

On Saturday morning he was at the bus stop outside the pub in time for the earliest bus of the day. By late morning he was inside the bus station café having a nerve-calming cup of coffee before heading to the Deans' home.

There were two familiar cars on the driveway. He rang the doorbell. To his surprise it was Tilda who opened the door. She gave an involuntary yelp of delight when she saw Luke standing there. They both stood rooted to the spot. Seb happened to be coming downstairs, his hair tousled and looking as if he'd just woken up.

'Luke,' he exclaimed, 'what the hell...?'

But Luke saw, to his relief, that Seb had a grin on his face.

'Come on in,' he said, 'tell us what you're up to these days. You did me a big favour, even though you don't know it. Do you want a coffee or something?'

Tilda shut the front door, and the three of them went into the kitchen, where Ros was sorting out the washing. She looked up briefly and gave Luke a friendly nod.

Seb and Luke talked about their respective jobs, each pleased that they were not in the other's shoes. Tilda sat and listened, hanging on Luke's every word. She got the impression that he had not found a new girlfriend, which gave her a reassuring feeling. Eventually Luke found an opening in the conversation to ask Seb if he'd heard any more from Helena. Ros had left the kitchen by now. Seb shook his head.

'But what we *have* been doing,' Tilda chipped in enthusiastically, 'is some research into the Georges on our family tree.' Luke gave her an enquiring look. 'The name George seems to crop up all over the place,' she continued, 'and we've got four or five ancestors called George, so we're not sure who to concentrate on.'

'And it's possible that none of them is the George that Helena and Mishka have been pursuing us about,' said Seb, 'but thank heavens I've had no more phone calls recently, so perhaps they've given up at last.'

'I wish they had,' said Luke gloomily, and he told Seb and Tilda about Mishka's recent visit to the pub. Luke was still at a loss to know how Mishka had traced him.

Tilda was having difficulty controlling her emotions. She found herself doubting whether Luke was telling them the whole truth about Mishka's visit.

Perhaps they had been in contact with each other all the time. Perhaps Luke was trying to get information out of Seb and her to give to Mishka. He hadn't tried to get in touch with her, Tilda, so perhaps he was back together with Mishka and was just pretending that he wasn't. And so Tilda's thought processes continued. She was churning up ever more feelings of jealousy and doubt.

Eventually she blurted out, 'Why have you *really* come here, Luke?', giving him an accusatory look.

Both Luke and Seb stared at her, aghast. Luke had been longing to see Tilda again, and she had initially seemed pleased to see him, but now she was viewing him with blatant mistrust. He didn't know how to respond. He was completely dumbfounded.

'Well,' asked Tilda aggressively, 'did this Mishka tell you to come here?'

Seb and Luke were both astounded at Tilda's venomous tone.

There was a tense silence, until Seb said, 'I think you two have some private issues to sort out, so why don't you go out for a walk and take old Zeus with you? Then we can all start again with this George business... how's that?'

Luke looked doubtful, but Tilda grabbed Zeus's lead and the dog immediately trotted and sat by the door. Tilda appeared to be on the point of tears, so Luke got up and followed her and Zeus out of the door. He gave Seb a puzzled look as he left, but Seb just shrugged his shoulders.

* * *

Luke and Tilda walked as far as the park in silence, with Zeus on his lead between them. Luke eventually looked over at Tilda and saw that tears were rolling down her cheeks. He moved across and stopped in front of Tilda, facing her. Zeus lay down, and Tilda hung her head. Luke tentatively put his hand under her chin and lifted her wet face. He hesitantly kissed Tilda on the lips, unsure whether this would be welcomed. She dropped Zeus's lead and flung both arms around Luke's neck. Zeus lay patiently on the path, his head on his paws.

Tilda felt as though a great weight had been lifted from her. Luke's kisses were reassuring… until she thought of Mishka again. *Had he been kissing her in the meantime? Was he just trying to keep the peace now? Was this all a charade?*

Tilda pulled away and looked questioningly at Luke.

'Is there something going on between you and that woman?' she asked quietly, unable to say Mishka's name. Luke had a hurt expression on his face.

'Of course not,' he replied, kissing Tilda on her neck, 'I don't want anything to do with her. I genuinely don't know how she found me at the pub. I wish I did. I've thought about you so much, but I wondered if you wouldn't want to see me again. I was scared stiff of coming here, in case you gave me the cold shoulder. But I'm really pleased I came… I've missed you so much.'

They walked on, holding hands and each deep in thought.

Eventually Tilda said sheepishly, 'Sorry for being a bitch earlier. I was jealous. I don't want to ruin things now you've come back.'

'Don't worry,' replied Luke with a smile, 'I won't let you!'

It was beginning to drizzle by the time they made their way home. They huddled close to each other, whistled for Zeus who had been chasing squirrels, and walked back, both feeling much happier. Martin was in the kitchen emptying the dishwasher, when Tilda and Luke came in.

'Good to see you again, Luke,' he said cheerfully, much to Luke's relief. 'Seb tells me that you had a tedious journey getting here today, so do you want to stay over and go back in the morning?'

Luke gratefully accepted the invitation, and Tilda tried not to look as pleased as she felt.

Forty-Four

'Bea's been telling me so much about her life, it's really interesting,' began Sadie, when Chloe came home from work. 'We'll be really good friends, Bea and me.'

Chloe looked around the kitchen and noticed that Sadie had done the pile of ironing which Chloe had a guilty conscience about. She had meant to do it days ago. And Sadie had moved Bea's chair over to the window, so that she could watch the children in the playground beyond the garden wall.

'Don't worry, Mrs Montgomery, I'll move the chair back again before I go,' said Sadie, worried that she shouldn't have moved it.

'I'm sure that Bea enjoyed looking at a different view,' said Chloe to reassure her.

Bea had fallen asleep, so Sadie made a cup of tea for Chloe.

'So what has Bea been telling you about herself?' asked Chloe quietly.

Sadie took the hint and answered softly, 'Well, she was telling me all about her son, Jacob. He sounds to have been such a lovely little boy,' said Sadie. Chloe was astonished but eager to hear more. 'He was a handsome young man, by Bea's account, and so kind to his mum. Then he worked abroad somewhere, Bea couldn't remember where, so she didn't see much of him for several years.'

Chloe thought she may have another explanation for his absences, but she didn't say anything to Sadie about that.

'She's sad that he hasn't ever got married,' continued Sadie, 'as she would really like to have had some grandchildren. But perhaps with all his travelling it's best that he stayed single.'

'And did Bea say whether she's had any contact with him recently?' asked Chloe, hoping that it sounded like an innocent question.

'She was a bit confused about that,' replied Sadie, 'I know that she was in The Willows, like my poor Maddie, but she seems to have forgotten all of that. She seemed much more certain when she was talking about long ago. She had a relation called Anastasia, but I couldn't work out where she fits in. Bea's face was all lit up when she talked about music and dancing and handsome young men! But I'm not sure if this was all real, or something she'd seen on the telly.'

Chloe smiled. 'Yes,' she said, 'we all get confused about this, but we think that Anastasia was a real person, and we'd love to know more about her. But it's difficult, as you say, to know what's fantasy. There's one person we certainly have met, though, and that's Bea's son, Jacob.'

Tony had wanted Chloe to make Sadie aware of the Jacob situation, at least in part. So, she took a deep breath and hoped that Bea was as fast asleep as she appeared to be.

'Actually,' began Chloe quietly, 'I need to tell you a few things about Jacob.'

Sadie looked surprised but keen to hear more.

Chloe continued, 'You remember that we asked you not to open the front door to anyone, and not to answer the phone?' Sadie nodded. 'Well, the reason for that is that Jacob has turned up here a few times, and he definitely isn't the nice young man of Bea's memory. He may have been a lovely boy, but he certainly isn't lovely now… or at least not to Tony and me, and not to Bea either. He accuses us of kidnapping Bea, which is nonsense, and he wants to take her to another home, or so he says. Anyway, you don't need to know the details now, perhaps another time, but you do need to know that he can be very unpleasant and threatening. That's why we don't want you to have anything to do with him, for your sake and Bea's. Please have a think about what I've said. It may change your mind about wanting to work here, but I really hope not.'

Sadie was quiet for a moment, and then, with a determined look on her face, she said, 'Don't you worry about that, Mrs Montgomery, no one bullies Sadie Smith and gets away with it. I'll protect Bea, the same way as I always tried to protect my poor Maddie when she was bullied at school. I'm much tougher than I might seem, Mrs Montgomery. I won't let any bully-boy get near my Bea.'

Chloe had to smile at Sadie's possessiveness of her new charge. She also felt reassured by Sadie's reaction.

Bea was now stirring in her chair, and Chloe felt relieved that she had broached the topic of Jacob without her hearing anything. Tony had been right that it was only fair to Sadie to explain the situation to her.

There was no knowing when Jacob might reappear at their front door.

Forty-Five

'I think we should concentrate on this wretched place called Minchford and on George Montgomery,' declared Seb. 'I hate the thought of the place, but it's cropped up too many times to be coincidental.'

'I'm afraid I agree with you, Seb,' replied his father. 'It must hold awful memories for you, but hopefully you're no longer of any interest to the police there. How would you feel about all of us going over there tomorrow, just to have a look at the place, and perhaps we can lay a few ghosts to rest? I wouldn't mind seeing the old folks' home where you were supposed to have murdered someone.'

Seb initially looked horrified, but he slowly came round to his father's idea.

The Dean family had been poring over the tattered family tree again, this time with Luke joining in too. Only Ros remained marginal to the activity and theorising. She had no desire to go and visit Minchford. She couldn't understand why everyone was so enthusiastically delving into the family's past. It was just a lot of fuss about nothing, as far as she was concerned. *The police had realised their mistake in respect of Seb, and that had closed the matter,* she thought. And she saw no reason to forage around after this man, George, whichever George it was.

***

So the following day Martin, Seb, Tilda and Luke set off by car for Minchford. Luke had phoned Mick, to ask if he could return to work on Monday afternoon, and Mick had readily agreed. Tilda was sitting next to Luke on the back seat, surreptitiously holding his hand and wishing it was a longer journey to Minchford.

Martin decided to park in the most central car park they spotted and then to explore Minchford on foot. He had brought the name of Charles Abbott's firm of solicitors with him. A quick internet search found the address and a map. They all headed in that direction, although Seb and Luke were at a loss to know why they were going and looking at some closed offices. But Martin and Tilda were very taken with the ancient gabled frontages of the buildings in the narrow streets. It only took a few minutes to find the offices of Brownlow and Noggs, with its gleaming brass nameplate by the entrance.

'Right,' said Martin with an air of triumph, 'that's the first landmark found!'

'How has that helped us?' asked Tilda, echoing the thoughts of the other two.

'Just getting a feel for the place,' replied her father, 'and if he ever contacts me again, I'll be able to picture his offices.' Tilda gave him a sceptical look but said nothing.

She wanted to wander along a few more of the narrow streets, looking at the quaint old buildings with their small leaded windows. Martin was happy to do this too. Seb and Luke followed along behind, each engrossed in something on his phone. They were soon in a street with more modern shops and offices. Tilda suddenly stopped and pointed to a stylish slate nameplate on the wall beside her. The top name read *Anthony Montgomery*.

'What were you saying yesterday about coincidences, Seb?' laughed Tilda. 'We get here, and one of the first names we see is Montgomery… pity he's not a George, though!'

Seb and Luke suddenly showed an interest. Seb took a picture of the nameplate on his phone.

'Might be useful,' he said. Tilda again looked sceptical.

The group sauntered further, until they were back in the market square, where they had parked.

'Anyone fancy a drink and a snack?' asked Martin. There was an inviting-looking pub facing the square, so they all headed there. Luke and Tilda went to find seats for them all, while Seb and his father waited to be served at the bar.

'Are you feeling OK, Seb, being back here?' asked Martin quietly.

'Yeah, Dad, fine,' Seb replied. 'I didn't exactly do any sightseeing while I was here before, I just remember a claustrophobic cell. But thanks Dad, I'm fine with it all.'

'Right,' said Martin, when they were all settled with their food and drink at a window table, 'Tilda, would you work out how we get to the old folks' home from here, please? Is it too far to walk?' She and Luke now had a reason to huddle together over her phone.

Martin watched them and gave Seb a questioning look. Seb just shrugged his shoulders, looking amused.

'It's on the other side of town,' declared Tilda after a couple of minutes, with a confirming nod from Luke, 'best to take the car.'

'Thanks, Tilda,' said Martin, 'just check out where the police station is too, will you? Can we drive past it on our way to the home?'

Seb looked horrified… that was one building he didn't want to see again.

'Don't worry, Seb, just research, we won't stop,' said Martin.

* * *

After lunch, they walked back across the market square to the car. Seb was feeling apprehensive. Was there really any need to drive past the police station? He couldn't figure out whereabouts in the town it was. He didn't want to know.

Tilda guessed how her brother was feeling. She was giving Martin directions from the map on her phone.

Suddenly she said, 'Oh whoops, sorry Dad, we've just passed the road where the police station is, it was off to the left back there.'

Martin was not deceived by Tilda's little 'mistake'. He was actually pleased that she cared about her brother's feelings.

'Not to worry, Tilda,' he said casually, 'let's keep going and not do a U-turn.'

Seb heaved a quiet sigh of relief.

A mile or so further on Tilda instructed her father to take the next left turn. Not far down this road The Willows should be on their left. Sure enough, a large sign, rather weathered and in need of repainting, indicated that this was indeed the home. Martin drove into the car park and reversed into a space.

'You three wait here,' said Martin, 'I'm just going to have a quick wander round the outside,' and he got out of the car. Seb, Tilda and Luke looked at each other, wondering what Martin was up to.

Another car pulled into the car park and stopped close to the front door. A young woman in a uniform came out of The Willows and helped the driver take a wheelchair out of the car boot and assemble it. An elderly woman was then helped out of the car and into the wheelchair.

Seb and Luke couldn't believe their eyes. They looked at each other in sheer amazement. But there was no mistake. The young woman in the uniform was undoubtedly Helena. Seb sank as far as he could down into his seat and shielded his face with his arms. Luke buried his face in Tilda's shoulder. Tilda was delighted but mystified. *Who were Luke and Seb hiding their faces from?* Tilda could only conjecture that it was the care worker. *But why?* At that moment her father opened the car door and got into the driver's seat. He looked surprised at the way Seb was sitting but thought better of asking him about it. Seb heard the other car drive off and carefully peered over towards the front door. Thankfully it was closed.

'It's actually much bigger than it appears from the front,' began Martin, 'and there's quite a nice garden at the side and the back. I wonder why that person was murdered here… it all looks so peaceful.'

Forty-Six

There were mixed emotions in the car as Martin drove home from Minchford. Seb was feeling bewildered at having seen Helena at The Willows… and in a carer's uniform! *Was that really the same gorgeous, sophisticated young woman, who had so easily seduced him at university? And how on earth had she landed up in godforsaken Minchford? And why did they have to visit at precisely the moment she came out of the front door? She still looked stunning, even when not in expensive clothes.*

Luke's mind was racing too. He was thinking about the bizarre coincidence of seeing Helena in this unlikely setting. Of course, he had not been emotionally involved with Helena, but thoughts of Mishka surfaced in his mind again. *Was she perhaps working at the home too?* He couldn't imagine such a trendily dressed young woman, whatever colour her hair was nowadays, looking after elderly people in need of comfort and care. *She was totally self-centred.* Luke was thoroughly confused.

Tilda was perplexed too. What had prompted Seb and Luke to hide their faces so dramatically? *It had to be that carer,* she thought, *but who was she? Could it possibly have been Helena, or even Mishka?* she wondered. She decided to swallow her curiosity for now and just enjoy holding Luke's hand beneath her loosened jacket.

Martin, though, was not so reticent.

'Come on then, Seb,' he began, looking across at his son in the seat beside him, 'what was all the hiding about back there? Don't tell me you were comfortable slumped down in the seat with your hands over your head.'

Seb turned to the backseat and gave Luke an enquiring look. Luke shrugged and nodded. Seb took this to mean that he should give some sort of explanation to his father.

'Well…' Seb hesitated, '… the long and the short of it is that we'd just seen Helena, bloody Helena. Looks like she's a care worker at that home. I couldn't believe my eyes, but Luke saw her too. There's no way we wanted her to spot us, so we were trying to hide our faces.'

Martin was taken aback. He had briefly speculated about possible explanations, but that had not been one of them.

Tilda silently congratulated herself on having guessed correctly, but she was also relieved that it was Helena, not Mishka.

Martin was thinking about what Seb had told him.

'Well,' he said, 'from what you've told us previously, this young woman certainly seems to lead a varied life. One minute a seemingly sophisticated young woman chasing after my son, and the next minute doing a job that isn't at all well paid and not many people are motivated to do. I wonder how long she's worked there.'

Martin paused, while he manoeuvred the car past a broken-down lorry. Once underway again Martin continued, 'Do you think that her presence in Minchford has anything to do with your arrest, Seb?'

Seb looked at his father, horrified by the thought.

'Sorry, Seb,' said his father, 'but we have to be realistic, and presumably it's at least a possibility.'

The journey home continued in silence, all four absorbed in their own thoughts. As they were approaching home, Martin asked them all not to mention the Helena incident to Ros. By all means tell her anything else about the day, but she would only worry if she heard that Seb and Luke had nearly been seen by Helena. They all agreed.

For some time Martin had been concerned by his wife's reaction to the recent strange events. Ros preferred to distance herself from it all, but Martin wasn't sure why.

Ros opened the front door when she heard the slamming of car doors.

'Had a good day, then?' she asked. The responses were a mix of 'mmm…' and 'yeah…' as they all came into the hall.

* * *

Zeus trotted out of the kitchen and sat beside Tilda, looking up at her.

'Haven't you had a walk yet?' she asked him. He thumped his tail on the floor. 'OK, then, let me get your lead,' she told him, hoping that Luke would join them.

'Won't be long, Mum,' she called out, and she, Luke and Zeus set off for a brisk walk. Once in the park, where Zeus could run around freely, Luke and Tilda wandered over to a large, gnarled oak tree. Tilda's back was pressed against the tree trunk as she and Luke kissed each other, their bodies eager for more than just a kiss. They finally parted when Zeus came and barked beside them.

'You're not jealous are you, old boy?' laughed Luke.

'More like exhausted,' said Tilda, 'come on then, let's get you home.'

Tilda felt reassured about Luke's feelings for her. She wished they could spend the night together, but it was all too risky with her mum and dad around. But this was the last night she would see Luke until… she didn't know when.

They strolled home slowly, arms around each other. Tilda cleaned Zeus's paws, and he went and lay down in his bed.

Ros was preparing the evening meal. She told them that Martin and Seb were having a chat in the sitting room, so Tilda and Luke went to join them.

'I was just telling Seb about a phone call I made from my study just now.' Martin lowered his voice, but he could hear an electrical appliance whirring in the kitchen. Ros wouldn't hear him.

'Just out of interest I rang The Willows. I asked to speak with Helena, as I was an old friend of hers.' Luke gasped. 'And I was told that no one called Helena works there, and never has, as far as this person knew. So what do we all think of that?' asked Martin.

Seb and Luke looked stunned. Tilda felt perplexed.

Forty-Seven

It was a great relief to Ros when family life resumed its usual routine the following day. Martin and Seb had left for work at the usual time, and Tilda had gone to college. Luke had caught a bus even earlier, so Ros and Zeus had the house to themselves.

Ros felt unsettled by the discussions during the previous evening. She realised that sometimes she was deliberately excluded, although Martin tried to reassure her that this was not so. More often she chose to be excluded. She had uneasy feelings about the other four being so interested in Minchford, especially when Seb had had such a dreadful experience there. And the discussions she'd overheard shed no light on this for her. She felt worried about how the future might play out.

***

During the morning Martin had a brief space between meetings, so he closed his office door and did some internet searching. He then made a phone call. At lunch time he called Seb into his office.

'I had an interesting conversation earlier with Anthony Montgomery… remember the name?' asked Martin.

Seb thought for a moment and nodded. His father was surprising him yet again.

'Why did you do that, Dad?' asked Seb.

Martin explained that he had felt disquieted by all the recent strange coincidences, and he wanted to get some clarity.

'I didn't honestly think that Anthony Montgomery would be linked to the whole saga in any way,' said Martin, 'but, believe it or not, he is. He was surprisingly open with me. But there've been some odd things happening in his family too. The weirdest of all was that he knew all about the murder at The Willows, and he was one of the people who found the woman's body there!'

Seb was dumbstruck. His face was pale, and Martin noticed that his son's hands were trembling.

'Are you OK, Seb?' he asked. 'Shall I tell you the rest later?'

'I'm fine,' replied Seb, although he clearly wasn't. 'Just carry on, Dad, I'll be OK.'

Martin decided to give Seb an abbreviated version of his long conversation. Tony, as he preferred to be called, had told Martin that his elderly aunt had been a resident in The Willows. She'd had a nasty fall which caused her to be hospitalised. Then the manager of the home was suddenly murdered, and Tony and his wife (whose name Martin had forgotten) decided to look after the aunt in their home. Then the girl who was paid to look after her was also murdered.

Seb blanched again, having visions of being questioned by the police about a second murder. Martin seemed to read his son's thoughts.

'Don't worry, Seb,' he said, 'no one's thinking you did it, I'm sure.'

Tony had gone on to explain to Martin that his aunt, Mrs Elsworth, still lived with them and was being cared for by the dead girl's mother.

Seb found this rather ghoulish, but he kept quiet.

'The other thing he told me,' said Martin, 'and here we have yet another coincidence, is that his aunt's solicitor is Charles

Abbott, the chap who contacted me. And he was with Tony when they found the murdered woman's body. So, if ever we needed proof that the world is a small place, I reckon this is it.'

'So does Tony still have any links with The Willows?' asked Seb, bracing himself in case Helena had been mentioned.

'I didn't ask him that specifically,' responded Martin, 'but I didn't get the impression that he does.'

Martin thought he had probably told Seb enough for now.

'So Tony and I agreed to be in touch again, if we need to,' he said. 'He came across as a pleasant, sensible sort of guy. But in case you're wondering, Seb, I only told him about the Montgomery link and our visit to Minchford on Saturday. I didn't say that you'd been there before.'

'Thanks, Dad,' replied Seb, the colour returning to his face.

'Oh yes, I nearly forgot,' continued Martin, 'Tony said he used to have an uncle George, who was also a Montgomery, but he had died a long time ago and he didn't know much about him.'

On their way home Martin and Seb agreed not to mention this phone call to Ros. She had reacted strangely whenever they'd all discussed 'George', and she hadn't really wanted to hear about their visit to Minchford. It saddened Martin, but he respected her feelings.

Forty-Eight

DC Hussein put the phone down after a long call, an exultant smile on her face. Her boss glanced up from his computer screen and asked, 'What was that all about then?'

Rita looked across at him and said, 'That was Simon from the fraud team. They're interviewing Charles Abbott. They had a warrant to search his offices following what Paula Trelawney had shown them at The Willows. Simon didn't give me the details, but he wanted us to know the general direction of their investigation.'

'And that is?' asked Baz, while Rita was ordering her thoughts.

'Their hypothesis is that Charles Abbott and Sally Jeavons were jointly running a financial scam and lining their own pockets with residents' money. They appear to have been syphoning off monthly fees into an illicit account, thereby diverting it from The Willows' account. But they only did this with a few residents' payments, presumably to avoid it being too obvious. Even so, Abbott and Jeavons may have netted a substantial sum of money each over a long period of time. Simon thinks there may have been another scam going on too. The likelihood is that Abbott will deny all knowledge of that too. At the moment he's placing the blame for any financial mismanagement firmly with Sally Jeavons. He acknowledges that he occasionally helped residents with legal

212

issues, and he admits that he visited The Willows regularly, but he states that he knew nothing about Jeavons' management of the home.'

'So do I take it that Simon thinks he may have hit upon a potential motive for the murder of Jeavons? Hence his telling you all this?' interrupted Baz.

'That's it in a nutshell,' replied Rita, 'what do *you* think, guv?'

'Well,' replied Baz slowly, staring at the ceiling, 'I think you've got some work to do.'

Rita groaned quietly, wishing he could just have said, 'Yes, that sounds like a possible motive!' But this was Baz, and she knew that she would have to scrutinise all the evidence again in the light of the new intelligence. *Baz was right,* she conceded silently, *they had to have a watertight case.*

* * *

Baz realised that he had burst Rita's metaphorical bubble, so he stood up, wiped a space on the whiteboard and said cheerfully, 'Right, Rita, brainstorm!'

Within a few minutes they had a checklist for Rita. What had forensics established about the time of Jeavons' death? Could Abbott have killed her and then returned to 'discover' the body? Was there any evidence linking Abbott with Smith's murder? Was anyone else implicated in the financial scam? and so the list went on.

Eventually Baz looked at Rita and grinned. 'Well,' he said, 'that should keep you going… today, at least. Have another word with Simon at the close of play, and update me before the morning briefing.' She was opening his office door to leave, when Baz called out, 'Get me a cup of coffee now, will you, I'm parched!'

Rita felt that she should be annoyed by Baz's request, but there was too much about him that she liked and valued, so she willingly complied.

Rita located the electronic records of the Jeavons investigation. Before going through them all again, she made some notes of the brainstorm with Baz. Now, thanks to Simon, she had a potentially new perspective on Charles Abbott. But Rita reminded herself that he had not been charged with anything yet… let alone been found guilty. *Keep an open mind,* she told herself.

The records reminded her that Jeavons had been dead for at least two hours by the time she was found by Abbott and the Montgomerys. *Potentially therefore,* Rita deduced, *Abbott would have had time to change his clothes and clean himself up before 'finding' the body.* Another thought occurred to her. *Did he know the codes on The Willows' doors, if he was a regular visitor and associate of Jeavons?*

She made a note to ask Paula Trelawney about the security system.

Rita was interrupted by Baz coming and standing by her desk.

'I'm wondering if Simon might do us a favour and ask some questions about residents' wills, valuables and so on, if you brief him carefully about the possible links between his fraud investigation and the murders. What do you reckon? I was just thinking about Mrs Elsworth's jewellery box, and I think someone said he has responsibility for her money too. Check all this out will you, Rita, and then talk to Simon. It may be more effective for his team to ask these questions. But I don't know how long they plan to keep Abbott here.' With that, Baz left the room.

Rita skimmed through the notes of their visit to the Montgomerys' home and all the records relating to Charles Abbott. She ordered her thoughts and went to talk to Simon.

Forty-Nine

Chloe was putting on her jacket, ready to leave for work, when she beckoned Sadie into the dining room.

'Just a quick word,' she said. 'Tony and I found some old photos, and we wondered if you would show them to Bea and see if she recognises anyone. We think they are members of her family, but we're not sure. Perhaps you could write the names on the back, but don't worry about the spellings, as there may be some strange names among them. Would you like to do that?'

Sadie was very enthusiastic and happily agreed. 'Perhaps she'll tell me more about Anastasia and all that dancing!' said Sadie, with a laugh.

* * *

Chloe drove to work thinking how fortunate they were to have Sadie looking after Bea. *And yet poor Sadie must still feel terrible at losing her only daughter, and in such a brutal way.* She rarely mentioned Maddie, but Chloe knew that the police investigations were still ongoing, and no one had yet been charged with Maddie's murder. Tears began to trickle down her face as she remembered Maddie. *Why would anyone want to kill*

such a caring young woman? And then dump her body in the woods?
Chloe's mood changed to anger when she recalled Maddie being
sacked by Sally Jeavons, apparently for having spoken to her and
Tony. The sight of Mrs Jeavons' lifeless body was suddenly in her
mind's eye. This was followed by a vision of Jacob, swearing and
intimidating her.

Chloe was passing a large supermarket, so she pulled into the
car park. She had to dispel these thoughts before arriving at work.
Chloe sat for a few minutes, closing her eyes and taking deep
breaths, until her heartrate slowed. So many horrific events in a
short space of time, but she must put them out of her mind and
compose herself for her day's work.

* * *

In the meantime, Sadie was preparing Bea's breakfast. She too
was thinking about Maddie, her lovely girl. She wanted answers,
but the police seemed to have forgotten about her. And Sadie
didn't like to impose on their time by asking questions. *But
why would anyone kill her harmless girl? What had they gained
by doing such a wicked thing? Had Maddie suffered before she
was killed?* It all made Sadie so sad, thinking about it. *Children
shouldn't die before their parents, should they?* Sadie sat at the
kitchen table, looking vacantly out of the window, when she
heard Bea's little bell. She wiped her eyes on her overall sleeve,
straightened herself up, and went to Bea's room trying to
appear cheerful.

* * *

In the late afternoon Chloe arrived home, exhausted after a
succession of challenging meetings. Bea was dozing in her chair,
but Sadie was bursting with news for Chloe.

'I've got so much to tell you,' she said to Chloe in an attempted whisper, in order not to disturb Bea, 'I must tell you it all, before I forget it!' They sat at the kitchen table, the old photos spread out in front of them.

'Well,' began Sadie triumphantly, but still trying to keep her voice down, '*this* is Anastasia! And *this one,* over here, is her husband, George. Don't you think that Anastasia is beautiful, Mrs Montgomery? And look at all the jewellery she's wearing! It must be worth a fortune!' Chloe nodded in agreement. Sadie's enjoyment was infectious.

'But Bea told me that George left his wife and little daughter at home while he went travelling on business, and that's how he met up with Anastasia. Bea said their affair went on for years, and she's not sure if they ever actually got married. They were always together, though. I wish I could remember George's first wife's name,' continued Sadie, 'I'm sure Bea mentioned it.'

'Her name was Juliana,' came a voice from the chair by the fire, 'but her daughter's name escapes me for now.' Chloe wondered how long Bea had been awake.

'We had a good natter about all this earlier, didn't we, Bea?' asked Sadie.

'Did we, dear?' replied Bea, 'is it teatime yet?'

Sadie went over to the sink to fill the kettle. Chloe went on looking at the photos, turning them over to see if Sadie had written any names on the reverse. Sure enough, one had 'Edgar' written on it, so that was Bea's late husband. There was another picture, of three young children sitting stiffly in a row, clearly in their best clothes, with a little girl in the centre. On the reverse was written, George, Bea, Arthur. *So this was Bea and her two brothers, and Arthur was Tony's dad,* thought Chloe.

'Bea,' asked Chloe, 'did your brother George have any children?'

'Oh yes,' came the reply, 'Dennis is my nephew, but I lost contact with him a long time ago. But Arthur was such a lovely brother to me, and then he and Mary were killed in that dreadful car crash. They'd have been so proud of Tony for looking after me, and you, of course.'

Chloe smiled. She felt sad that she'd never known Tony's parents, but the fatal accident had occurred a couple of years before she met him. She was pleased, though, that Tony now had such a strong bond with Bea.

'Here's your tea, dear,' said Sadie, putting the cup on Bea's tray-table.

Chloe didn't want to appear to be cross-examining Bea about her relatives, but she asked, as casually as she could, 'Did you ever meet Anastasia, Bea?'

'I most certainly did,' came the reply, with an assurance that surprised Chloe. 'But after George couldn't come back here, I didn't see Anna many more times. You see,' Bea continued, 'she didn't have any children of her own, and I was her only niece, so she always indulged me. She gave me lots of her jewellery and told me to look after it very carefully.'

Bea stopped talking, her shoulders slumped, and she started sobbing quietly. Sadie immediately went and held Bea's hand, trying to soothe her. 'But I've let Anna down, haven't I?' she said between sobs, 'I don't know where her jewellery is, do I? What will she say?'

Chloe didn't know how to respond, but Sadie sensitively diverted Bea's attention, telling Chloe about a television programme they had watched after lunch, all about sea birds. Bea had particularly enjoyed watching the puffins with little fish in their beaks. Bea perked up again on remembering this. For now, her concerns about Anastasia's jewels were forgotten.

After Sadie had left, Chloe involuntarily started to think about Jacob again.

Fifty

Luke and Seb had talked long into the night about having seen Helena at The Willows.

Luke, in particular, was feeling besieged by her and Mishka. It didn't seem to matter where he went, one of them would appear. And he still couldn't fathom why he, of all people, had been drawn into all this… whatever "all this" was.

Seb was feeling both angry and fearful. He now thought he knew how Minchford police had heard of him. But he didn't know what the hell Helena had told them to implicate him in a murder. *And he could envisage no less suitable person to be a carer in an elderly persons' home than that bitch Helena!*

* * *

The following morning, after little sleep, Luke had made the tedious journey back to The Ancient Mariner. Tilda had gone off to college feeling thoroughly miserable, wondering when she might see Luke again. But at least they could now keep in touch with each other.

Luke managed to catnap on the bus and train, but he still felt exhausted when he arrived at the pub.

'Looks like you've had a good weekend!' said Debbie cheerily. 'I've put some pizza slices in your kitchen, as I thought you probably wouldn't have done any shopping. Just bung them in the microwave for a couple of minutes, and they'll be fine.'

Luke thanked her and went up to his room. Debbie had been more generous than she had implied. There were some apples and a large slice of fruit cake, as well as the pizzas.

Luke ate an apple, put on his work clothes and went downstairs to start on some more painting. Tilda was never far from his thoughts. *If only they could be with each other more,* he thought, *but without a car that was difficult... and on his current pay a car was out of the question.* Notwithstanding his wandering and inconclusive thoughts, Luke made good headway with the painting. He stood back to look at his handiwork, when Mick came into the room, a bit breathless.

'Sorry, Luke, I forgot to tell you that your red-head friend came here again yesterday. She was disappointed that you weren't here, but just left a message that she'd see you soon. You really are a dark horse, aren't you? Debbie thought you'd gone off somewhere to be with her this weekend, but we were obviously wrong. We don't mind if you want her to come and stay with you... we're very broadminded, you know!'

Mick laughed, but he quickly realised that Luke didn't look amused. 'Sorry, Luke, did I say something wrong?' he asked.

Luke hesitated, wondering how much to tell Mick. He had no reason to distrust Mick; he and Debbie had been very kind to him.

So Luke began, 'Can I tell you something confidentially, Mick? But I really don't want it to go any further than you and Debbie.'

Mick nodded reassuringly.

'Don't worry, Luke,' he said, 'landlords like us have to keep confidences all the time... especially when alcohol loosens lonely tongues! Debbie and I can keep quiet when we need to.'

Luke put the roller down in the paint tray.

'Well Mick, that red-head is not a friend of mine at all, in fact she's more like a stalker.' Mick looked surprised. 'She inveigled her way into my life at uni, but I've never been really sure why. She looked quite different then, and she had a strong foreign accent. I genuinely thought she was from eastern Europe somewhere, but that seems to have been an act. She was just using me, but I've never been able to fathom out why. Anyway,' Luke paused, 'she has somehow always been able to find me. I thought I'd been so careful when I moved here, but, damn it, it hasn't taken five minutes for her to find me. It scares me.'

Luke decided not to mention the link to a murder. Mick seemed to be sympathetic to his situation, but mention of a murder, or worse still two, might prompt Mick to sack him. Mick, after all, was trying to build up a reputable business.

Mick thought for a while, before looking at Luke. 'I don't envy you having to deal with that, mate,' he said with a rueful expression. 'Although I have to say that she certainly turned a few heads in the pub. She's a looker, isn't she?' Mick laughed. 'Seriously, though, how can Debbie and I help?'

'To be honest,' replied Luke, 'I haven't a clue. I just wanted you to know the situation, in case she tries to manipulate you into disclosing my phone number or fixing up a meeting with me.'

Mick was quiet again. 'You hear about cases like this on the telly, don't you? I'm sure that stalking's against the law, so should you keep notes, just in case the police ever have to be involved?'

It was Luke's turn to be quiet. 'One thing you could do,' he then said slowly, 'if you really don't mind being involved…'

Luke was hesitating, so Mick said, 'Of course I don't.'

'Well,' continued Luke, 'it might help to know what car she comes here in. I've seen her twice with an older bloke in an upmarket car. I don't know the make or the reg, but the police would be able to trace it, if ever they were involved. So, how would you feel about surreptitiously taking some pics on your phone, if she comes here again? It's asking a lot of you, I know, especially if the chap in the car sees you and gets nasty.'

'Don't worry about that, Luke, we landlords are used to dealing with belligerent customers!'

Luke felt relieved at having opened up about Mishka. *It didn't actually solve the problem,* he thought, *but he had enough faith in Mick and Debbie, once she knew the situation too, to think that he had at least some protection. And wasn't her message that she would be back again soon?* Luke dreaded that prospect, so he would keep well behind the scenes in the pub and trust that Mick and Debbie would be as good as their word.

Fifty-One

Rita worked long into the evening. She was determined to have positive developments to report the following morning. *Progress is so slow,* she thought, ... *we just need that one piece of luck... that unexpected breakthrough.*

Her phone rang. It was Simon reporting on the interview with Abbott. Initially he had appeared cooperative and unconcerned by a police interview. He seemed to think that he could outwit the police and rely on his intellectual powers and legal knowledge to wrong-foot the officers questioning him. Gradually, though, his demeanour changed, and he retreated into a sequence of "no comment" answers. So at present Simon had little firm intelligence to offer Rita.

Disappointment swept through her. But Abbott was still being questioned, and something of importance might yet emerge.

Rita returned her focus to the Tradovic family. Her phone rang again.

A tentative voice said, 'I hope I'm doing the right thing, phoning you. You probably won't remember me, but I'm Sadie Smith... you came to my house not long after my Maddie was found... you know... in the wood.'

Rita was now fully alert. Trying to sound encouraging, she asked, 'So how can I help you, Mrs Smith?'

There was a pause.

'Well,' she replied, 'I'm looking after old Mrs Elsworth now, just like my Maddie did, at Mrs Montgomery's house. I asked Mrs Montgomery what I should do, and she thought you should know about this.'

There was another silence. Rita was wishing that Mrs Smith would get to the point.

'And what do you wonder if I should know about?' asked Rita calmly.

'Well,' said Sadie, 'I settled Bea, Mrs Elsworth, in her chair by the kitchen window. She loves watching the birds on the feeder from there.' Rita sighed. 'So I thought I'd give her bedroom a real clean, thorough-like, while I could. I took the seat cushion out of her favourite chair, and I found something slipped down under the cushion. I knew it straightaway, and it gave me quite a turn. It was my Maddie's phone, you see. I knew it from its lovely stripy pink and white cover. I told Mrs Montgomery about it, and she thought I should tell you too.'

Rita silently punched the air. *Was this the start of a breakthrough at last?*

She thanked Mrs Smith and arranged to be with her within an hour to collect the phone.

In the meantime, Rita was determined to find out more about Petra and Katya Tradovic. She trawled through the police database, trying to find a match with either name. No luck on the names Petra and Katya. But the name Tradovic did have one match. A fifty-eight-year old man, Oscar Mikhail Tradovic, had several convictions recorded, the last of which was around six years ago. Most of his convictions were for minor offences of dishonesty and violence, but one had resulted in a custodial sentence. Rita reminded herself that there was nothing at present to connect this man with Petra and Katya, but she nevertheless felt elated. *There's an outside chance that it could be significant,* she thought. She would ring her colleagues in his area tomorrow to find out more about Oscar Tradovic.

The following morning Rita arrived at work earlier than usual. There was a spring in her step. The data analysts were working on Maddie's phone. *Please, oh please, find a missing link,* she prayed. But even if she had nothing conclusive to report to Baz yet, there had been significant steps forward. She hadn't yet managed to contact any colleagues about Oscar Tradovic, but at least she could mention that possible lead to Baz too.

So she reported to him feeling more confident and upbeat than usual. To her relief, Baz was pleased with her progress, but inevitably he wanted more.

* * *

A couple of hours later Rita's phone rang. It was Simon to say that Charles Abbott had left the police station, having been informed that he may be required for further questioning. His arrogance had resurfaced when the interviews concluded.

Simon also told Rita that the offices of Brownlow and Noggs had been searched, and paper and electronic items had been removed. He assured Rita that he would inform her immediately, if anything significant emerged.

Fifty-Two

Tony felt exhausted. Chloe had come downstairs a couple of times, saying it was time he came to bed. He had been determined to finish sorting out all the financial papers in Bea's cardboard box. At least they were now in date order. There were invoices from The Willows, bank statements for several accounts, letters about Bea's will, some other investments (which Tony felt sure Bea would not recall), some ancient savings accounts, and correspondence about a house she had bought many years ago. *What a mess,* thought Tony.

'I'll just make a start on the bank statements,' Tony told Chloe. 'I want to reconcile them with The Willows' invoices and other bills.'

Chloe decided to leave Tony to it. Once he set his mind to a task, he would not rest easy until it was finished.

All the invoices were signed by Mrs S Jeavons, which unsettled Tony initially. The image of her lifeless body flashed across his mind.

Pull yourself together, he told himself sharply, *don't be so feeble.*

Tony's plan was to look thoroughly at all transactions over the past two years, and if he found anything of concern in those, he would take his search back further. Invoices had been sent on a monthly basis. *But who had actually been responsible for paying them?* Tony wondered. He was certain that Bea knew nothing about online banking, and her statements gave no indication of direct debits. Chloe and he had found no cheque books in Bea's name. *So how were the invoices paid?* Tony made a note to ask Charles Abbott. After all, it had been his suggestion that Tony should look after Bea's affairs.

Tony then had second thoughts about this. He knew that Chloe had niggling doubts about Charles Abbott.

Suddenly his telephone conversation with Martin Dean came into Tony's mind. *After all,* he thought, *he has an interest in the whole saga too. Hadn't Mr Abbott contacted him not long ago? And hadn't Martin been over to Minchford quite recently, although Tony couldn't recall the reason. Perhaps they should meet for a drink and compare notes again.*

Tony decided to phone Martin in the morning. He placed the sorted piles of papers neatly on a bookshelf with a heavy encyclopaedia on top, ready for further perusal the following evening.

* * *

A few days later Martin Dean and Tony Montgomery met for the first time. They had decided on a pub halfway between their two homes. It was fairly empty when Tony arrived. There was only one man sitting on his own, so it wasn't difficult to identify Martin. They shook hands warmly, and Martin offered to buy some drinks.

'My children and I,' began Martin, 'have been trying to work out how you and we are related. We've found an ancient family tree, but unfortunately it's in a very tattered state and not easy to decipher. But we reckon that your aunt Beatrice is a second cousin to my late mother Lisbet. Does that sound feasible to you?'

Tony laughed.

'I have no idea,' he said, 'and to be honest, I'm not too bothered! Let's just accept for now that we are long-lost relatives, and I'm really pleased we've found each other. My main concern is to find out how poor old Bea fits into two local murders. Finding that woman's body in her office was one of the worst experiences of my life, but it's equally awful thinking that Bea may be unwittingly caught up in it.'

During the next hour Martin and Tony exchanged all they knew about The Willows, the murders of Sally Jeavons and Maddie Smith, Seb's interrogation by the police, Bea's unpleasant son Jacob, Charles Abbott, the sinister women Helena and Mishka, and an unidentified George.

'And there's something else,' said Tony after fetching a round of drinks, 'Bea has a bee in her bonnet, if you'll excuse the pun, about an aunt of hers called Anastasia or Anna. Does the name mean anything to you?'

'Aha,' replied Martin, 'the enigmatic Anastasia had a long passionate affair with Bea's uncle, while he was working abroad. I reckon that was in the early decades of the twentieth century. He was a George, and he really fired up the lurid imagination of my daughter. But her interest was more in the salacious details, I'm afraid, than in solving our various conundrums!'

They both laughed. Tony felt a moment's regret that he and Chloe didn't have any children.

'Well,' said Tony after some thought, 'Bea tends to get in quite a state when she thinks about Anastasia. But her mind is often confused, so we're never sure what is real memory and what's not. Anyway, Bea talks about how wealthy Anastasia was, and how she'd given Bea valuable jewellery to look after. She always used to wear a key on a chain around her neck, which was said to be the key to the jewellery box which Anastasia had given Bea eons ago for safe keeping. Chloe and I now have the key, but it's still a mystery where the box is, or even if it still exists. There was a theory at one stage that it might be in a Norwegian bank vault, but we haven't really looked into that, although Chloe was all for booking a short break in Oslo!'

'Well, well,' chuckled Martin, 'when I heard from Abbott, the solicitor, about George Montgomery, Tilda's immediate reaction was that a long-forgotten relative had died and left us loads of money! I told her not to get her hopes up, but perhaps she wasn't far from the truth, at least about the existence of wealth in some branch of the family way back.'

'Your daughter sounds like a bright spark,' said Tony, and Martin nodded in agreement.

A short pause followed, during which each man pursued his own thoughts. Martin then asked, 'I don't suppose you have any pictures of Jacob, do you Tony?'

Tony thought for a moment.

'I don't think so,' he replied, 'the only ones I've seen are of Jacob as a child. Poor old Chloe has seen him recently, of course, but my only direct contact has been him ranting down the phone at me. Why do you ask?'

'Maybe just an idle thought,' said Martin, 'but if Helena and Mishka change their personae and looks, I wondered if Jacob does too. It might be helpful to make sure we're all talking about the same person. Or is my imagination too much like my daughter's?'

Both men laughed again.

'Well, in all honesty,' said Tony, 'I wouldn't fancy asking Chloe to get Jacob to face her phone camera and say "cheese"!'

More laughter, but this time with a sinister edge to it.

'I take your point,' was Martin's heartfelt response.

After a couple of hours it was clear that Tony and Martin had enjoyed each other's company, as well as having mutual interests. They were both keen to keep in touch about any developments and to exchange any relevant photos.

As he was getting into his car, Tony's phone rang. It was Chloe. Bea had got up out of her chair unassisted, while Chloe was upstairs for a few minutes. She must have lost her balance, fallen to the floor awkwardly, hitting her shoulder and arm on the edge of the kitchen table. Chloe hadn't been able to lift Bea, who was very distressed, so she had called for an ambulance and Bea was now on her way to hospital. Chloe was about to follow in her car.

Fifty-Three

'Right, guv,' said Rita, scarcely able to conceal her enthusiasm, 'things are moving at last.'

Baz looked across at her, raised his eyebrows and asked, 'Well?'

Rita steadied her voice and began, 'I've been talking to an officer in the Midlands who knows Oscar Tradovic. It seems he's been in the frame for more than he's been convicted of. He's a slippery character by all accounts. Primarily known for theft and minor violence. But the offence he went to prison for involved a knife. Now here's the interesting bit, guv, he had a co-defendant… one Jacob Elsworth, and they served their sentences in the same prison. I need to do some double-checking just to make sure it's our Beatrice Elsworth's son, but the age seems about right, it's quite an unusual name, and he pushed the Montgomerys' neighbour pretty hard into a thorny hedge, so he's not averse to a bit of violence. I've asked the officer to send over all he's got on Tradovic and Elsworth.'

'Good work, Rita,' said Baz, 'anything else?'

'Oh yes, guv, there's more. The tech team have given me preliminary findings from Maddie Smith's phone. She apparently didn't use it much. There were quite a few texts to and from her girlfriends and her mum, just the usual stuff. But then they found some threats to Maddie. They've only given me two examples so far, but the gist of the first one is that "being a snitch is dangerous", and the other one told Maddie to "get her sodding hands off old Bea Elsworth or she'll get it". No prizes for guessing who sent that one,' said Rita and immediately regretted it, seeing Baz's disapproving look.

'He's cropping up a lot, isn't he?' said Baz. 'Looks like we'll be hauling him in soon for a chat. Keep pushing the data analysts, though, as there may be more to find. Is that the lot then, Rita?'

'Just a couple more things,' said Rita, knowing that her report was pleasing Baz, and wishing to prolong her moment of satisfaction. 'Simon tells me that Abbott appears to have deleted a lot of files and history from his office computer recently, but it should be possible to retrieve most of it. Simon is focussing on the possible fraud, of course, but they've got our investigation in mind too.'

'And the final thing?' asked Baz.

'Not really to do with the investigations, guv, but a friend of mine met Paula Trelawney at the gym. Apparently old Bea Elsworth has had another fall and is back in hospital. I don't know what damage was done. She's had a tough time, hasn't she?'

Baz appreciated Rita's kind nature. She hadn't yet developed the hardened cynicism which he knew was in himself.

Fifty-Four

Luke had finished all the painting in the new restaurant area and felt proud of the result. Mick also thought that Luke had made a good job of it. He was sitting on an upturned bucket, wondering what Mick would want him to do next, when his phone alerted him to a new message. It was from Debbie, who was only a few metres away from him in the pub, behind the partition.

The message read, 'Red-head here. Stay there.'

Luke's heart sank. Surely Mishka wasn't here again, so soon after her last visit. Luke sat motionless, his thoughts and heartbeat racing.

Meanwhile Debbie decided to keep the red-head talking, confident that Luke would stay where he was. She offered the woman a drink "on the house" in view of her numerous unsuccessful visits to see her friend. Debbie suggested that Luke would be so disappointed to miss her yet again. The red-head accepted a small glass of white wine.

* * *

Mick was also behind the bar and realised what Debbie was doing. He wandered outside, took his phone out of his pocket and began taking pictures of the pub and its surroundings. One of the regular customers strolled into the car park and asked Mick what he was up to.

'Just want some new shots for publicity purposes... it looks quite different from the old photos,' Mick explained in a loud voice.

While doing this, Mick glanced around the car park. He recognised most of the regulars' cars, but one in particular caught his interest. It was clearly the most expensive car there, and a man was sitting in the driver's seat engrossed in something on his phone. Mick took his chance and caught the registration plate and some side views of the driver. To Mick's concern, the man then stepped out of the car, phone still in hand. He appeared just to be stretching his legs. Mick continued taking pictures of the pub, ensuring that a couple included front views of the man. He then started to walk to the door, when the red-head came out.

Mick nodded at her and called out, 'Have a safe journey'. She looked up, surprised, and then gave him a stunning smile. The man by the car was beckoning to her, obviously keen to leave, so she quickened her step. Just before she got into the passenger seat, Mick unobtrusively took a sequence of photos of her and the man, who was leaning on the car.

He immediately went inside to show Luke his pictures.

'I've taken dozens of all sorts of things, so as to not cause any suspicions,' he explained to Luke, 'but there may be some that you want.'

Luke was keen to see them. There was absolutely no doubt that the woman was the transformed Mishka, but he didn't initially recognise the man.

Then a thought struck him. 'I've seen him with her before,' said Luke, 'when I was still at uni. I'm sure I took some pictures of them then. I just hope that I uploaded them onto my laptop, as I've changed my phone since then... all because of her, of course,' he told Mick ruefully. 'Thanks, Mick,' he continued, 'you're a real mate.'

Mick grinned, gave Luke a friendly punch on the arm, and suggested that they have a chat with Debbie, as it was thanks to her that Mick had been able to take the photos.

There were not many customers in the pub, so Debbie told them quietly about her conversation with the red-head, as Debbie always referred to her. She had explained to Debbie that she and her best friend had been really close friends with Luke and his mate, Seb. They'd had such great times together, but somehow they'd lost contact after Seb and Luke had finished at uni, and she *so* wanted them all to meet up again. Perhaps they could all come for a meal at Debbie's pub?

Luke was fuming as he heard this version of events.

'The lying, scheming bitch,' he exclaimed, trying desperately to keep his voice down. 'I just can't believe it! It was nothing like that, and I certainly don't want to meet up with her and bloody Helena for a cosy meal. What the hell is she playing at? Why won't she bugger off and leave me alone?'

Debbie was astonished at Luke's reaction. She'd never heard him speak so forcefully before. His anger, or was it fear, was almost palpable.

'Well,' interjected Mick, 'we can't stop her coming here, unless she or her friend start making a nuisance of themselves, but we can do our utmost to keep her away from you, Luke.'

None of them was sure how this could be achieved, but it was reassuring for Luke to know that Debbie and Mick were definitely on his side.

That evening Luke sent some of Mick's photos to Seb. He was concerned about how Tilda might feel on seeing the glamorous Mishka, but there was nothing he could do about that. After several texts back and forth, it was agreed that Luke, Seb and Tilda would meet up the following weekend for a strategic talk.

Fifty-Five

Martin and Seb were taking another look at Luke's pictures of the man and Mishka. They were discussing everything, ahead of Luke's arrival tomorrow, sitting side by side on the sofa. Ros came into the lounge and gave an involuntary gasp when she saw the image on Seb's phone. She quickly composed herself. Seb continued scrolling down the pictures, unaware of his mother's presence, but Ros's reaction did not escape Martin. He was puzzled. The image she had seen, was of the man leaning on a car facing the camera.

What was it about the image which had caused Ros to gasp like that? Why had she immediately tried to cover up her reaction? He decided to ask Ros about it later, privately.

* * *

The following day Luke made the irksome journey to the Deans' home, but the expression on Tilda's face on seeing him made it worthwhile. Ros was concerned about her daughter's obvious adoration of Luke, but she decided that there could be little harm in it, as long as Luke continued to live some distance away and her college work didn't suffer.

As lunchtime approached, Martin suggested that they all go to The Black Horse for a meal. Seb, Luke and Tilda were all in favour of this, but Ros declined, saying that she had a headache and wanted to lie down for a while. Martin was sceptical about Ros's excuse. She had shown no signs of feeling unwell ten minutes ago. He wondered if it was connected with her reaction to the picture yesterday evening. She knew that they would all talk about their "obsession", as she called it, and perhaps she wanted no part in it.

In the pub Martin asked, 'So that's the beguiling Mishka, is it?'. He immediately wished that he had phrased the question differently, when he saw his daughter's expression.

'Well,' replied Luke quickly, 'that's the current version of her. She looked quite different when we were at uni, didn't she, Seb? And then she had a strong foreign accent, which has completely disappeared now.'

Tilda was clearly uncomfortable while the focus was on Mishka, so Martin asked, 'But this man… what do we know about him?'

Seb and Luke both looked blank.

'But I have seen him before,' said Luke. He searched for a couple of moments on his phone. 'Look,' he continued, 'I found this photo on my laptop, and I'm sure it's the same guy. I just happened to see them both in the street when I was going to the cinema one evening. That was the first time I'd seen Mishka looking so different.'

'So, they've obviously known each other for quite a while,' said Martin.

The food arrived, but Tilda didn't seem hungry now. She felt miserable and vulnerable while the conversation centred on Luke's ex-girlfriend.

If that's the type of girl Luke's attracted to, she thought, *I have no hope of holding onto him.*

But Luke sensed what Tilda was thinking and squeezed her hand under the table. She looked up at him with a wan smile.

Martin's brain, though, was working fast.

'It's a long shot,' he said between mouthfuls, 'but I wonder if Tony would recognise this chap. After all, his aunt Bea was in the old folks' home where we saw Helena. So Mishka may have been there too… and she seems to rely on this chap as a chauffeur, so perhaps Tony has seen them.'

Seb looked up at the ceiling, thinking his father's imagination was running wild.

'Well,' continued Martin defensively, 'I think it's worth a try. You haven't come up with any better suggestions.'

Martin continued his meal.

A few minutes later he said, 'That's done, so now we wait and see what happens.'

Tilda was less interested in the pictures of the unknown man than in the prospect of Mishka turning up at the pub again, and next time possibly meeting up with Luke. She couldn't bear the thought.

As if reading her mind, Luke told them all how fortunate he was to have Mick and Debbie looking out for him.

'They're good at dealing with unwanted customers,' he said, 'and they won't let her near me, if they can help it,' he said, with a reassuring glance at Tilda and another squeeze of her hand beneath the table.

Martin was just finishing his last mouthful of delicious sticky toffee pudding, when his phone rang.

'I'll just take this outside,' he said when he saw who the call was from. With that he left the others, suggesting that they order coffees, and went out into the pub's garden.

'Typical Dad,' grumbled Tilda, 'even on a Saturday his work is more important than we are.'

'Come on, sis, be fair,' retorted Seb sharply, 'he is trying to help us sort out this mess. He could've been bloody furious at me being questioned about a murder, but he hasn't been. Don't forget what a state I was in when you came and rescued me here.'

Tilda looked shamefaced.

'Sorry,' she muttered quietly, 'I know you're right.'

Martin's coffee was cold by the time he returned to the table. He had a triumphant look on his face.

'I'll get you a hot coffee,' offered Tilda, trying to make amends for her thoughts about her father.

'Thanks, Tilda,' replied Martin, 'but don't bother. This cold one will do.' He sipped the coffee. 'Well,' he beamed at the three expectant faces, 'that was Tony and, would you believe it, we have an identity for the man in the photos… easy as that!'

Martin took several more sips of cold coffee.

'Come on, Dad, spill the beans,' said Tilda impatiently.

'Well,' said Martin, 'it's quite a story.'

'All we need's his name,' blurted out Tilda. She knew this trait in her father, spinning out a story to maintain suspense.

'Hang on, Tilda,' he said, 'you should know a bit of context too.'

Tilda sighed quietly and waited for her father to explain.

Martin reminded them all of Tony's link with The Willows, and how he had been one of the people to find the murdered woman's body.

'We know all this,' interrupted Tilda impatiently.

Martin ignored the interruption.

'Tony's elderly aunt, Bea,' Martin continued, 'had been a resident there, but now she's living with Tony and Chloe. They were actually on their way to the local hospital to see Bea, when Tony received our photos. Tony was driving, so Chloe opened up the pictures and gasped, "I don't believe it!" He looked across and saw how shocked Chloe was, so he pulled off the road as soon as he could. It transpires that the photos are of Bea's son, Jacob, and apparently Chloe has had some very unpleasant encounters with him recently. He's been to their home, making all sorts of demands and threats. He's really frightened Chloe by the sound of things. So poor Chloe was really shocked when she saw a picture of the dreadful man on Tony's phone.'

'Poor woman,' said Tilda sympathetically, 'that must've been awful for her. I hope she's feeling alright now.' Luke gave Tilda a loving look.

'Right,' said Seb, 'so we know who he is, but what can we do about it?'

'Well,' replied his father, 'Tony also told me that the police were called to their home, when Jacob made a nuisance of himself and was threatening Chloe. But I can't see anything wrong in his connection with Mishka. It's all very strange how those two know each other, but until one of them commits some sort of offence, I don't think we can actually *do* anything. I think you're just going to have to ride it out, Luke, I'm sorry to say.'

'But the link still seems to be George, doesn't it?' asked Tilda.

'Quite right, Tilda,' replied her father, 'we mustn't take our eyes off that ball.'

On the way home, Martin asked the others not to talk about Jacob in front of Ros yet. He felt sure that her headache had been fabricated, but he didn't say that to his children or Luke. He wanted to have a private conversation with Ros about her reaction to the picture of Jacob Elsworth.

* * *

As they parked in the drive, Seb saw that the front door was wide open. He went in first and immediately knew that something was wrong. Zeus didn't come out to welcome them, as he usually would. He called to the others, who were dawdling in the drive.

Martin saw the scared look on Seb's face. He rushed into the kitchen, where Zeus lay slumped on the floor. He opened one eye, briefly looked at Martin, wagged his tail slightly and closed his eye again. Martin called out to Ros, but there was no reply.

He charged up the stairs, past the other three who were standing, bewildered, in the hallway. All the bedroom doors were wide open, and most of the cupboard doors too. Clothes were strewn all over the carpets. Ros was lying on the floor of the smallest bedroom, apparently unconscious and with her hands bound behind her back with one of Martin's neckties.

'Seb,' he shouted, 'call an ambulance and the police, we've been burgled and your mum's hurt.'

He knelt down beside his wife, in a state of shock.

Fifty-Six

Rita Hussein put the phone down.

'*Yes,*' she said in an emphatic tone. She gathered her thoughts and went straight to Baz's office. As usual he was tapping on his keyboard, looking stressed.

'I hope it's good news, Rita,' he said, his eyes still on the screen.

'It certainly is, guv,' she began, 'he had to make a blunder at some stage, and it seems that he has.'

'Just give it to me straight,' muttered Baz impatiently.

'Sorry, guv,' replied Rita, 'well, Jacob Elsworth is in custody, being questioned about a burglary and an assault. Not on our patch, though. His car was caught on CCTV at, believe it or not, the home of Sebastian Dean, the young man we questioned about the Jeavons murder.'

Baz looked at Rita, clearly more interested now.

She explained that an emergency call had been received from a member of the Dean family. They had come home to find that the house had been burgled and Sebastian's mother, Rosalind Dean, had been assaulted. She refused to go to hospital to be checked over, but she was not thought to be seriously hurt. The Deans have no CCTV, but luckily their neighbours do, and their camera covers the entrance to the Deans' driveway. The car belonging to Jacob Elsworth, which Katya Tradovic was caught speeding in previously, was clearly visible waiting at the entrance to the driveway at the relevant time. The whole family, except Mrs Dean, had been out having a pub lunch at the time. She hasn't been interviewed yet.'

'Hmm,' said Baz, 'does the CCTV show who was actually driving the car? Does that model have tinted windows?'

Rita was annoyed with herself. She hadn't asked the officer about that, and she should have done.

* * *

Rita returned to her office to write up her records. She had difficulty concentrating on the task in hand. Baz had been right that Jacob Elsworth repeatedly cropped up in their investigations. But *why* did he?

Think, Rita, think, she told herself, *what have you missed?*

She decided to focus first on the connection between Jacob Elsworth and the Tradovic family, to see what needed further investigation. *There was the prison connection between Elsworth and Oscar Tradovic. There was a link between Elsworth and Katya Tradovic, sufficient for him to lend her his car. Was there any evidence that Elsworth and Oscar Tradovic were still in contact with each other, or even offending together again?* Rita's head was beginning to spin.

Her phone rang, much to her relief.

The caller identified himself as Tony Montgomery, nephew of Bea Elsworth. Rita was surprised but, quickly gathering her thoughts, asked him how his aunt was after her recent fall. Tony was taken aback. *How did the police know about that?* he wondered.

'She's back at home now, thank you, she'll be fine,' replied Tony. 'But the reason I rang you was more about her son. It may not be of any significance to you, but I thought I would mention it to you anyway.'

'What did you want to tell me, Mr Montgomery?' asked Rita, silently praying that a missing link was about to be disclosed.

'Right,' continued Tony, a little uncertainly, 'you remember that Jacob Elsworth has been to our house, causing a disturbance and making threats to my wife?'

Rita made a confirming 'mm… ' sound.

'Well, a distant relative of mine sent me a couple of photos earlier today to see if I could identify the man in them. The girl in some of the pictures has apparently been stalking a young friend of theirs and making a real nuisance of herself. Well, I didn't recognise the man, but my wife Chloe did, and it gave her a horrible shock. It was my aunt's son, Jacob Elsworth.'

Rita's brain changed up a gear.

Eventually she said, trying to sound calm, 'Two things, Mr Montgomery. Would you please send the photos to me, and also ask your relative to send any more relevant photos which he has. If there are some of the girl with Jacob Elsworth, that would be really helpful. Secondly, would you give me details of this relative of yours, as we may need to contact him.'

'No problem,' replied Tony, relieved that he appeared to have assisted DC Hussein. 'My relative's name is Martin Dean. I'll check his contact details and get back to you.' The call ended.

Rita was really fired up now. *Another thread tying Jacob Elsworth into possible criminal activities. And it had to be the same Martin Dean, but she would need confirmation of that. But what was this stalking allegation all about? And what was Elsworth's role in that, if any?*

Rita got up and went to Baz's office. It was empty. She guessed that he had gone outside to have a cigarette, in need of some nicotine to keep him going. Rita put a clean chart on the wall, and this time the name Jacob Elsworth was written in the centre. Rita liked working visually when there were a multitude of strands to pull together. By the time Baz returned to his office, revitalised, Rita was standing back, examining her work. Beneath the chart she had listed her professional contacts and their roles in all this. There were also columns listing potential suspects, informants and victims.

Baz stood next to her. 'Good work, Rita,' he said, 'but should another name be on there?'

Rita's heart sank. *Why did Baz always go straight to something she had left out?*

'Who's that then, guv?' she asked, hoping she had a good reason for the omission.

'I can't see that solicitor Abbott's name,' he replied, 'don't you think there's a link there somewhere? What about Elsworth's old mum being at The Willows? Do Elsworth and Abbott know each other?'

Rita groaned. *She was trying so hard to cover all bases, and wretched Baz immediately spots a flaw!*

'Don't worry, Rita,' said Baz with a sympathetic grin, 'they always say that two heads are better than one.'

Baz's phone rang. It was Tony Montgomery, wanting to speak to DC Hussein again. Baz handed the phone to Rita, flicking the switch so that he could listen in on the conversation.

'Sorry to bother you again,' began Tony, 'but you seemed to be interested in Bea's son, so it got me thinking. I know that you interviewed both me and my wife after we found Mrs Jeavons' body, but I can't remember if I told you about a remark the solicitor made just beforehand. Chloe has just reminded me of it. It seemed odd at the time, and I really can't remember if I mentioned it. We were both pretty shaken up, as you know. Anyway, in case it helps, Mr Abbott happened to say to me that he thought Jacob Elsworth had once had a car just like the one we saw leaving The Willows, as we arrived. I don't know if that's true, of course,' continued Tony, 'it's just what Mr Abbott said.'

After the call ended, Baz said, with fake smugness in his voice, 'Great... that confirms that Abbott's name should be on your chart!'

Rita smiled slightly and held up her hands in a gesture of defeat.

Fifty-Seven

It was Sadie's birthday, so Chloe arrived home early with a large sponge cake with 'Happy Birthday' written in pink icing on the top. She had also brought a bottle of sparkling white wine.

Sadie looked so pleased, and Bea said, 'We'll have to sing for you, Sadie,' and clapped her hands. Chloe managed to find three candles in pink holders and placed them in a triangle on the cake. She lit them. When Chloe and Bea had sung 'Happy Birthday' to her, Sadie blew out the candles and beamed.

'I don't remember when I last had my own birthday cake,' she said, discreetly wiping a tear from her eye.

The pop of the cork made Bea jump, and they all laughed. Sadie was reluctant to have any wine initially, but Bea egged her on. Chloe proposed a toast to Sadie and told her how much they appreciated her. She suddenly realised that she was on sensitive ground, as it was only due to Maddie's death that they had found Sadie. But it was Sadie who rescued the situation.

'Is it alright if we have a toast to my lovely Maddie, may she rest in peace?'

Chloe raised her glass, feeling relieved. 'To lovely Maddie,' she echoed.

Chloe had alerted Tony to the birthday party, and he arrived home early too. He gave Sadie a box of assorted chocolates, which the shop had decorated for him with a multicoloured ribbon. Sadie looked overwhelmed.

'All this, just because it's my birthday! I can't thank you enough,' she said.

'Well,' said Tony, 'just one more treat. Whenever you're ready, I'll take you home in the car. We can't have the birthday girl hanging around waiting for a bus, can we?'

Sadie protested, but Tony insisted.

* * *

While Tony was driving Sadie home, Bea, who was slightly tipsy, started talking to Chloe about Anastasia.

'She had such beautiful jewellery, and she looked like a princess when she went to parties. Perhaps you could borrow it when you go to a party like that,' said Bea in a slightly unsteady voice. Chloe laughed softly.

'I don't think I'd dare to,' she replied, 'and I don't often get invited to parties like that. Tell me about Anastasia's parties,' but Bea had nodded off.

Tony soon arrived home, and Bea was still asleep in her chair. 'Looks like everyone enjoyed the party,' he whispered to Chloe, 'are you squiffy too?'

'There's a bit left in the bottle, if you want to finish it,' replied Chloe, and Tony poured himself the last half-glass.

'Perhaps I ought to remain clear-headed anyway,' he said. 'I'm sure I read something in Bea's old papers about her buying a house, so I want to check it out.'

'That sounds a bit unlikely, doesn't it?' asked Chloe. 'Has Mr Abbott mentioned a house to you? Why on earth would Bea have a house that you don't know anything about?'

'They're just the sort of questions that I am hoping to answer, but to answer one of them, no, Abbott has never mentioned her owning a house.'

Tony was right. There were several letters and other documents relating to a house purchase by Bea. They were all dated around twenty years ago. At that stage Tony wasn't in regular contact with his aunt. He wondered when Bea's husband, Edgar, had died, but Tony couldn't recall seeing a death certificate for him. What did strike Tony, though, was that Abbott's firm of solicitors, and indeed Abbott himself, was central to Bea's affairs even then. Tony hadn't appreciated just how long they had been her solicitors, although he did remember her referring to them as "her family's solicitors".

Chloe joined her husband at the dining room table, where Bea's papers were spread out.

'Right,' said Chloe, 'let's find out where this mystery house is. Of course, it's quite possible that Bea subsequently sold it again... she's an unlikely property tycoon, isn't she?'

Tony laughed.

'If she did do that,' he replied, 'we can guess which firm of solicitors was involved, and who holds those documents.' Chloe groaned.

They continued looking through the papers. They quickly found the details of the house. It was in the village of Great Fordington, a short drive from Minchford.

Chloe gasped, and suddenly Tony realised why. Maddie's body had been found in the woods just beyond Little Fordington. And Sadie continued to live in Great Fordington.

Chloe was upset by memories of Maddie flooding in. *Perhaps the residual effects of the wine are not helping either,* thought Tony.

She stood up, telling Tony that she would check on Bea and then start preparing their supper. Tony nodded. Chloe needed time alone with her thoughts.

He went back to reading Bea's papers. He suddenly thought, *maybe Jacob is aware of this house, if Bea still owns it, and he stands to inherit it. It must be worth a lot more now than when she bought it. Perhaps Jacob thinks that I have designs on his inheritance, hence his determination to wrench Bea away from Chloe and me.*

Tony was feeling out of his depth, and not for the first time. This whole saga had begun with an impulsive visit to his aunt one day, on his way home from work. And now he felt embroiled in a series of traumatic events, which he couldn't understand. And poor Chloe was being affected by it all too. The only good aspects were that he had found a new relative, Martin, and that he and Chloe were able to give Bea a comfortable home for as long as she needed it.

* * *

The following morning, after a restless night, Tony decided to phone DC Hussein again.

After brief pleasantries, Tony told her that he might have stumbled across a motive for Jacob Elsworth's harassment of his wife and aunt. Rita listened sceptically until Tony mentioned Bea's house in Great Fordington.

'We had no idea she had bought it all those years ago, but we also don't know if she still owns it. Oh yes, the solicitors involved were Brownlow and Noggs, if that's of any importance,' concluded Tony.

Rita thanked Tony for his call.

Very interesting, she said to herself.

Fifty-Eight

Tony couldn't find anywhere to park near his office this morning, so he drove around the nearby side streets hoping to come across a suitable space. Thankfully he did, but he was frustrated at wasting time like that. He wound his way on foot through the maze of narrow streets and found himself passing the offices of Brownlow and Noggs. He noticed a sheet of paper on the inside of the door, stating that the offices were closed until further notice and offering apologies for any inconvenience caused. Tony wondered what that was all about.

He settled down to the backlog of work which had been accumulating while he was preoccupied with matters concerning Bea. His plan was to stay at the office late that evening and make substantial inroads into the outstanding workload.

His office phone rang. Tony cursed, but then answered it.

'Sorry to disturb you at work, Mr Montgomery, this is DC Hussein. I'm hoping you can help us. We are aware that, before the murder of Mrs Jeavons, you passed some pictures you took in The Willows to Mr Abbott for safe keeping. My colleagues have retrieved some images of what we believe to be Mrs Elsworth's room there, but there seem to be a few distorted images taken at the same time, which we hope you still have on your phone. Would you be able to send me the sequence of pictures you took at that time?'

Tony was astounded. *Why would the police want those?* He picked up his mobile phone and searched through his pictures. Sure enough, he still had the images of Bea's room which, according to the late Mrs Jeavons, was being "spruced up" ready for Bea's return from hospital. In Tony's opinion it was being thoroughly searched.

'Yes, I've just found them,' Tony told DC Hussein, 'do you want them all?'

'As many as you have,' she replied, 'and thank you for your cooperation.' And the call was ended.

Tony looked through the pictures again. He hadn't given them any thought recently. He remembered deliberately including Mrs Jeavons in some of them because he was so incensed at her treatment of Bea's room and her obstruction of himself. But now he noticed that one of the carers was in the room too, presumably following Mrs Jeavons' instructions. Tony wasn't sure which carer she was.

He had a sudden thought. He sent the picture of the carer to Martin with the message, 'Long shot, Seb's friend?'

Within minutes a reply came back from Martin, 'Yes, Helena. Talk later.'

Tony wondered if he should tell DC Hussein who the carer in the picture was, but he thought better of it. The police could always identify her through the manager of The Willows, if they needed to, so he should let them do their job.

Tony now tried to exclude all else and concentrate on his work.

* * *

Meanwhile Chloe was in her office, similarly trying to clear a backlog. She felt confident that Bea was safe in Sadie's hands at home. Sadie tried to think up stimulating things for Bea to do during the day. Maddie had sometimes told her that the old ladies and gentlemen at The Willows just sat in their chairs and dozed most of the day, if they didn't have visitors or organised activities. Sadie thought that was sad. *When the weather was better,* she decided, *she would take Bea in her wheelchair to the park for a change of scenery. Today, though, with a blustery wind outside, they would stay at home together.*

Fifty-Nine

Ros was fully conscious when the ambulance, and then the police, arrived at her home. She was very shaken, but not badly hurt as Martin had at first feared. Her wrists had been bound with one of Martin's neckties. He took a pillow off the bed and gently raised Ros's head onto it. As he did so, she saw the mess in the room and burst into tears.

Martin wanted Ros to go to hospital for a thorough check-up, but she was adamant that it was not necessary. She was sure that she had passed out briefly because she was afraid, not due to any injury. So, it was agreed that Ros should rest at home and only seek further medical assistance if she needed to. The paramedics watched her go downstairs and get settled on the sofa, and they then left.

While the police got on with their forensic work, Tilda turned her attention to groggy Zeus. Luke was trying to make helpful suggestions, but he had never owned a dog. Tilda was pleased that he was there in the kitchen with her, though. She rang the local vet for advice and he offered to call round to examine Zeus. Tilda stroked the dog's head, and he responded with a half-hearted thump of his tail on the floor.

* * *

Seb was upstairs watching the police as they forensically examined the two bedrooms which had been disturbed.

One of the officers turned to Seb and asked, 'Do you know who this phone belongs to? It was lying on the floor under these clothes.'

Seb looked across at the phone and said that he didn't recognise it. It was in a silver, tan and black, faux snakeskin cover. It certainly didn't belong to either of his parents, and the cover wouldn't be to Tilda's taste.

The officer slipped the phone into a plastic evidence bag and sealed it. 'I'll show it to your parents before we leave,' she told Seb.

* * *

A few hours later the Dean household was returning to normality. The police had left, and Tilda had quickly tidied the bedrooms. Nothing seemed to have been damaged or stolen. The intruders had just thrown clothes all over the place, which Tilda couldn't understand. The vet had examined Zeus and reassured the family that he would recover soon.

Tilda noticed that the vet had spoken to the police on the driveway as he left. *Poor old Zeus,* she thought, *I wonder what they tempted you to eat.* But Zeus was back on his feet before long, albeit unsteadily.

Martin had a quiet chat with Ros and then phoned for a takeaway Chinese meal, hoping that this might cheer everyone up. He opened a bottle of Ros's favourite Chardonnay wine, although he wasn't sure whether she should be drinking alcohol after her frightening experience.

They were finishing their meal when Ros, who had eaten and drunk very little, suddenly said, 'I need to say something to you all.'

Martin looked surprised. This was out of character for Ros, so they all waited quietly for her to continue.

She took a sip of wine, looked at the expectant faces around the table, and began. At first her voice was shaky, but it became stronger as her story unravelled.

'I'm sure this wasn't a random break-in,' she said, 'and I'm sure that they knew you were all out at the pub. They didn't seem interested in stealing anything, they just wanted to frighten me, and they certainly did that. Their faces were covered with masks, with just eye slits, and they were wearing work overalls, so I wouldn't recognise them again. They tied up my hands, just so I couldn't phone you or the police, I suppose. They didn't say anything, they just communicated with each other or me with gestures. It was all very frightening, though, and I think I must've passed out. The next thing I remember is you all arriving home, thank heavens.'

Everyone was silent while Ros was speaking.

After a short pause, she continued. 'There's one other thing too,' she said, 'which happened yesterday. You, Seb, and Dad were looking at some pictures on your phone. I'm sure they must be linked to all the strange goings-on recently, which I haven't wanted to get involved in. Well, now I am involved, like it or not.' Ros hesitated and took another sip of wine. 'I only saw one picture, but I couldn't believe my eyes.'

Martin recalled Ros's sharp intake of breath as she walked behind the sofa yesterday. He said nothing.

'I think I used to know that man,' she said.

Seb gasped, and Ros looked at all their bewildered faces.

'You must have got it wrong, Mum,' said Seb, 'you can't possibly know him. You can only have seen the image briefly. You must've mistaken him for someone else.'

'Well,' replied Ros, 'there's one way to check that... show me the picture again!'

While Seb went to fetch his phone from the lounge, Martin gently tried to dissuade his wife from looking at the image again.

He'd been aware of her reaction at the time, and he felt it was unwise for her to look at it again, bearing in mind what she'd been through today. But Ros was adamant.

Seb found the picture and, after an enquiring look at his father, showed it to his mum. Ros blanched.

'Yes, it's him alright,' she said, nodding as if to emphasise her certainty.

Seb and Martin exchanged puzzled glances.

'He was a horrible boy,' continued Ros, 'mean and spiteful. He went to my school, just for a year or two, while he was in a home for delinquent adolescents. He was a dreadful bully. There was a girl in my class that he bullied cruelly, just because she had a squint. He tried to ensure he didn't have any witnesses, but one day a friend and I saw clearly what he was doing. The girl was too scared to tell our teachers, but I decided that the staff should know. So I reported him, and when it all came out, he was excluded from our school. After that he sometimes waited for me to leave school in the afternoon and threaten me with being beaten up by his gang, but I didn't ever see him with a gang. Then, a few weeks later he just disappeared. But I remember his face clearly, and I'm certain this is an older version of that face. After I'd left school there was a picture of him in the local paper. He'd been in court for some reason, but I don't remember why. It was a horrible shock to see him on your phone, Seb. So what's that all about? Why have you got a picture of him? He's not a friend of yours, is he?'

By now the events of the past few hours had been overtaken by Ros's surprising disclosures. Martin's immediate reaction was that Ros was confusing the man in the photo with a teenager she remembered from her schooldays. It all seemed too coincidental. He knew that Ros had been unsettled by the family pursuing the 'George' business, by Seb's arrest and the weird phone calls. He wondered if today's burglary was one trauma too many for her.

Seb, though, was taking his mum's story at face value. There had been so many inexplicable coincidences recently, that he was inclined to believe yet another one. And no one had mentioned anything to Ros yet about the connection between the man in the picture and Helena or Mishka. She had no reason to link him with the family's investigations.

Seb was becoming increasingly unnerved.

Sixty

Rita was bounding up the steps to the side entrance of the police station, two at a time, when Simon from the fraud team called out from the car park.

'Hey, Rita, a meeting's been called for ten o'clock in my office… you'll want to be there!' He got into his car and drove off. Rita was intrigued.

Simon proved to be right… it was a very useful meeting. Rita took copious notes and was eager to share them with Baz. The only downside was that there was still no one in the frame for the Jeavons or Smith murders. But after the meeting she went straight to Baz's office, only to find that he too had been called to a meeting… with the DI. Hopefully Rita's news would cheer him up.

After a few minutes, Baz came into his office, where Rita was creating yet another wall chart.

'Well, Rita,' he said, 'you seem a helluva lot more upbeat than the boss was. What have you got?' Rita beamed.

'The long and the short of it, guv, is that Charles Abbott is about to be charged. Not with murder, I'm afraid… sorry to disappoint you there, guv. He was brought in for another interview. He soon realised that the evidence found on his various devices roundly condemned him. So, after placing all wrongdoing firmly with Sally Jeavons, and being adamant that he'd innocently become embroiled in something he didn't understand, he gradually began to acknowledge that they were possibly both culpable, but he, of course, to a lesser extent. Then, when it began to sink in just how much evidence we have, he couldn't start confessing fast enough. There's still a lot of follow-up to do, but by the end of his interview, he looked to Simon like a broken man. Maybe it was dawning on him that he stands to lose everything, his reputation, his professional status, his liberty possibly, and quite probably his family and friends.'

Rita paused to gather her thoughts. Baz sat quietly, waiting for Rita to continue.

'At one point the interviewing officers left the room and watched Abbott through the two-way glass. He had his head in his hands, with his elbows on the table. After a few minutes they went back into the room and restarted the recording machine. By then Abbott had regained his composure and his usual arrogance. The officers had anticipated this, so they feigned interest in Abbott's attempts to manipulate and bargain with them. He was willing to tell them more, he said, in return for no charges being brought against him. He claimed that no court would believe that a well-respected lawyer, such as himself, would have participated in a murky fraud unless under considerable duress. Anyway, he had probably defended half of the jurors at some stage, so he wouldn't be convicted!'

Rita paused again.

'You can imagine what Simon was thinking by then, guv. He was seething when he told the meeting. But Abbott's cockiness apparently increased as he thought he was winning over the officers. So,' she concluded, 'he'll probably end up with more charges, not less.'

Baz decided to ignore Rita's final remark, although he could see her point.

'So, Rita,' asked Baz, 'what exactly has Abbott been up to?'

'Well,' she replied, 'to be honest, guv, I don't understand all the accounting details, but, if I've got it right, he and Jeavons were targeting certain old people at The Willows, the ones who didn't have any interested relatives or friends. They persuaded these old folks to make a new will. And they'd all seen Abbott visiting The Willows regularly, so he was the obvious choice of lawyer to help them and to be their executors, when the time came. All sewn up! This had apparently been going on for years, with money being left to fictitious beneficiaries, who were actually Jeavons or Abbott by some devious route. As this was proving to be quite lucrative, they got greedier and set up other scams too... like residents' invoices being payable to other account numbers actually held by Abbott, who shared the proceeds with Jeavons. But, as Simon said,' continued Rita, 'none of this would've been possible if The Willows had been properly managed and audited. Abbott claims that he originally wanted no part of it, and it was all down to Jeavons' greed. He says that she was blackmailing him, and he couldn't extricate himself from it. She had him over a barrel, or so he claims.'

'So, has he explained what he meant by that?' asked Baz.

Rita skimmed a few pages in her notebook, gave Baz an enigmatic smile, and said, 'Well, guv, you may have to use your imagination a bit now.'

Baz looked surprised and asked, 'We are sticking to facts, aren't we, Rita?', but his expression betrayed his interest in where this was leading.

'We certainly are,' she replied, 'these are the facts as given by Abbott.'

She continued, 'Abbott states that Jeavons claimed to have found him and one of the care staff in the laundry room at The Willows in what he termed a "compromising situation". This is said to have been a few years ago. Jeavons sacked the carer, who admitted having an affair with Abbott. When asked to give more details about the "situation", Abbott's face turned scarlet, and he clammed up.'

'So this isn't the first time that Abbott's reputation has been threatened,' mused Baz, 'and this has been hanging over him, if he is to be believed, for quite some time. And Jeavons was the constant factor all that time.'

Baz leant back in his chair.

'Would this constitute a motive for murder, Rita, d'you think?'

Rita didn't answer immediately. This possibility had been discussed in the meeting in Simon's office. Whilst her colleagues had been sifting through a huge amount of evidence relating to Abbott's fraudulent activities, they had not yet found anything which unequivocally pointed to Abbott planning to get rid of Jeavons. It was becoming clear, though, that there were increasing tensions between them prior to her death.

Rita had been standing by the window, looking through her notes, but now she turned to face Baz again.

'Well, guv, this possibility was mooted at our meeting, but at the moment it remains just that… a possibility. As you always say, guv, where's the evidence to support this? So far it's circumstantial only.'

Baz nodded slowly, deep in thought.

Sixty-One

Paula Trelawney was returning to her office after dealing with an altercation between two kitchen staff, when she heard her phone ring. It was DC Hussein. She wanted to know if Paula had heard anything about a carer being sacked by Mrs Jeavons for having an affair with a visitor to the home a few years ago.

Paula thought for a while.

'No sackings immediately come to mind,' she told Rita, 'or at least, only poor Maddie Smith, and you know all about that, don't you? The staff records I inherited here are in a dreadful state, but I can do some checking, if that would help you.'

Rita thanked Paula and assured her that it would be helpful.

Paula racked her brains. There were often rumours and gossip circulating among the staff, which Paula sometimes came to hear about. But most of the talk recently had been about the murders of Sally Jeavons and Maddie Smith. Staff didn't tend to stay in their jobs for very long, so Paula doubted if she would glean much history from current staff. Her only option was to look through Mrs Jeavons' staff records. Paula sighed.

After half an hour of searching, Paula was beginning to think that her pessimism was justified. She speculated that Mrs Jeavons probably wouldn't have kept a record of her sacking someone anyway.

* * *

There was a confident knock on her office door, and Petra Tradovic came in.

'Well, Petra,' asked Paula, more brusquely than usual, 'how can I help you?'

There was always something about Petra's manner which put Paula on edge. Petra would smile at residents, but not at Paula. She wondered if she'd behaved like that with Sally Jeavons too.

'Well,' replied Petra, 'Rosie Carter in Room 3 is saying that she wants to write a will, but she's got no one to help her with it. There's been a rift in the family, so she wants someone outside of the family to advise her. In the past we usually suggested that the old chap Abbott should come and talk to residents with that sort of request, but he doesn't seem to be around at the moment, does he?'

There was a smirk on Petra's face, and her tone was challenging. Petra appeared to think she had the upper hand in this conversation and was loath to lose it. Without allowing Paula the time to respond, she continued, 'Seems he's in a bit of bother and been a naughty boy.'

She was looking Paula straight in the eye, watching for a reaction.

Paula was sorely tempted to encourage Petra to tell her more, but she realised that Petra was testing her. She was determined to remain professional and not get drawn into gossip, however interesting that might be. She knew that her priority must be to help Rosie Carter with her request for advice about her will.

Paula was fond of Rosie, who had been a talented artist. There were several of her watercolours hanging on the walls of her room, but nowadays her eyesight was beginning to fail, and her hands were too shaky for her to paint as beautifully as before. But Rosie was always cheerful. Paula decided to go and have a chat with her as soon as Petra left the office.

'Right, Petra,' she said, 'thank you for letting me know about Rosie. I'll go and see her in a few minutes,' and she did so.

* * *

After returning to her office, Paula's thoughts returned to what Petra had said about Mr Abbott, and her manner while saying it. *There was an air of triumph in Petra,* she thought. *Did it stem from her sensing that she knew more about Mr Abbott than Paula did, or was she perhaps exulting in his apparent fall from grace? There could be lots of other explanations too.*

But whatever the reason, Paula was left feeling uneasy.

She continued her search among Sally Jeavons' records for the information Rita Hussein had requested. It proved a fruitless task, and Paula eventually decided to ring DC Hussein and apologetically admit defeat.

'Thanks for looking anyway,' said Rita, 'my colleagues have just informed me that they've found the name from another source. I appreciate your help though.'

Rita ended the call, and Paula was left frustrated for the second time at hearing partial information and wanting to know the rest.

Look on the bright side, she told herself, *at least some more of these wretched files have been sorted out.*

Sixty-Two

'Right, guv,' began Rita, 'it's all coming together, thank heavens.'

'I'd rather you said, "thanks to your excellent police work",' replied Baz with a laugh. Rita and Baz were both pleased with their recent progress, and DI Buchan would be too.

'Starting with Jacob Elsworth,' said Rita. 'He has a cast-iron alibi for the time of the burglary at the Deans' house. It's all been checked out, but he may still be an accessory to the burglary. At first he claimed that his car, which was seen on the neighbour's CCTV, had been stolen on the previous day, but eventually he admitted that he'd lent it to a friend. He couldn't recall the friend's name, but after being reminded that we knew that Katya Tradovic had been caught speeding in the same car not long ago, he conceded that it was her. He had no idea that she intended to commit a burglary, or so he said.'

'Great,' said Baz, 'what else have you got?'

'Well,' continued Rita, 'lucky for us, Katya Tradovic was a careless burglar. She dropped her phone in the Deans' house, presumably while she was chucking clothes out of cupboards, and didn't realise that she'd left it out of sight on the floor. It's apparently a mine of information. It's amazing how much stuff about themselves that people put on phones and social media! Anyway,' continued Rita, noticing a raised eyebrow from Baz, 'going back through the phone's history, the data analysts have found well-established connections between Katya, Elsworth, her sister Petra, and Charles Abbott. There's also evidence that Katya was liberal with her sexual favours, with both Elsworth and Abbott. What's not clear yet, though, is why. What information did they have that Katya wanted?'

'So, are you saying that Katya was the carer in the laundry room? With Abbott? And did she get sacked by Jeavons?' asked Baz. 'And is it certain that she and Petra are sisters? And both are Oscar Tradovic's daughters?'

Rita laughed.

'Any more questions, guv?' she asked.

'There will be,' he replied.

'Well,' said Rita, 'the answers so far are yes, yes, yes, yes and yes!'

But Rita had more to report.

'As far as the burglary is concerned,' she said, 'Mrs Dean states that there were two females in the house. They were dressed in black overalls and had balaclavas covering their hair and faces, so she didn't think she would recognise them again. One of the intruders gave the dog something to eat, which made him drowsy, while the other one took her upstairs and tied her hands together. Other than that, they apparently didn't touch her. But she had to watch while they both ransacked cupboards and drawers, and scattered the family's clothing all over the bedroom floors. Mrs Dean was terrified, and she still doesn't know what they were looking for. She didn't hear either of them talk, they only communicated by gestures. The offenders were only in the house for a matter of minutes, and that's confirmed by the neighbours' CCTV. But if one of the intruders was Katya Tradovic, then I thought that perhaps the other was Petra. So I rang Paula Trelawney, and sure enough, on the day of the burglary Petra wasn't on duty. But before you say anything, guv, I know that doesn't confirm that she was at the crime scene.'

'This is all good intelligence,' said Baz slowly, 'but we seem to be unearthing crimes which aren't necessarily our business.'

Rita's heart sank. Baz made a valid point, though.

'So how does all this link with our major concern, the murders of Sally Jeavons and Maddie Smith?' asked Baz, just thinking aloud.

'Time for a coffee?' asked Rita hopefully. Baz nodded.

'Ten minutes,' he said, taking a cigarette out of its packet and heading for the door. Rita wandered along to the coffee machine, deep in thought and wishing that she could suddenly have a "Eureka!" moment.

* * *

Back in Baz's office, ten minutes later, Rita suggested that they switch the focus away from people, just for the moment, and look at things differently.

'Firstly,' she said, 'there's Elsworth's car. According to Abbott, it may have been Elsworth's car he saw leaving The Willows just minutes before he and the Montgomerys found Jeavons' body. We have no independent verification of this. There's no CCTV coverage. Then we have Katya Tradovic being caught speeding in Elsworth's car. She gave the police false details of her address, etc. And then, on another day, the same car is caught on CCTV miles away linked to a burglary. Elsworth admits that he'd lent it to Katya Tradovic.'

'OK,' said Baz, 'so we have sound intelligence that there are links between Katya and Elsworth, Katya and Abbott, Katya and Jeavons, Katya and Mrs Dean (as burglar and victim), Katya and Petra Tradovic, Katya and Elsworth's car, and, of course, Katya and The Willows. Agree, Rita?'

She nodded.

So where does that take us? wondered Baz.

There was a lengthy silence, while each thought about the links.

Rita then said hesitantly, 'Well, I would suggest that the key relationships are between Katya and Elsworth, and Katya and Abbott. My reasoning is that both men possibly know something, or have access to something, which Katya is willing to go to any lengths to get. By all accounts she's an attractive woman, but I suspect she's ruthless too.'

Rita paused, taking time to think before continuing.

'Both men have links to The Willows, so this is where we get back to the murders. Elsworth's mother lived there, until she had a mysterious fall, and Abbott was lining his pockets from his joint scams with Jeavons.'

Rita paused again.

'You see,' she said, 'I find it strange that Katya Tradovic worked in a care home so far from her family home. There must be masses of places nearer to her family, so what made her choose to work specifically in The Willows? So, I surmise that the link is Jacob Elsworth, who knew her dad and served a prison sentence with him. Elsworth may have said things to Tradovic about his mum, and for some reason the Tradovics decided it would be advantageous to get to know her. Perhaps Mrs Elsworth is the key to all this.'

Another pause.

'I realise that's mainly speculation, guv, but it could fit, couldn't it?'

'Hmm…' replied Baz, 'if you're right, then I think Jeavons has to be brought into the mix too… posthumously, of course. Don't I recall you saying something about Mrs Elsworth's jewellery box going missing at some point, and her nephew being suspicious of Jeavons and how she'd treated his aunt? I may have got that wrong, so please check.'

Rita nodded.

'There must be more to the Tradovics' interest in Mrs Elsworth than a jewellery box, though, mustn't there?' asked Rita. 'We have evidence that Abbott busied himself persuading the residents to change their wills, to his and Jeavons' advantage. So perhaps Mrs Elsworth was one of these victims. After all, we know she had this mysterious jewellery box, but Tony Montgomery also told us that she owned a house, so who knows what else she might have. Perhaps only Abbott knows the true extent of her wealth. But a bit of pillow talk with Katya and the genie was out of the bottle! What do you reckon, guv? Worth pursuing?'

Baz had an amused look on his face.

'What's so funny, guv?' asked Rita.

'Well,' Baz replied, 'I hope you'll choose your words more carefully when you're giving evidence in court!'

Much to her annoyance, Rita blushed.

Baz waited a few moments and then said, 'How about seeing if Simon's team has found a copy of Mrs Elsworth's will among Abbott's office records? Then perhaps another visit to the Montgomerys' home?'

Sixty-Three

The following Saturday morning, by prior arrangement, Baz and Rita arrived at the Montgomerys' home. Rita had assured them that it was just a matter of confirming some facts about Mrs Elsworth's dealings with Charles Abbott.

Rita and Baz sat at the kitchen table with Tony and Chloe, and Bea sat in her chair by the window. Chloe had forewarned the police that Bea's mind sometimes wandered, but at other times she remembered the past with remarkable clarity. She hoped the police would take this into account when speaking to Bea.

As it happened, Bea responded confidently to the questions from the police. She talked about how Charles Abbott had been the family's lawyer for many years, but she added, in a whisper, that she wasn't sure that he was completely trustworthy. She thought he'd asked strange questions when he was helping her to review her will. In her view he'd wanted to know too much about her uncle George and his wife Anastasia. He'd known years ago that Bea had inherited things from Anastasia, so why did he want to go over the past again?

There were tears in Bea's eyes as she spoke of Anastasia, so Rita changed the subject. She asked about the house which Bea had bought several years ago.

'Yes,' said Bea quietly, 'Charles had a hand in that too. It was supposed to be a good investment for Jacob's future, but I don't know what's happened to it. I don't know what Jacob is up to these days either.'

Baz gave Tony a questioning look.

Rita thanked Bea for talking with them, and she beamed in response. 'Do come and see me again,' she said.

Rita and Baz were just leaving when Tony asked if he could speak to them in the dining room. Chloe stayed with Bea in the kitchen.

'There's something that's been plaguing me for a while,' began Tony diffidently, 'and I haven't been sure whether or not to ring you about it.'

'Is it linked to The Willows by any chance?' asked Baz.

Tony nodded.

'Best tell us then,' continued Baz.

Tony thought for a few moments.

'Well,' he began, 'it's actually quite a long and convoluted story, and I'm not sure how much of it would be of any interest to you.' He paused.

'Let's just start with the part that's troubling you most,' suggested Rita, willing Tony not to take too long.

'Right then,' began Tony, 'you recall asking me for the pictures I took at The Willows before Mrs Jeavons was killed?'

'Yes,' said Rita, 'carry on…'

'Well,' continued Tony, 'I'd been having a long talk about our extended family with a relative of mine. There'd been a lot of strange happenings involving his son, the son's friend and a couple of foreign young women. This was all at university.'

Rita was becoming impatient, but suddenly she was fully tuned in.

'Sorry,' said Tony, 'but this *is* relevant. There'd been so many odd coincidences in the whole story, that I decided to send one of the pictures you've got, the one with a carer in, to Martin, to see if his son recognised her. I didn't really expect him to, but it *did* turn out to be his former girlfriend. He knew her as Helena. Anyway, Martin thought he'd check her out, and tell her to stop pestering his family. So he rang The Willows, only to be told that no one called Helena worked there and never had. As I say, it's been playing on my mind, for what it's worth.'

Baz and Rita exchanged meaningful glances.

Just as they were leaving, Baz turned to Tony again and asked, 'Do you by any chance know if Helena has a sister?'

Tony looked surprised, thought for a moment, and replied, 'I think she has a close friend, but I'm not sure that they are sisters.'

'A name perhaps?' asked Baz.

'I think it's Mishka,' said Tony, 'and she was the girlfriend of Luke, Martin's son's friend.'

'Just one last thing,' said Rita from the porch, 'am I right in thinking that the son's name is Sebastian?'

Tony nodded in confirmation.

He closed the front door and leaned against the back of it. The police had seemed to know what he was talking about. The thought struck Tony that he should phone Martin and tell him about his conversation with the police. Perhaps they would contact him too.

Sixty-Four

'Whew,' exclaimed Rita, 'what tangled webs people weave!'

Baz glanced up from his screen. She had just come into his office looking pleased.

'Well, guv,' she began, 'I really wonder how we ever got results without the assistance of offenders living their lives on their phones.'

Baz suddenly felt old, and he didn't want to pursue Rita's train of thought.

'So, what's been found?' he asked.

'Well,' replied Rita, 'the techies have finished their initial analysis of Abbott's phone, various electronic devices and paper records. They apparently had to wade through masses of pornography on his office computer, all legal stuff, thank heavens.'

Baz raised an eyebrow but said nothing.

'But what's of interest to us,' continued Rita, 'as well as the frauds committed with Jeavons, is his connection with Jacob Elsworth. You remember Bea told us that she had reservations about Abbott, because he asked strange questions when reviewing her will... he seemed too interested in her relative George and someone called Anastasia?'

Baz nodded.

'Well, he certainly was interested in George, but even more interested in Anastasia. He'd done a lot of genealogical research on her a while ago. It seems that she came from an aristocratic family, but she'd had to flee her own country when there were rumblings of revolution against the ruling elite there. But Abbott believes that she moved her wealth out of the country before she fled. Then she met and fell for an English international businessman, George Darwin, who divorced his first wife and married her. All this was the best part of a century ago.'

'So, are you telling me,' asked Baz, 'that Abbott was trying to track down this Anastasia's fortune, if it still exists, through Bea Elsworth? and he aimed to get his own hands on it by drawing up an artfully worded will?'

'That seems to be the nub of it, guv,' replied Rita. 'There's evidence that he was also using Jeavons to pump Bea for information while she was at The Willows. And you remember her fall in the garden? Well, that was planned between Abbott and Jeavons, just to frighten Bea and loosen her tongue. That plan backfired, though, because they hadn't reckoned on Tony Montgomery removing Bea from The Willows. So that's when Abbott started using Jacob Elsworth more.'

'More?' asked Baz.

'Yeah,' drawled Rita, deep in thought, 'Abbott has known Jacob since he was quite young. He knows about Jacob's criminal past and desire for money. But what he didn't know was that Jacob was independently trying to locate Anastasia's wealth, which he vaguely knew about from his mum. Whilst Abbott and Jeavons were relying on Bea Elsworth for clues about it, Jacob was trying other routes. He thought that other branches of his family might know something. But he didn't want to alert them to anything, if they'd never heard of Anastasia. We haven't got the details of that yet. The evidence so far just relates to Abbott putting pressure on Elsworth to get information out of Tony and Chloe Montgomery, hence the visits to their home. Some of the communication between Abbott and Elsworth seems to indicate mutual blackmail, with Abbott trying to use Elsworth's criminal history as ammunition against him, and Elsworth using at least one known sexual indiscretion against Abbott. And in interviews they've both tried to present themselves as victims of the other's activities.'

The phone on Baz's desk rang. It was a member of the forensics team, trying to find Rita. Baz handed her the receiver and flicked the switch so that he could listen too.

It was only a brief call, but when it ended, there was a triumphant cry of 'Yes' from both of them. Jacob Elsworth's car had been forensically examined. It had apparently been thoroughly cleaned recently, but one hair had been found embedded in the back seat. DNA testing determined an exact match with Maddie Smith.

'Right,' said Baz, thumping the desk with his fist, 'let's get him in, and this time there's no room for errors.'

Sixty-Five

Tilda was becoming increasingly anxious. No matter what time of day she tried to contact Luke, his phone was always turned off. And he hadn't sent her any messages for over a week. Once again, she was losing confidence in her relationship with him. She felt that she just couldn't compete with stunning Mishka. *Was Luke telling her the truth when he said that his relationship with Mishka was firmly in the past?* she wondered.

Tilda tried Luke's number again. No response, and no messaging service.

* * *

When Seb came home from work that evening, Tilda asked him if he'd had any contact with Luke recently. Seb could see that his sister was very worried, so he offered to ring Luke's boss, Mick, to make sure that Luke hadn't had an accident or been taken ill. Tilda gave Seb a brief hug, much to his surprise.

'I'd better ring him now,' said Seb, 'before the pub gets too busy.'

A few minutes later Seb ended the call, looking puzzled.

'Well, sis,' he said, 'Mick doesn't know where Luke is either. It seems that he asked Mick for a couple of days off, packed a bag, and they haven't seen or heard from him since. Mick seemed very surprised, as Luke had always been so reliable and open. While we were talking, Debbie nipped up to Luke's room and came back to tell Mick that it looked as though most of Luke's belongings had gone with him. So they are as bewildered as we are. I guess we just have to wait until Luke gets in touch,' Seb concluded.

'If he ever does,' sobbed Tilda.

Sixty-Six

Tony Montgomery and Martin Dean had a long phone conversation after the police had visited Tony's house. He wanted to update Martin. He had felt uneasy, as he suspected that he was simply confirming details which the police knew already. But Tony had also briefly mentioned Luke and Mishka, and he wanted Martin to be aware of this. Tony, of course, knew neither of them and regretted saying anything about them, but it had happened.

Martin listened attentively, but when Tony mentioned Luke's name, he interrupted.

'Tony,' he said, 'I'm not sure what to make of Luke. He strikes me as something of a puzzle. He appears to have left his job, and he doesn't answer his phone. Tilda is absolutely distraught. But, more seriously, I wonder how much he knows about all the odd events in our family.'

'Well,' replied Tony, 'I'm afraid I've now mentioned his name to the police, but I don't know his surname, do you?'

Martin reminded Tony that he had interviewed Luke for a job in his business, and he'd been given his personal details then.

'His surname's Carmichael,' said Martin, 'or so he told me.'

'You really think he might have lied?' asked Tony, astonished.

'I'm not sure what I believe, at the moment,' replied Martin.

Later in the conversation Tony explained what he had learned about Bea's house and the role Charles Abbott had played in its purchase. In Bea's mind it was intended as an investment for Jacob. But Abbott was now under investigation by the police, and his offices were closed, so Tony wasn't sure whether or not she still owned the house. It was in Great Fordington, a village not many miles from Minchford, so Tony was contemplating driving over there to have a look at it, just out of interest.

Following the phone call Tony's mind was at ease about his mentioning Luke and Mishka to the police. He'd previously had the impression that Luke was well liked in the Dean household, particularly by young Tilda, but Martin seemed to be changing his tune. Tony wondered why.

* * *

The following evening, after leaving his office, Tony drove to Great Fordington. He decided not to tell Chloe about his detour until he got home. He was concerned that Jacob might be living in the house, and that would really unsettle Chloe.

Great Fordington consisted of a church overlooking a small village green, a pub, a shop and a few hundred houses. The village was surrounded by farmland and woods. If this was Great Fordington, Tony wondered just how small Little Fordington was. And this thought brought poor Maddie to his mind. *It was,* he recollected, *in the woods beyond Little Fordington that her body had been found.*

Tony soon located the house which Bea had bought so many years ago. He drove slowly past it, turned the car and parked on the opposite side of the road with a clear view of it. He sat and cast his architect's eye over the property. It was a solidly built, detached house which Tony assessed as being at least a hundred years old. The exterior suggested that it was in need of modernisation, and the garden was neglected. *But all in all,* thought Tony, *a desirable property, which would certainly attract buyers, if it were to be sold.* Tony reminded himself, though, that it may not belong to Bea anymore.

He had a sudden thought. He turned, lifted his briefcase off the back seat, and took out his sketchpad and pencils. He sat in the driver's seat and did several quick sketches of the house. His plan was to show them to Chloe, and perhaps to Bea when the time seemed right.

He was startled by a gentle tap on the window next to him. He looked up to see Sadie, who had got off the bus a short way up the road. Tony lowered the window and greeted her. She was looking at his sketches.

'That's a lovely house, isn't it, Mr Montgomery,' she began, 'are you thinking of buying it?'

Tony gave a little laugh.

'Oh heavens, no,' he replied, 'this is just to do with my work. Do you know who lives there?'

Sadie shook her head.

'Well, 'bye then, Mr Montgomery, I must get home and make my Mervyn's tea,' she said and strode off down the road.

While they were chatting, Tony noticed someone else walking towards him from the bus stop, on the opposite side of the road. Before reaching his car, though, she turned into the driveway of Bea's house. She hesitated at the front door, looked around and went in.

I'm sure that was her, Tony said to himself, *I'm sure that was Helena.*

He pulled out his phone and rang Martin.

Sixty-Seven

'That was a productive hour, wasn't it, Rita?' said Baz, as they were walking up the stairs from the interview room back to his office.

'Hmm…' replied Rita, 'he struck me as one frightened man. Not surprising, though, when you alluded to two potential murder charges. He wasn't expecting that, judging by his reaction.'

Baz and Rita had been questioning Jacob Elsworth. When confronted with forensic evidence from his car, linking him with the murder of Maddie Smith, his eyes looked scared. He vigorously denied knowing anything about the murder. But it gradually dawned on him that the police knew more about his associates than he had anticipated. They had clearly pieced together his links with Oscar Tradovic and his daughters, but he wasn't sure just how much they knew. They told him that his mum's lawyer, Abbott, was in custody, being questioned too.

Jacob felt powerless. *What were they all saying to the police? How much guilt were they shovelling onto him? If only he could get a message to Katya, or even Oscar, but he couldn't.*

* * *

'What threw him most,' began Rita, when they reached Baz's office, cups of coffee in hand, 'was the mention of this woman

Anastasia. He seemed to accept that we would work out his links with the Tradovics and Abbott, but the fact that we're aware of Anastasia came as a real shock to him. Trouble is,' she continued, 'that *we* don't actually know much about her, except that she's Bea Elsworth's exotic aunt, allegedly very wealthy, and several people are after that wealth.'

'But going back to the Tradovics for a moment,' said Baz, 'wasn't there something you wanted to tell me, before we saw Elsworth? What was that all about?'

'Hell, sorry guv,' replied Rita, looking guilty, 'I meant to say something before we interviewed him. It just slipped my mind. Sorry, guv.'

'Well,' said Baz, more sharply than usual, 'you'd better tell me now.'

Rita gave her boss a concise account of a phone call she'd received earlier that day from the data analysts. Evidence on the phone found at the Deans' home confirmed that the two burglars were Katya and Petra Tradovic. Trawling back through the phone's records revealed that earlier messages to the Deans' number were of a threatening nature. Other messages were found, to Sebastian Dean, with demands for information, mostly relating to someone called George.

'They haven't completed all their analysis yet, but they hope to by tomorrow. I really do apologise, guv,' said Rita, 'I should've told you sooner.'

Before Baz could ask any more questions, his phone rang. He answered it and listened for a short while. Then he punched the air.

'Great work,' he said, 'thanks for that,' and ended the call.

'Quicker than we expected,' he said to Rita. 'There's a message on the phone from Katya to Petra instructing her, in a coded way, to ring us anonymously and put Sebastian Dean in the frame for Jeavons' murder, and then to ditch the phone. Embarrassing thing is that we acted on that tip-off without checking it out properly… gave him an unjustifiably hard time. The flip-side is that we can now link the Tradovic women more firmly to Jeavons' murder.'

'And the finding of Maddie Smith's hair in Elsworth's car may tie them into her murder too,' suggested Rita. She heaved a sigh of relief.

Rita wiped a space on one of the whiteboards and wrote 'Katya' in the centre. The phone rang again.

'For you, Rita,' said Baz, holding out the receiver, 'Paula Trelawney wants a word.'

There was a brief conversation, during which Rita gave Baz a 'thumbs up' sign. 'Thanks for letting me know, Paula. Just remind me of Petra's address, will you… fine, thanks,' and Rita put the phone down.

'Well, guv, Paula wanted to tell me that one of the carers, Lucy Kingdon, had just rung her. Lucy was in a state of shock. She apparently lives in Great Fordington and was walking home from the bus stop, when she saw someone being brought out of a nearby house and put into a police car. Lucy could hardly believe her eyes… it was the carer, Petra. Apparently, Petra glared at Lucy and quite frightened her. So when she got home she rang Paula.'

'Presumably in connection with the burglary?' surmised Baz. 'Maybe next time *we'll* be arresting her in connection with murder?'

Sixty-Eight

Paula Trelawney was about to lock her office and go for a work-out at the gym, when she hesitated. She had a niggling feeling that there was something important which she had to do, but it escaped her for the moment. Suddenly she remembered.

Can I leave it until the morning? she asked herself, knowing that she really ought to do it now. So, she went back into her office, closed the door and rang Tony Montgomery's number.

'Hello Mr Montgomery, it's Paula Trelawney from The Willows,' she began. 'I have some good news for you.'

Tony was surprised. News from The Willows was rarely good.

'Yes,' continued Paula, 'I had reason to go down to the basement earlier today, something which I've only done a couple of times before. Anyway, in amongst everything else, I noticed an old filing cabinet which looked as though it hadn't been touched for years. In one of the drawers there were two wooden boxes. Well, Mr Montgomery, the long and the short of it is that I believe that one of them belongs to your aunt.' She heard a sharp intake of breath on the line.

'But I thought that Bea's jewellery box was kept in the safe in Mrs Jeavons' office. At least, that's what Maddie told us, just before she was sacked,' said Tony, 'so why do you think that this box is Bea's?'

'Well, can I ask you a question first, please?' asked Paula. 'Do you happen to know if your aunt has any middle names?'

Tony thought for a moment.

'Yes, yes, I'm sure she has… half a tick… yes, she's Beatrice Georgiana Elizabeth, that's it. She was named Georgiana after her mother's brother George, and Elizabeth after her own mum. I'm sure that's right. Why do you ask?'

Paula explained that one of the boxes was inscribed on top with four initials, BGEE, which seemed fairly conclusive. The box must belong to Bea.

'I felt I should ring DC Hussein about finding the box, just in case it was significant in her investigations. She was in her car at the time, so she came here, took a look and gave me the all-clear to let you know about it. I'm off to the gym when we finish talking, so shall I drop the box off at your home afterwards? It's not far out of my way,' said Paula.

* * *

When Tony arrived home from work, he gave Chloe the news.

'Did she say if it's locked?' asked Chloe immediately, 'Bea will be so pleased to see it again. I just hope that the key fits it.'

Tony nodded absentmindedly. The real significance of Paula's find was only just dawning on him. He thought back to the lifeless body of Sally Jeavons. He remembered the ransacked safe in her office and wondered if the murderer had really been looking for Bea's jewellery box among all the other valuables belonging to the elderly residents. Or was it just a coincidence that the jewellery box couldn't be found, and the burglary was nothing to do with Bea at all?

Tony was becoming increasingly confused. Then he recalled the "sprucing up" of Bea's room when he visited The Willows unexpectedly. That was undoubtedly a search and almost certainly, in his mind, to find Bea's precious key.

* * *

Paula delivered the box to the Montgomerys' home, as arranged.

'It seems to be locked,' she said cheerfully, as she handed it over, 'so I hope it will hold some nice surprises for Bea.'

Chloe thanked her, and Paula left.

Bea was now asleep, unaware of the evening's developments. Chloe was inspecting the box and the decorative initials on a silver cartouche on the lid. The silver was tarnished, but that could soon be rectified. She shook the box gently, but it made no sound. And Paula had been right… it was locked. Chloe was very tempted to fetch the key and have a look inside, but Tony was adamant that Bea should unlock it, so that wouldn't be until tomorrow. Chloe agreed reluctantly.

'You know,' she began, 'it's not at all how I expected it to be. Don't get me wrong, it's beautiful in its own way. The wood is lovely, and I love the rounded edges and globular feet, but somehow it's less showy than I thought it would be. If only it could talk… I'd love to know more about when Anastasia gave it to Bea, and what's inside it, of course!'

Tony laughed.

'Yes,' he said, 'it holds a lot of family history, I guess. I hope it jogs Bea's memory. But I can't help thinking that it's probably linked to Mrs Jeavons' murder, and more sadly to Maddie's murder too. We mustn't forget that in all the excitement of returning the box to Bea. But I'm not suggesting we remind Bea of those events,' he added, when he saw Chloe's horrified expression.

'I should hope not!' she said.

* * *

The following evening, after Sadie had gone home, Tony signalled to Chloe that they should now show Bea her jewellery box. Chloe was hiding the key in her hand. At first Bea seemed uncertain, but suddenly she recognised the box and beamed. She looked up at Tony and tears started rolling down her cheeks.

'Oh,' she said quietly, 'my darling Edgar's box, how lovely.'

Chloe and Tony looked bewildered. This was not what they had expected to hear.

'Would you like to see inside…' asked Chloe, hoping that this might jog Bea's memory, 'shall we try the key?'

Chloe held out the key to Bea, who had difficulty putting it in the lock. Tony offered to help, but he couldn't make it fit either. Chloe's heart sank.

They fiddled with the key and the lock for a while but had to admit defeat. It clearly wasn't the right key. Bea suddenly chuckled.

'My Edgar was such a tease,' she said, 'he told me that I would lose a key, so he had a hidey-hole made for it.'

Tony and Chloe wondered what Bea was talking about.

'See if you can find it,' she laughed, revelling in their puzzlement. Eventually Chloe realised that there was a false base built into the box, and in one corner there was a concealed compartment.

Bea chuckled again and said, 'Well done, Chloe, you've found it! Wasn't my Edgar clever?'

Tony then gave the box back to Bea, and she slid the compartment open. Sure enough, the key was inside, and it fitted the lock. Chloe held her breath as Bea opened the box. Slowly she took out the contents. There were old coins wrapped up in tissue paper, some pieces of jewellery which looked to Chloe like gold set with seed-pearls, and a couple of pendants. But mainly the box contained old photographs and letters.

Tony was watching his aunt as she gradually emptied the box onto her tray-table, each item evoking memories in her. He felt so pleased that the box was in her possession again.

But Chloe, after initial feelings of relief and pleasure, was beginning to feel uneasy. She didn't say anything to Bea or Tony. She saw that they were enjoying the moment. But Chloe was in a daze. If the key and the box, which had been found after so much effort and at a considerable price, didn't fit together, then what *did* the key fit?

Sixty-Nine

Rita burst into her boss's office without knocking. Baz looked up, clearly annoyed.

'This had better be good, Hussein,' he told her in a warning tone. Rita cursed, asking herself when she would ever learn to contain her enthusiasm.

'Sorry, guv, I know I'm in the wrong again,' she said, appearing contrite and holding up her hands.

'If you tell me you've cracked two murder cases, I'll forgive you,' he offered, now with a more sympathetic look on his face.

'Not quite, guv,' replied Rita, 'but if ever we needed confirmation that there's no honour among thieves, we've certainly got that! They're singing their little hearts out in the interview rooms!'

'Just get on with it,' snapped Baz, 'and cut the poetic stuff!'

Rita guessed that Baz was under renewed pressure from above.

'Sorry, guv,' she apologised again. 'Right, firstly Abbott. He is wriggling furiously and distancing himself from any dealings with Elsworth and Katya Tradovic. As the evidence is put to him, though, he accepts some part in the financial offences at The Willows with Jeavons. It's apparently a watertight case as far as his syphoning off money from elderly residents is concerned, and all his unethical dealings with their wills, and so on. He's minimising his responsibility and trying to place most of the blame on Jeavons. He's very remorseful, or so he says. He insists that Jeavons was blackmailing him, and this caused him to act out of character. He is adamant that he did not have a sexual relationship with Katya… that allegation was just Jeavons trying to discredit him and have a tight hold over him, he says. But as soon as the murders of Jeavons and Smith were mentioned, he was equally adamant that he had nothing to do with either. His fear was almost palpable apparently. So at the moment there's not enough evidence to tie him conclusively into the murders, but they haven't finished interviewing him yet.'

Rita paused, allowing Baz an opportunity to ask questions.

'Carry on then, Rita,' he said.

'Secondly, Elsworth,' continued Rita. 'He's not as canny as Abbott. He's more of a 'punch first, think later' sort of guy. And by that stage he's out of his depth. Like Abbott, though, he's keen to heap guilt on others and exonerate himself. But he's nowhere near as adept at it as Abbott.'

Rita paused again, wondering if Baz would tell her to stick to the facts, as he usually did.

But he didn't, so she continued.

'Elsworth has one big regret in his life. No, correction… ' she hesitated, 'two big regrets. The first is that he couldn't protect his mum from the wiles and greed of Abbott. Elsworth claims that his mum's very wealthy, she inherited a fortune he says, and Abbott knows this. He says that Abbott has been manipulating Bea to change her will and cut him, Elsworth, out of it. Of course, he is only trying to protect his mum from Abbott's greedy hands. No thought of his own inheritance potentially going down the drain, or so he says. He only has his mum's best interests at heart.'

Rita's contempt for this version of events was scarcely concealed, so Baz said calmly, 'Let's remain neutral, eh, Rita? Carry on.'

Rita skimmed through a couple of pages in her notebook and continued.

'The officers questioned Elsworth about his relationship with Katya Tradovic, and they put it to him that he and Tradovic were conspiring to divert his mother's money to them. They also suggested that Elsworth, Tradovic and Abbott were all conspiring to get their hands on Mrs Elsworth's wealth. Elsworth went into a rage at this apparently and had to be restrained. Once he'd calmed down and had time to think, he gave his version of events. And this brings us to his second big regret.'

Rita paused, took a few sips from her bottle of water, and resumed her feedback.

'While he was in prison, Elsworth stupidly bragged to his co-defendant, Oscar Tradovic, about how wealthy his old mum was. She'd inherited a fortune from a foreign relative, but no one was sure where the wealth was or how to access it. Over the months, Tradovic gradually got more information out of Elsworth. He says that, unknown to him, Tradovic was feeding all this to his two daughters during visits. By the time Elsworth was released, Katya and Petra had well-laid plans. He says that he didn't realise at first what was going on, and he thought that Katya really fancied him. Now he knows that "the conniving bitch", his words, was just using him. And he fell for it, driving her around and even lending her his car. She seduced him, mocked him, tried every trick in the book to get information out of him. If only he had been able to keep his mouth shut. And all he wanted to do was to protect his old mum.'

Baz raised a sceptical eyebrow, hoping that Rita wouldn't notice.

'So what does Elsworth claim that the Tradovics planned to do?' he asked.

'Well,' said Rita, 'once the Tradovic sisters knew the situation, as well as Abbott, Elsworth had lost control of everything.

They seem to be a lot brighter than he is, and they think more strategically. According to Elsworth their idea was to ferret out other relatives of his mum and him, and through them to trace this rich relative and locate the wealth. At the same time, though, one of them was to work in The Willows and get as much information as possible out of Bea herself. Working there would also give her plausible excuses for going through Bea's personal possessions. So that was Katya, to start with.'

Rita paused, hoping for some reaction from Baz. None was forthcoming, so she continued.

'But Katya had her own ideas too, and she was happy to spread her sexual favours to achieve what she wanted. Not only was she Elsworth's lover, or so he thought, but she was also caught in The Willows' laundry having sex with Abbott. So Jeavons sacked her. But whatever Elsworth may have thought about that situation, he desperately needed to keep track of Katya and her sister. They simply knew too much. He bitterly regretted ever bragging to Oscar Tradovic, but he couldn't change that now. What was done was done.'

By now Baz was leaning back in his chair looking at the ceiling. He was reviewing what Rita had said and trying to fit all the pieces together. It was best to leave him to it.

Eventually Baz asked, 'But can we link either him or the Tradovic women firmly with the murders? I get the picture of all of them setting their sights on old Mrs Elsworth's supposed wealth, but what's coming out about the murders?'

'Well, guv, later in the interview Elsworth was asked to explain how his car came to be linked to two murders and a burglary,' said Rita. 'He reacted furiously apparently, trying to up-end the table and threatening the officers. He had to be restrained and taken back to a cell. He was making a helluva commotion and kept shouting, "Find Luke". So they haven't finished interviewing him yet.'

Rita sat down and heaved a sigh. 'Sorry, guv,' she said, 'I can't tell you that we've cracked either murder, but there are two men in custody who are shitting themselves with fear.'

Baz tried to stifle a surprised laugh. Such language was unusual from Rita.

He briefly cast an affectionate look in her direction.

Seventy

Not for the first time, Tilda thought her world had come to an end. *Were relationships always such a rollercoaster ride? What had she said or done to make Luke disappear again?*

Seb was as perplexed as she was. And there was no one she could talk to about it all… *parents just don't understand,* she reasoned. So she withdrew into her own thoughts, only sharing them with Zeus as they walked through the woods. Zeus seemed to give her sympathetic looks as they ambled along.

* * *

Unknown to Tilda, Luke was many miles away by now. He couldn't cope with all that was going on in his life, and, as was his way, he distanced himself from it all, both literally and emotionally. His sudden and secretive departure from The Ancient Mariner had taken everyone by surprise. He knew he was letting Mick and Debbie down… and Tilda. There was some deep-seated instinct in him, though, which always chose 'flight' over 'fight'. *There would always be people hurt by his actions,* he told himself, *but that was just how he was. He had tried so hard with Tilda, but yet again he had shown himself that he couldn't maintain a close relationship.*

Luke had convinced himself long ago that he would never change. The psychological damage inflicted on him during his childhood would always be there. The various types of therapy he had undergone then hadn't made a lasting positive impact, and he couldn't face seeking any more. Most of the time he interacted with other people in ways which gave few clues about what he had endured or how he was feeling inside.

But in the last few weeks Luke had begun to wonder how much more pressure he could take. In his mind the root cause of everything which was wrong about his life lay with someone whom he hadn't seen for many years… his father. As a last resort, he decided to confront his father.

Why should his life be forever blighted by the actions of his father?

So he had finally made arrangements to visit him. Luke was plagued by apprehension and temptations to cancel the visit.

* * *

As a small boy, Luke had had the terrifying experience of seeing his father kill his mother. He remembered the spine-chilling screams, followed by an eerie silence, and the sight of his mother's lifeless body slumped on the floor. Luke could still recall his cowering in a corner, too bewildered and frightened to move. His father had ignored him and stormed off out of the house. That was the last time he had seen his father, until this visit.

Luke had been taken to live with an aunt and uncle, whom he hardly knew. His father and mother were rarely mentioned. Unknown to Luke, his aunt had kept his father informed occasionally of important milestones in Luke's life. The only information they gave Luke was where his father was. They neither encouraged nor discouraged Luke as far as making contact with him was concerned.

Luke's aunt and uncle had cared for him well, and encouraged him in his schooling. His uncle, Charles, took Luke sailing and enjoyed seeing his nephew develop a love and aptitude for the sport. But nothing could erase from Luke's mind the sheer horror of what he had witnessed, and no one had ever explained to him why it had happened. As a child he had had terrifying flashbacks and uncontrollable rages. Nowadays he had times of desperate sadness, especially when he realised that he could scarcely recall his mother's kind face.

After Luke had started at university his aunt and uncle moved to France, an ambition they had long held, and contact with Luke had gradually waned and almost ceased. Luke thought they were probably glad to be free of their responsibility for him. But this had left him alone in the world, in terms of family… apart from his father, who probably still had many years in prison ahead of him.

* * *

Luke had never been into a prison before. He found it daunting from the moment he set foot inside. He alternated between telling himself that coming here was all a big mistake and being determined to get some answers out of his father.

But it was his father, Stan Carmichael, who immediately took the initiative in the conversation. He knew that the visit was time-limited, and there were things he wanted to say to the son, whom he hardly knew. The murder of Luke's mother was not on his agenda, though.

When the bell rang, signifying that visits had now ended, Luke felt confused and angry. He had none of the answers he had hoped for. His father had given him no space for awkward questions. But he had told Luke about things which had been playing on his own mind.

A few years ago, he told Luke, he had been talking with another inmate, name of Tradovic, about Luke. This man, Tradovic, had been boasting about how clever his two daughters were, and, not to be outdone, Stan had talked about Luke. He was proud that his son was planning to go to university, the first member of his family to do so, and he boasted about Luke's prowess as a sailor. Stan only knew these things from one of his sister's brief, infrequent letters. He had never seen Tradovic again.

Not long ago, though, word had reached Stan on the prison grapevine that Tradovic's daughters were in trouble themselves. He'd heard that they'd been grooming university students with a view to a large-scale theft. Stan didn't know any of the details, but the university mentioned was the same one as Luke had been planning to attend. So Stan had been concerned about whether there was any connection with Luke, knowing that he had bragged about his son to Tradovic. He wanted reassurance that Luke had not been drawn into any trouble.

Luke had listened to his father with scepticism. *It all seemed too coincidental, but how and why would his father have made up such a story... what would he have to gain?*

Luke didn't believe that his father felt any concern about him. He came across to Luke as totally *self*-centred. Luke said nothing, but he was relieved when the bell sounded and visits ended. He needed time to think it all through.

Luke and his father parted from each other without so much as a handshake. Neither showed any emotion, but Luke's mind was in turmoil.

But one thing was certain... he had no intention of ever visiting his father again.

Seventy-One

'You'll be pleased to know, Mr Elsworth, that your mother's jewellery box has been located. That's good news, isn't it?'

The officers watched his reaction closely. Jacob Elsworth looked stunned, and there was a glimmer of panic in his eyes.

Was this a trap? he asked himself. *What did they know about her jewellery box? Abbott must have said something, the bastard. Or were they just bluffing? He must control himself.*

He sat on his hands, motionless, and waited for the officers to speak again.

'Luke's a good sort of chap, isn't he?' asked the other officer.

Elsworth tried to disguise his surprise. *Had they really spoken to Luke? How had they found him?* He cursed himself for having stupidly shouted out Luke's name. *Why the hell had he done that?*

He continued to sit upright and still, but his brain was in tumult.

As he made no reply, the first officer continued, 'Good-looking, intelligent young man with the world at his fingertips, wouldn't you say? Good talker too, it seems.'

Elsworth was reaching bursting point, but he willed himself not to be provoked. Having been restrained by them twice already, that was enough for him.

It must all be bluff. They couldn't know that he and Katya had stalked Luke and tried to put the frighteners on him. Luke wasn't

important, just a means to an end. But had they really spoken to him?
Worse still, had they spoken to Katya… he had to find out, but how?

Elsworth hated the powerlessness of being in police custody. He wondered how much longer they would keep him there.

'One last thing,' said the first officer, 'we've made sure that your mother's house in Great Fordington is secure. That's good, isn't it? The tenant has been arrested, you see. And, oh yes, just to let you know that we have a warrant to search the property… just so you know.'

Elsworth's face turned puce, and he leapt to his feet. But he quickly regained his self-control and was taken back to a cell. He would be given time to think about what he had just been told.

Seventy-Two

Luke left the prison feeling alone in the world.

He hated his father and wanted nothing more to do with him. He was guilty of the unforgiveable and brutal murder of Luke's mother, and he didn't express any remorse even after all this time. But Luke now knew too that his father was responsible for Mishka infiltrating and disrupting his life. His father had made it sound accidental that he had boasted to another inmate about Luke.

But he had never before shown any signs of being proud of Luke, so why then?

Luke just wanted to get away from the prison. He decided to walk the couple of miles to the bus station rather than wait for a visitors' shuttle-bus. He needed to keep moving.

When he finally reached the bus station, it struck him that he actually had nowhere to go. All his thoughts had been focussed on getting to the prison and seeing his father. Now he realised that he was friendless and homeless. He sat on a bench, having collected his bags from a locker, and wondered hopelessly what he should do. He hadn't got much money left either.

Finally, Luke decided to swallow his pride and text Mick. He knew that Mick and Debbie had helped him out cheerfully in the past, several times, but he knew that he had really let them down this time. He had disappeared without a word. It was a long shot that they would even talk to him. But Luke thought it was his only hope. *Even if they didn't want to give him his job back, they might at least let him stay at the pub for a night or two, while he sorted himself out.*

Mick responded to Luke's text within minutes. It was a brief reply, but Mick told Luke to get back to the pub, so that they could talk. He felt a huge surge of relief. *That was a start, at least. It gave him some breathing space,* he hoped.

It was mid-evening by the time Luke arrived at The Ancient Mariner. Debbie immediately saw that Luke was in a bad state, so she told him to put his bags in the corner and sit at a table. She brought over a beer and let him choose a meal. It was clear that Luke hadn't eaten much that day, and she began to wonder where he'd been. It was quite late by the time she and Mick could finally sit and talk to Luke.

Mick brushed aside all the apologies and thanks that Luke was expressing. He said that he and Debbie had been very worried about Luke, particularly bearing in mind the red-head and all that saga. And Luke's friend, Seb, had been worried too and had phoned Mick to see if Luke was OK.

'I had no idea anyone would be worrying about me,' said Luke, clearly surprised by the thought.

Why is his self-esteem so low? Debbie wondered to herself.

Gradually Luke explained to Mick and Debbie where he had been, and why. They both listened, by turns astonished and concerned. Neither interrupted Luke's story. It had been simply spilling out of Luke's mouth, and neither Mick nor Debbie doubted the truth of what he was telling them.

Eventually Mick said, 'Well, Luke mate, I reckon you ought to get some shut-eye, and then you can see how things seem in the morning. You've got a lot to think about. Take your things up to the flat, and we'll talk again in the morning. Just no disappearing overnight, OK?'

Mick gave Luke a playful punch on the shoulder and grinned at him. Debbie gave Luke a sisterly hug. Luke was overcome with emotion at the warm reactions of both Mick and Debbie. He gathered up his bags and went up to the flat before his tear-filled eyes became obvious to them.

Luke had a restless night. He tossed and turned. Different recent events became muddled in his dreams, and he woke with a start, convinced that he'd been visiting Mishka in prison and that the officer watching them was Tilda in a uniform. In the early hours Luke decided that he didn't want to try and sleep anymore. He listened to some music and tried to work out whether he would ever be brave enough to contact Tilda.

If he did, what would her reaction be? he wondered.

* * *

In the morning, the smell of coffee drifting up from the pub tempted Luke downstairs. Debbie, cheerful as ever, gave him a mug of coffee.

'Did you sleep alright?' she asked, but the dark rings beneath Luke's eyes were all the answer she needed. 'When Mick comes in, we'll tell you our thoughts on your situation... no pressure, you can reject them all if you want to.' She smiled.

Luke drank his coffee, while Debbie continued to get the bar ready for the day.

Mick joined them a few minutes later and poured himself some coffee.

'Had any thoughts then, Luke, about what you're going to do next?' he asked. 'I know we didn't say much to you yesterday evening, but if you want to stay here and carry on working, that's an option you can put into the mix. Now we know what's been going on in your life, you're very welcome to stay here longer, if you want to.'

Luke felt as though an enormous weight had been lifted from his shoulders. He had doubted that Mick would offer him that option. It would give him some short-term security, at least. Debbie noticed the relief spreading across Luke's face.

'We had another thought too,' she chipped in, 'but perhaps you want to think about Mick's suggestion first?'

Luke shook his head. 'I don't need to,' he said, 'I just can't believe you're such good friends to me.'

Debbie went and put her arm round Luke's shoulders. 'Come on, Luke, friendship is always a two-way street… you've more than gone the extra mile for us with all that work, and you've never complained… well, not to us, anyway!'

'We mentioned yesterday,' said Mick, 'that your friend, Seb, had rung here after you disappeared. Now that we know where his family fits into the whole story, we wondered if you might want to tell them a bit more about yourself? It's your decision, of course, but perhaps it would be a good idea for Seb's family to understand what's been happening to you? It sounds like they're genuinely nice people, and you can't have too many friends, can you?'

Luke was beginning to look doubtful, so Debbie picked up Mick's thread.

'We were thinking,' she began, 'that you could invite them over here next Sunday for lunch. You could show off your handiwork, and we could make a small area in the restaurant nice and private for you, and I'll prepare a special lunch. I won't charge you anything… just leave me a colossal tip, eh?' Both Mick and Debbie laughed. 'I know it's a horrible journey for you to go to their home, but it would be much quicker for them by car. So that's just something else for you to think about, Luke… OK?'

Debbie went and put a couple of croissants on a plate, with a tub of jam, filled up Luke's coffee cup and said, 'Sorry, folks, but I must go and do some stock-taking before the delivery guy arrives. Enjoy your breakfast, Luke.'

Mick also had work to do. Before going down to the cellar, he said quietly to Luke, 'Think about what we've told you, Luke… we're both pleased you're back.'

As he opened the door, Mick turned around, and gave Luke a grin. 'And you know where the paint-brushes are!' he said.

Seventy-Three

'Well done, Rita,' said Baz, 'excellent work', as they were walking back to his office from a multi-team briefing. 'In fact, it was so good, I'll get you a coffee… just this once!' Rita gave her boss a sideways look and laughed.

'Wow!' was all she replied.

Baz went further along the corridor to the nearest coffee machine. He had been genuinely impressed by Rita's succinct presentation of their evidence and perspectives in relation to the murder investigations. For once the DI had praised their work.

Baz realised, though, that he was developing other feelings for Rita too. He knew that he must suppress those. He reminded himself that he was her boss, and that must preclude a close personal relationship. But it was difficult.

Rita was standing, looking out of his office window, when Baz arrived with the coffees.

'The search of old Mrs Elsworth's property in Great Fordington was certainly productive, wasn't it?' commented Rita.

Baz nodded and said, 'Interesting too what the fraud team had found out about Abbott trying to get his hands on the house. It seems he was trying to manipulate Mrs Elsworth into selling it, on the pretext that she needed the money to pay for her fees at The Willows. And all this behind her son's back. And the money wouldn't have gone to The Willows at all, but into his and Jeavons' pockets. Mrs Elsworth's fall in the garden really threw a spanner in the works, didn't it? That may have been engineered by Jeavons, to make Mrs Elsworth talk, but it resulted in no more easy access to her for Abbott. And then other interested parties appeared on the scene.'

Baz gave a satisfied-sounding laugh.

'I was thinking, though,' said Rita, 'about what was actually found in the house. That's more relevant for us, isn't it?'

'You're right, of course,' replied Baz, 'I got a bit side-tracked. Let's pray that the unused syringes they found can be matched to the injuries on Jeavons and Smith. There's no evidence that either of the Tradovic women is a drug-user, so it makes me wonder who else was on their potential murder list.'

Rita shuddered visibly.

'Let's hope that evidence is found linking the syringes to The Willows. They've already established that the drug is sometimes prescribed to residents there,' continued Baz.

'It makes me sad,' said Rita, 'that Maddie Smith seems to have been an innocent victim in all this. From what they've found on her phone and social media accounts so far, she unwittingly got to know too much about what Jeavons was up to, and about the circumstances of Mrs Elsworth's fall. It seems she was bullied and blackmailed, but the tech team have more work to do on this. We need more firm evidence yet to establish it as a motive. But that really seems a petty reason for murdering her, doesn't it, guv?'

Baz looked across at Rita. He wished he could hug her.

Seventy-Four

Luke was becoming increasingly nervous. The Deans were on their way to The Ancient Mariner to have lunch with him. He had wavered for a couple of days about whether or not he should go along with Debbie's suggestion. Eventually she had offered to ring Seb on Luke's behalf, just to gauge his reaction. But Luke then decided to summon up his courage and make the call himself. He was relieved when Seb agreed to come, with his parents and Tilda.

In fact, Luke's greatest concern was seeing Tilda again. He had no idea how she would feel about him now. He couldn't blame her if she wanted to end their on-off relationship. He seemed to do nothing but hurt her, even though he didn't want to.

Debbie welcomed the Dean family to The Ancient Mariner. She hoped it would ease things for Luke, whom she knew had mixed feelings about the reunion. True to her word, she had reserved a discreetly placed table for them all, where they could have a conversation without being overheard.

Martin was very complimentary about the pub, which pleased Debbie.

Tilda was quiet, unsure whether this meeting with Luke was a good idea. *After all, that woman Mishka had been here looking for Luke, hadn't she? Would she turn up again today?* she wondered. Tilda scarcely made eye contact with Luke as she battled with feelings of jealousy. Luke was finding it difficult to catch Tilda's eye, as he tried to fathom out what she was thinking.

Debbie brought two bottles of wine to the table, hoping that this might relax them all. It was clear that there was tension in the air. But after a few minutes of inconsequential chat, Luke decided that he had to bite the bullet and explain his disappearance to the Deans. He hoped that they could all then enjoy their meal.

Luke looked at the tablecloth or out of the window while he told the Deans about his family background and the visit to his father. He did look at Seb, though, when he was explaining how Mishka and Helena had infiltrated their lives. Luke tried to conceal his anger towards his father, but Martin sensed it and sympathised with him.

Debbie arrived with their meals. This gave Luke some respite from telling his story.

Martin was silently recalling the time when Seb confessed to the family that he had failed his exams and had to return to university. That was excruciatingly difficult for Seb, and Martin guessed that Luke was having similar feelings now. *Having concealed his story for so many years,* thought Martin, *it was a brave move on Luke's part to disclose it now. No wonder his behaviour had been unpredictable and odd at times.*

'Well, Luke,' said Martin, trying to sound supportive, 'you've shown a lot of trust in our family, telling us so much. You're also helping us to understand some of the strange events in recent times.'

Luke nodded slightly, feeling relieved. *Perhaps he had done the right thing after all.*

'So I hope it might ease your mind a little, Luke,' said Martin, smiling, 'to know that Petra and Katya Tradovic, or Helena and Mishka as you know them, are likely to be charged with offences connected to the break-in at our house... you know, while we were all at The Black Horse, except poor Ros, of course. They were caught on our neighbours' CCTV, or at least the car was, and one of them stupidly dropped her phone in the house, and the police found it. So I guess that there may be incriminating information on that. They'll be questioned about other offences too, or so the police told us. One of them has apparently been arrested, but I'm not sure which one. They're still trying to track the other one down. But hopefully neither of them would be stupid enough to try and contact you or Seb again.'

Luke began to feel even more relieved. He briefly glanced over at Tilda. She too was beginning to relax, and he gave her a hesitant smile.

Tilda blushed.

Seventy-Five

'If people realised how much information their online footprint tells us about them, they'd never use phones or social media!' exclaimed Rita, as she ended a long phone conversation with data analyst, Louise. Baz looked up at her, waiting for more.

'Well,' Rita continued, 'it seems that Katya Tradovic is the tactical thinker, as far as the sisters are concerned. But she's made two big mistakes… firstly, in dropping her phone in the Deans' house, and secondly, in trusting her social media accounts to protect her privacy. As we know, she uses two identities, Katya and Mishka, and Louise has unearthed masses of incriminating data in both names. She's certainly been harbouring vengeful ideas about Sally Jeavons ever since she was caught having sex with Abbott at The Willows all that time ago. She's had great difficulty accepting that Jeavons sacked her. Katya sees herself as superior to Jeavons it would seem, and she can't cope with the ignominy of being sacked by an inferior person. It was sheer greed that made her work at The Willows, based on what her father had told her about Bea Elsworth's wealth. Katya saw her as an easy target. She thought there might be other wealthy residents there, so she tried to worm her way into their lives too, for eventual personal gain. She had to swallow her pride to do this and temporarily put up with the "demeaning work", as she saw it. But then she worked out that

311

Abbott and Jeavons had scams going already, so her plans had to become more complex.'

Rita paused for breath.

'And Louise got to know all this from her phone and so on?' queried Baz, looking surprised. He silently began wondering what data analysts might make of the vitriolic exchanges between him and his ex-wife a few years ago, if they accessed his history. But he kept quiet about that.

'Go on then, Rita,' he said.

'Well,' she resumed, 'once Katya had been kicked out of The Willows, she enlisted her sister Petra to go down other routes to acquiring Bea Elsworth's money. Firstly, she got Petra to take a job at The Willows. Apparently Jeavons found it so difficult getting staff that she ignored the link with Katya. Then, she also thought that Sebastian Dean would be a good target. She'd worked out somehow that there was a family connection between him and Mrs Elsworth, so she persuaded Petra to pursue Sebastian at university on her days off, and basically to inveigle him, by any means, into giving away details about Mrs Elsworth's supposed wealth. Katya found out about a useful intermediary, Luke Carmichael, from her dad during prison visits, so she went after him and then set up the "affair" between Sebastian and her sister.'

'So do I take it that Katya put Sebastian Dean in the frame for Jeavons' murder? On a phone that was only used for that purpose?' asked Baz.

'Exactly,' replied Rita, 'Louise says that Katya and Petra used a form of code when they were communicating with each other about their various plans, but it was fairly rudimentary, to Louise at least. So, she says there's no doubt about all she found, and Katya was behind that call, even if Petra actually made it.'

'I don't suppose Louise discovered a confession of murder, or even better, two murders, did she?' asked Baz hopefully, but only half-seriously.

'Nothing quite that explicit, I'm afraid,' replied Rita with a rueful smile.

Baz shrugged his shoulders.

'So, we need to find Katya and bring her in,' he said, 'and perhaps her sister is the best place to start. Katya seems to be eluding questioning with regard to the driving offences and the Deans' burglary from what I hear. So, a bit of pressure on Petra perhaps?'

'Before we do that,' Rita said quickly, 'there's more that you should hear.'

Baz looked across at her, his eyebrows raised. 'More from Louise, you mean?' he asked.

Rita nodded.

'Remember that her team has had Maddie Smith's phone for a while,' began Rita, 'so Louise gave me those interim findings too.'

'OK,' said Baz, 'fire away.'

Rita skimmed through her hastily scribbled notes.

'Right then,' she started, 'Maddie Smith didn't use her phone very much, as we already know. But now that the links and history have been searched a bit more, it's clear that she was on the receiving end of threats, and these came from the Tradovic sisters. They were convinced that Maddie had sussed out the scams being run by Jeavons and Abbott, so not only was she a threat to them, but also to the Tradovics' plans. So, when Petra saw Maddie talking to the Montgomerys just after Bea Elsworth's fall in the garden, they feared that she might open some cans of worms and incriminate them. Those fears increased when Maddie went and looked after Bea in the Montgomerys' home. Eventually, Maddie had to be silenced.'

Baz had dealt with many murderers in his career, but he was still shocked by what Rita was telling him. He thought he was immune to such feelings, but the current evidence showed this to be a cruel premeditated killing, apparently motivated by greed and self-preservation. *How could these two young women create such an inhuman trail of destruction? Such evil is difficult to comprehend, no matter how case-hardened I've become,'* he thought.

'Guv,' said Rita, realising that Baz's thoughts were elsewhere, 'just one more thread.'

Baz nodded.

'Well,' she continued, 'Louise's team looked at the links between Katya and Jacob Elsworth. In brief, they described the relationship as an "unequal partnership", but I think we'd worked that out already. The communication history shows Katya calling all the shots. She's just been using Elsworth. Basically, she was constantly putting pressure on him to elicit information from his mum, about her wealth, of course. There are apparently texts from Katya which are scathing about his ineptitude and his manhood. And recently she's been playing her strongest card, which scares him shitless,' (a raised eyebrow from Baz) 'namely the DNA evidence in his car.'

Baz leaned back in his chair and cast his gaze to the ceiling, in thinking mode.

'Time for a coffee?' asked Rita hopefully.

Baz nodded, but said nothing.

Seventy-Six

Sadie was just about to leave after her day's work, when she gestured to Chloe to follow her into the dining room, where she quietly closed the door. Chloe was mystified.

'I just want to tell you what Bea has been saying to me today, in case it's important,' she explained. 'You've always said I should mention anything she tells me about Anastasia… well, out of the blue, Bea talked about her today.'

Chloe listened carefully as Sadie described, in a rambling way, Bea's latest reminiscences about Anastasia and the box she had given Bea "for safe keeping". In amongst memories of George's colourful life, Bea had enthused about Anastasia's beautiful jewellery and the balls she wore it to. Sadie appeared to be swept along by Bea's memories, so Chloe tried to keep her on track. She was hoping that Bea had disclosed something about what had happened to the jewellery box, if that was what the mysterious box really was.

Sadie took so long describing it all to Chloe that she missed her bus home. Fortunately, Tony arrived while she was finishing off the story, and he offered to drive her back to Great Fordington. In the car she told Tony all about her lengthy conversation with Bea too.

* * *

Later that evening, when Bea had gone to bed, Tony and Chloe discussed what Sadie had told them. Some of the details about George and Anastasia had varied in the telling, but that seemed unimportant. Tony and Chloe focussed on Anastasia's box and its possible whereabouts. There had been no mention of Norway or bank vaults in the story relayed by Sadie. This was a relief to Tony, as his researches in that respect had led him nowhere.

'Right,' said Tony, 'so what have we got that's new? We've actually heard lots of this before, so what do we know specifically about this wretched box?' Chloe looked at him askance. 'Well, think about it, Chlo,' he continued, 'Anastasia's supposed wealth has caused nothing but misery in many people's lives.'

'So, do you think we should stop trying to find it?' asked Chloe.

'Of course not,' snapped Tony, rather sharply, 'we owe it to Bea to see all this through. But part of me wishes we'd never heard of it.'

Chloe realised that her husband was tired and that was probably the cause of his tetchiness, but she persevered.

'The most significant part of Sadie's story for me,' she said brightly, 'was Bea telling her about how the box was hidden. Bea didn't want to sell the jewellery but to keep it for Jacob, so that he would be financially secure after she's gone. Frankly, I wish she'd traded it all in and had a good time with the proceeds! Jacob certainly hasn't inherited his mother's kind nature.'

Tony smiled and nodded in agreement.

'So, Bea has told Sadie that the box was carefully wrapped up and put in a safe place. Even Abbott doesn't know its whereabouts. That must be galling for him… ' said Tony with a sardonic laugh.

'But it doesn't help us either,' replied Chloe.

'True,' said Tony, 'but we now know that the hiding-place was chosen because the box could remain there long-term… secret and secure.'

'Yeah,' Chloe picked up the thread, 'somewhere that no one would come across it by chance.'

'I've just had another thought,' said Tony, 'if she really does have lots of valuables, she would surely have mentioned them in her will. But I suppose that was drawn up by Brownlow and Noggs years ago, and probably by creepy Abbott.'

Chloe gave her husband an astonished look.

'Well,' he said, with a sheepish expression on his face, 'I've come round to your way of thinking as far as that man is concerned. I wish I'd trusted your instincts sooner.'

Chloe took Tony's hand and gave it a loving squeeze.

'Another thing Sadie mentioned was that Bea talked about something being bricked up, but it didn't make any sense to me. And the trouble is, that if we talk to Bea about it tomorrow, she'll probably have completely forgotten her conversation with Sadie, and she'll wonder what on earth we're going on about,' said Chloe. 'But going back to Bea's will,' she continued, 'do you remember that when Maddie first spoke to us at The Willows, and that was the biggest mistake the poor girl ever made, she said something about a lawyer having been to talk to Bea about her will, or that was the rumour anyway?'

'Hmm...' mused Tony, 'we know who that was, and we also know that the police have subsequently raided his offices and taken stuff away. I wonder what documents they've been looking at, and whether they perhaps contain wills. Worth pursuing, Chlo?'

'I'm never sure what's of interest to the police, and what isn't, when we speak to them,' replied Chloe, 'but yes, why don't you have a word with DC Hussein tomorrow morning? She seems OK, doesn't she?'

Seventy-Seven

The morning briefing was more upbeat than it had been for weeks. Even the DI managed to look pleased. At last this double murder investigation was coming together. He could not justify many more resources being allocated to it.

The phone was ringing when Baz reached his office. Rita was fetching some coffee for them both. The call was from Tony Montgomery, asking to speak with DC Hussein. Baz put him on hold until Rita arrived.

It was a lengthy call, concluding with Rita saying, 'Thank you for letting us know, Mr Montgomery. I'll be at your house in half an hour.' Baz looked across at her, wondering what necessitated a visit to the Montgomerys' home.

As Baz was driving along the bypass around Minchford towards the Montgomerys' house, Rita told him the salient points of her conversation with Tony.

'This could be something or nothing,' she warned Baz, 'we have to hope that old Mrs Elsworth is having one of her lucid and communicative times.'

Baz was beginning to think that this might be a wild goose chase, and that the DI would consider it a waste of his valuable resources. But Rita seemed hopeful that a positive new lead may emerge, so Baz was willing to back her judgement.

'Essentially,' Rita explained to Baz, 'Tony wonders how far back we've gone in searching stuff from Brownlow and Noggs. He thinks that Abbott may have begun manipulating Bea Elsworth's will, to his own advantage, decades ago. But from what Bea was saying to her carer yesterday, Abbott has never known where her inherited wealth is held, much to his annoyance. Originally only he knew the Anastasia saga, but once Bea moved into The Willows, and people took an interest in the chain and key she always wore, the cat was out of the bag, so to speak. Abbott was losing control of the situation. Well, that's Tony's take on things. What do you reckon, guv? A motive for the murder of Jeavons?'

Baz seemed less than impressed.

'He's quite the amateur sleuth, isn't he?' he remarked, with more than a hint of sarcasm in his voice. Rita's heart sank, thinking it was a mistake to arrange a visit to the Montgomerys' home without running it past Baz first. She tried to retrieve the situation.

'The second reason for Tony's call was something else which Bea Elsworth talked about yesterday,' she said. 'Before you say anything, guv, I know it's very vague and might not lead us anywhere…'

'Come on, Rita, don't get defensive before you've even told me,' cut in Baz, keeping his eyes on the road.

'Well,' she continued hesitantly, 'Bea was saying how this Anastasia's jewellery box had been wrapped up and hidden somewhere safe. Bea was saving it to provide her son, Jacob, with a substantial inheritance.'

Baz muttered something about some people having too many jewellery boxes, but Rita ignored him.

'Anyway,' she carried on undeterred, 'Bea started talking about bricks and hiding the box in a secure place, where it would be safe for a long time. Tony can't make any sense of all this. He thought, though, that as the contents of this box seem to be mixed up in people being murdered, he should tell us. He hopes that Bea might remember what she was saying yesterday and that we might get more out of her… and that it might be useful for our enquiries.'

Baz found a parking space near the Montgomerys' house.

'Right, Rita,' he said, 'let's keep this as short as possible. You'll do a better job than I will with old Mrs Elsworth, so it's over to you.'

Seventy-Eight

'I thought Tony was actually quite an astute amateur sleuth, didn't you?' asked Rita, as she and Baz were driving back to the police station. She gave a cheeky laugh.

'OK, OK,' replied Baz, 'don't rub it in! You were right… just this once!' He glanced across at her. He thought that Rita had handled the meeting with Tony, Chloe and Bea very well.

'Probably the most helpful part was Tony putting the sketches he'd done of the Great Fordington house on the table. Without any prompting Bea identified the house as the one she'd bought ages ago, and that seemed to trigger other memories for her. But the proof of the pudding will be in what we decide to do about that,' said Rita. 'Do you think the DI will sanction another search based on Mrs Elsworth's memories, guv?'

'The only way to find that out is to put a convincing case to him,' replied Baz, 'so we'll see if he's available when we get back.'

Rita's phone pinged. A message from Catriona in forensics. "Interim report ready. Call me."

'Sounds like more progress, guv. Let's hope forensics have found something,' she said.

'No time like the present,' he replied, 'give Catriona a call.'

Rita listened carefully to Catriona's verbal report. When the call ended, she could contain her excitement no longer.

'We've got 'em,' she shouted, 'the whole bloody lot of 'em!'

Baz looked at her with amusement and wished he could hug her.

'Eyes on the road, guv,' said Rita with a grin.

Duly admonished, Baz asked, 'Well, are you going to enlighten me then?'

'The short version is this,' Rita began. 'Forensics have got DNA matches for both Jacob Elsworth and Katya Tradovic on the clothing Maddie Smith was wearing when she was found in the woods. Catriona said that they'd tried to obliterate any of their DNA on her, but it would have been well-nigh impossible, as they'd carried her from their car to the place she was found. We know they'd tried to clean the car thoroughly, but that didn't work either. There'll be more detail in the full report. They can also positively identify where the serrated knife came from, the one which was left in Maddie's hand. It was the only one missing from a set of knives in the kitchen of the Great Fordington house where, of course, Petra Tradovic has been living. None of her DNA was found on it, though, only Katya's.'

'So we can link Elsworth and Katya Tradovic to the movement of Maddie's body, but what about the actual act of killing her?' asked Baz.

'Catriona had another call waiting while she was speaking to me, so she had to end our call. But she did say that the report also covers the syringes and drugs used. So we'll just have to wait to see those results,' said Rita, still buzzing.

'And in the meantime, we need to debrief about the meeting we've just had,' said Baz, 'and not be totally side-tracked by all the forensic news, however encouraging it is. So, Rita, how do you assess the meeting, and what actions have come out of it?'

Rita forced herself into the reality of the present again. Baz always managed to get her to focus on the immediate priorities. She was quiet for a couple of minutes, ordering her thoughts.

By now Baz was turning into the car park at the police station, so the debrief would have to wait until they reached his office. Rita was relieved to have more thinking time.

'My overall impression of Bea,' she began, when back in the office, 'was that she was more on the ball than I had expected, and what she told us came out of genuine memories, not some sort of fantasy. She was surprisingly definite about things. What did you think, guv?'

'Yeah,' agreed Baz, 'but how do we convince the DI that searching the house again may provide evidence of motives for two murders?'

'Well,' she answered, 'it'll strengthen our hand if Catriona's forensics report tells us more about the syringes and drugs found in the house, won't it? I can see that just saying that we want to look for a jewellery box, which may or may not exist, is flimsy to say the least! But put in the context of Abbott's seized documents, the evidence from Katya's phone, the forensics, and everything else, as well as all the interviews, that surely makes a good case, doesn't it?'

'Leave it with me,' said Baz, 'and you go through Catriona's report, with a fine toothcomb. Find out too, which of our suspects, if any, are still in custody. I'd like to keep track of where they are.'

Rita set about her tasks, but her feelings of elation were diminishing.

Would she ever be able to establish high enough standards of evidence to ensure convictions? she wondered.

Seventy-Nine

No advance warning was given. This was not a social call. The key element was to surprise any occupants.

Just before dawn, police vehicles and personnel were quietly assembling in the vicinity of the Great Fordington house. All possible escape routes from the house were covered. Baz and Rita sat in a car nearby, waiting for the signal that they could enter the house. Rita was excited, but apprehensive too.

Suddenly the air was filled with the noise of shouting, 'Police, police,' and the ramming of the front door. A team of officers in dark clothes and flak jackets barged into the house, still shouting. Watching this, Rita's pulse was racing. Baz gave her a protective glance, knowing that this was her first experience of a dawn raid.

After a few minutes, the all-clear was signalled, and other teams could now set about their work. Rita was relieved that the waiting was over. At least there appeared to be no people in the house, so they could focus on their search uninterrupted. Baz had tutored Rita in avoiding compromising the work of the forensics officers. She remained in the downstairs rooms while they were working upstairs. She looked around the old-fashioned kitchen, careful not to touch anything, but just to make mental notes. She noticed the block of kitchen knives and recalled Catriona's forensic report, which she had been reading until late into the night. She felt sure that it had stated that the serrated knife had been the only one missing from the set on the kitchen worktop. Rita looked again at the block and saw that there were two gaps. She would mention this to Baz.

Nothing else alerted her attention in the kitchen, so she moved into the dining room with its French windows overlooking an overgrown back garden. *The whole place needs a good makeover,* she thought. Looking around, Rita thought that this was probably the most used room. A television was there, magazines were lying around, there were dirty cups on the table, and a uniform, which Rita recognised as one from The Willows, hung on the back of the door. An ironing board leant against one wall. There didn't appear to be any central heating in the house, but this room had a modern gas fire.

Rita went out into the hallway and turned left into the sitting room. She could hear the hum of voices from the officers upstairs and wondered if their search was any more productive than hers. She was unsure where Baz had gone.

Now think, Rita, she told herself, *go through what Bea told us.*

She stood surveying the sitting room. Apart from a threadbare three-piece suite, a dated coffee table, a bookcase filled with probably untouched books, a couple of watercolours of pastoral scenes hanging on the wall, and a faded rug on the floor, there was little to see. She tentatively lifted one corner of the dusty rug. The floor was solid, not the sort with floorboards which could be lifted and used as a hiding space.

Rita was on the point of deciding that the downstairs rooms held no secrets. She thought she would go and find Baz, to tell him about the missing knife. Then a thought struck her. There was no gas fire in this room. In fact, there was no visible form of heating. *The chimneybreast has been blocked up and plastered over,* she thought.

Now what did Bea say about something being bricked up? she asked herself, trying to contain her growing excitement. She looked more closely. The bookcase covered where a fireplace would originally have been, and Rita couldn't see behind it. She knew that she shouldn't move things, so she called up the stairs to Baz to come down.

'Be with you in a moment,' he replied.

Rita crouched down at one end of the bookcase, trying to peer behind it. She felt certain that she had found what they were looking for. She heard someone come into the room and assumed it was Baz.

'Take a look at this, guv…' she started, but she got no further.

She felt an excruciating pain in her back. She struggled to her feet, only to see a figure, dressed all in black, lunge towards her with a bloodied knife in her hand. It was Katya Tradovic. She thrust the knife into Rita's chest, muttering obscenities. She then turned on her heel and disappeared. Baz had heard a commotion and rushed into the sitting room to see Rita writhing in agony in a pool of her own blood. He shouted for assistance and an ambulance was called. The search was no longer a priority for him. He was distraught at the sight of Rita on the floor.

Baz sat on the floor beside her and cradled Rita's head in his lap, not thinking whether or not this was medically the right thing to do. This was his colleague, and it dawned on him just how fond he was of her. He couldn't lose her.

Rita seemed to want to say something. Baz put his ear nearer to her mouth as she struggled to whisper, 'Fireplace', and then she lost consciousness. Baz looked up and immediately realised what Rita had meant. He leant over and softly kissed her forehead.

By now, Catriona, the lead forensic officer, had come into the room. She was taken aback by the scene which greeted her. She gently coaxed Baz away from Rita and calmly began to assess her injuries. She was in no doubt that they were serious, and the sooner Rita was transferred to hospital the better. Catriona was determined to do all she could to keep Rita alive in the meantime.

Baz sat on the floor a little way from Rita, an uncomprehending expression on his face.

Meanwhile, all hell had broken loose in the rest of the house and garden. Orders were being shouted, as it became known that an officer had been stabbed. It would be established later how this had happened... for now, the offender must be sought and apprehended. And were there any more potential assailants in the house?

Eighty

Baz was sitting in a reclining chair next to Rita's hospital bed. PC Nicola Robertson had volunteered to be on duty outside the room, which was a little distance from the main ward. She had always got on well with Rita, and, on hearing about the attack on her, she immediately offered to do hospital duty. It felt as though she was helping Rita in a small way. Nicola had also wanted to keep an eye on DS Underwood, who had given her sound advice on several occasions, particularly when she was applying for promotion. He looked as though he needed a friend at the moment.

Baz was clearly exhausted. He had been sitting at Rita's bedside each day since Katya Tradovic had stabbed her so viciously at the Great Fordington house. She had tubes and drips attached to her, and a monotonous bleeping sound came from one of the machines behind her. She looked peaceful, and her eyes were closed. Her hands were placed palm down on the bedclothes. Baz gently held her left hand, occasionally stroking it.

The nurses encouraged Baz to take breaks, to go for a stroll around the gardens, or browse in the newsagents in the hospital foyer. But he was adamant that he wanted to stay with Rita, other than a few hours each night, when he went home to sleep and change his clothes.

Nicola had got permission to give updates on the two murder cases to Baz each day. Whenever he received new information, he would quietly tell Rita about it.

'Do you remember telling me, love, that "We've got the whole bloody lot of 'em"? Well, you were absolutely right. I'm so proud of you.'

Baz hoped for even the smallest sign of comprehension from Rita, but there was none.

He told her quietly, a little at a time, how Anastasia's precious box had been found. The discovery was all down to Rita's good detective work, he said, as sure enough it was hidden in the bricked-up chimney breast. Forensics confirmed that it would have been there untouched for many years. It was still locked. Much to Baz's amazement, the DI had taken the box to the Montgomerys' home, so that Bea Elsworth herself could be the first to open it with her treasured key. Baz hoped that this unexpected show of human kindness by DI Buchan might be enough to prompt a reaction in Rita. It didn't.

* * *

However, the DI came to the hospital and quietly told Baz the rest of that story himself. He had made an appointment to meet with Bea, Tony and Chloe at their home. When he arrived, the whole Dean family was there too. And Luke Carmichael. So the opening of the box became quite a ceremony. When it was unwrapped from its layers of hessian protection, which forensics officers had carefully replaced, Bea had gasped with joy.

'Anna's box!' she had exclaimed.

The DI had been concerned, he told Baz, that the discovery might be all too much for Bea, and that she might have a heart attack. But no, she took the key, which Chloe was holding out for her, and carefully put it in the lock. To everyone's relief, it turned easily. Chloe helped Bea lift the domed lid of the beautifully carved wooden box. On the inside of the lid was a silver cartouche, with just one word inscribed on it in old-fashioned script, *Anastasia*. Thus, for the DI, any residual doubts about the ownership of the box were dispelled.

There was a strange silence in the room, particularly in view of how many people were present. Each had his or her own thoughts. This box and its contents had been at the root of so much human misery.

The DI told Baz that even he had been aghast at the beauty of the jewellery in Anastasia's box. Each item was individually wrapped, and it took Bea quite a while to lay them all out on the table in front of her. She hesitated several times, as if trying to recall which pieces she had seen before. The DI, who by his own admission knew little about jewellery, thought they must be worth a fortune. Tilda Dean had wanted to try some of the necklaces on, but the DI had said, with regret, that they must all be wrapped up again and retained by him until the pending court proceedings were completed.

The DI had one last piece of feedback for Baz. Before he left the Montgomerys' home, he had asked for a private word with Sebastian Dean. On the drive outside, the DI had apologised to Seb for what had proved to be his unjustified arrest. Seb had shaken the DI's proffered hand.

After the DI's visit to the hospital, Baz leant back in the chair, hoping that Rita had heard at least some of the story. He was beginning to view his boss in a more positive way.

* * *

Two nurses came in to change Rita's drips, so Baz left the room and chatted with Nicola. She updated him in hushed tones, and without naming any names, about the murders. There had been

330

a confession! Baz was suddenly more alert. He found a scrap of paper in his pocket and Nicola scribbled 'P' on it.

'Just one offence?' he asked, and Nicola nodded.

Baz was desperate for more details. But he had refused to have any electronic devices with him at the hospital. He simply wanted nothing to do with them, having spent weeks sifting through electronic evidence and seeing what evil could be generated by their use. So he asked Nicola to meet him outside the main entrance to the hospital when her shift ended. Nicola agreed.

When Baz returned to Rita's room, PC Nick Seymour was sitting outside. The two men nodded at each other, and Baz went in and sat by her bed again.

'Rita, love,' he whispered, 'Petra has confessed to the murder of Jeavons.'

Baz felt certain that he noticed one of Rita's eyelids flicker.

'Yes,' he continued quietly, 'she admits giving Jeavons the lethal drug dose. She's finding all sorts of mitigating factors, or so she and her lawyers think, but no matter how much she tries to implicate her sister and Abbott, she admits actually administering the drug with a syringe.'

Baz was sad and frustrated. Rita *so* deserved to hear the outcomes of their work. She had put *so* much effort into trying to seek justice for the victims. And now she was a victim, fighting for her own life. Baz looked at her lovingly and sobbed quietly.

Eighty-One

'DI Buchan is on the phone for you, Seb,' called out his father. 'Don't worry,' said Martin quietly, when Seb came downstairs, 'he just wants to tell you about developments. You're very honoured… I've never heard of a DI phoning anyone like us before!' Martin grinned.

A few minutes later Seb came into the kitchen, where his parents and Tilda looked at him expectantly.

'Well,' he began, 'my new friend, Gordon,'… a half-stifled giggle from Tilda… 'as I was saying,' continued Seb, 'he said it was a courtesy call to inform me that someone has been charged with the murder of the manager of The Willows and appeared in court this morning. He thought I should know, before I read it on social media, that the accused is Petra Tradovic, in other words my ex-girlfriend, Helena. Not only that, but her sister has been charged with the attempted murder of a police officer, and other charges may follow.'

'So, you mean Luke's old girlfriend?' asked Tilda nervously.

Seb gave her a confirmatory nod.

'Well,' said Martin, after a pause, 'I think that his call was probably over and above the strict call of duty, so I'm very grateful to him. But just before you text Luke, Seb, I want to tell you about a call I had from Tony earlier. It's about the officer who was hurt very badly, in fact she's still fighting for her life. Tony told me that it's DC Rita Hussein. Katya Tradovic, or Mishka, stabbed her, while they were trying to locate Bea's jewellery box. So, while we are all very relieved that issues are being resolved for us, I think we should spare some thought for DC Hussein, don't you?'

There was a subdued hum of agreement.

* * *

Back at the hospital, Baz continued his solitary vigil. Nicola updated him whenever there were developments. He now knew that Katya Tradovic had been charged with attempted murder, *but how,* he asked himself, *did that help Rita?* He tried to console himself with the thought that at least Katya and her sister would be 'banged up' for many years. And that was without all the charges against Katya, and perhaps Petra too, which could follow at the conclusion of the investigations into Maddie Smith's murder.

Baz looked at Rita and squeezed her hand gently, but there was no response. She appeared so peaceful, unaware of the turmoil being experienced by Baz. *How long would he need to sit here before there were hopeful signs? He wanted to tell her of his feelings for her, but would he dare?*

Baz forced his thoughts back to the investigations. It was increasingly clear that once all of Abbott's fraud and conspiracy activities, including possibly conspiracy to murder, had been sorted out, then he wouldn't walk the streets of Minchford for a long time. And then there was Jacob Elsworth. He'd been stacking up offences too. Nicola reported to Baz that Elsworth continued to wriggle like a fish in a net. He was firmly implicated in Maddie Smith's murder. Then there was the stalking of Luke Carmichael, with Katya, still to be fully investigated. If Ailsa Rudd pressed charges, there was the assault on her too.

Baz's brain was beginning to ache.

Why don't I just leave all this to our colleagues? he asked himself. He felt *so* tired. He wondered if this feeling was what the nurses had been talking to him about. They'd said something about people's reactions to trauma or loss, and what sorts of therapy might be available. But Baz had never thought of himself as the type of person to need therapy.

If only Rita would open her eyes, just briefly... Baz could hardly keep his own eyes open.

'Please, please, love, give me some sort of sign that you'll be OK,' he implored her.

But the only response was a rhythmic bleep... bleep... bleep...